THE JASMINE MAN

The Jasmine Man

Lola Lemire Tostevin

KEY PORTER BOOKS

Canadian Cataloguing in Publication Data

Tostevin, Lola Lemire
    The jasmine man

ISBN 1-55263-321-7

I. Title.

PS8589.O6758J37 2001   C813'.54   C00-933141-7   PR9199.3.T67J37 2001

The Canada Council | Le Conseil des Arts
for the Arts | du Canada
since 1957 | depuis 1957

The publisher gratefully acknowledges the support of the Canada Council for the Arts and the Ontario Arts Council for its publishing program.

We acknowledge the financial support of the Government of Canada through the Book Publishing Industry Development Program (BPIDP) for our publishing activities.

ACKNOWLEDGMENTS

My deep appreciation to my daughter, Lisa, who pored over the final drafts and offered valuable suggestions. Also to my husband, Jerry, and my son, Peter.

Thanks to Susan Folkins and Susan Renouf at Key Porter Books, Hilary Stanley at Westwood Creative Artists and Irene Niechoda.

Early excerpts appeared in *Westcoast Line*, PUBLIC, and *The Ottawa Citizen*.

I am grateful to the Toronto Arts Council for its support.

Key Porter Books Limited
70 The Esplanade
Toronto, Ontario
Canada M5E 1R2
www.keyporter.com

Electronic formatting: Jean Lightfoot Peters
Design: Peter Maher

Printed and bound in Canada

01 02 03 04 05 06   6 5 4 3 2 1

For Caleb and Ethan
And for Gregory in loving memory

Contents

Assalama: Hello

A MAN IN A TURBAN PEERS AT ME. I have seen this stamp before, the cancellation mark across the face, the familiar handwriting on the envelope.

I doubt, however, that this letter will begin like all the others. *My dearest Aimée. My very dearest Aimée. How I long to see you again, hold you in my arms.* Nor is it likely to sign off, like all the others, *Habib who loves you still. Habib who always will.*

His English handwriting, his strokes and flourishes, don't quite camouflage the elegance of his own language. Once, when I hadn't written to him in a long time, he sent a three-page letter entirely in Arabic to let me know he was still out there, thinking of me, making himself known yet inaccessible. But the letter wasn't as inaccessible as he'd planned. I couldn't read it, of course, but from the day we met, all Arabic translated into our story. Intimate yet withholding. Gestures unexpectedly flickering into memory: a hand on a shoulder as we walked, tilting the heart's axis; the timbre of his voice as he tried to teach me a few Arabic words: *Assalama*, hello. Knees and ribs amongst sheets, those faithful guardians of rooms in which lovers sleep, talk and love. *Ashnooa ahwalik*, how are you?

"You've never eaten fresh figs?" he asked the first time we met. "How can that be? People have eaten figs from the beginning of time. They should have been the forbidden fruit in the garden of Eden."

Except he didn't say "forbidden." He used some other word, his English awkward, translated from Arabic and French, and we began to laugh, the attraction between us already palpable. Two strangers trying to maintain a little decorum in spite of mouthfuls of pulpy figs.

9

I could have told him that I was familiar with the symbolism of figs, the numerous and suggestive allusions to them in literature, but I must have thought the subject too provocative to bring up with a stranger. In any case, it was unlikely we read the same novels. Two foreigners in Paris, our differences converging on our foreignness, giving us the fleeting impression we had everything in common. Until *salaama*, goodbye. The subtle taste of figs forever grafted to my tongue, flooding my mouth now and then like a small oasis.

His first letters puzzled me. I wanted conversation, news about him and his work, his life and his thoughts. But the letters retreated from the facts I craved, his sentences becoming as mannered as the collection of the medieval stories he read to improve his English: translated Arabic tales so rhymed and conscious of their form they imparted virtually no information, only effusive declarations of intangible love. I remembered him as always cheerful so how could I trust this despair and loneliness he always wrote about? Had he not met anyone else yet?

"If you think my words are not trustworthy," he wrote back, "then you must think the same of my sentiments. I swear, Aimée, they are sincere and unchanging."

We inhabited different vocabularies. As far as he was concerned, language required certain conventions: the more worthy the person addressed, the more artifice the person deserved. Love could only express itself through excess. The overflowing heart. And I do admit that, in the beginning, the experience of receiving one of his letters was as close to the experience of levitation as seemed humanly possible. A one-line postcard was a magic carpet that could carry me to Paris, or to the small country on Africa's Mediterranean coast at the edge of a desert. The two of us nibbling honey-soaked *makroudh* on a terrace above the sea, the stars out in armfuls, the moon a crescent *baa'*. The first time I saw the Roman mosaic of Oceanus in the Bardo museum in Tunis, his hair and beard filled with shells, weeds and crustaceans, it reminded me of him. I had not yet learned to draw the line between mythological creatures and ordinary humans.

He eventually did meet someone else, and he married. More than once, in fact. My initial resentment at hearing about his first marriage through someone else gradually gave way to relief. Especially after the birth of his first daughter, when I sent my congratulations and offered a few tips of parental wisdom: "Now that you are a proud father, you'll want to forget about us and get on with your life." I even resorted to the language he understood best: "The time has come to let our story fade like footprints in the sand." It's almost inconceivable to me now that I once wrote such phrases. The whole affair disintegrating into melodrama.

"Our story may fade," he wrote back, undeterred, "but once a story is written, it can never be erased. Just as you were part of my past you will be part of my future because you remain with me always. Our story is bigger than the two of us. It will live out its full destiny whether you want it to or not."

Destiny. It is written. The belief in the preordained pattern of our lives with which he justified almost everything. How casually he always brushed aside any notion of faithfulness that was unlike his own. And what was this story he kept referring to? Lovers fixed in time, as in a sculpture or on a movie screen? A fate to be relived over and over because it can't find its way to a happy ending?

"You cut your hair!" he exclaimed a few weeks ago, when we last met.

"It's easier," I said, suddenly self-conscious about my gray-flecked hair.

"It is unfortunate," he said, too mournfully.

He too had changed, of course. His hair had even more gray than mine. Lines were beginning to crisscross his fore-head. He'd shaved his beard but kept a mustache, his lower face no longer as sharply defined as it once was. Expensive suit and tie.

"The prosperous businessman worked over by the winds of the Sahara," I teased.

"Or by twenty years of trying to forget," he said, his right hand tracing the air before finding its way to mine. The gaze that once threatened to follow me to the end of myself. The insolent smile.

"Still a dreamer," I said.

"To my grave," he laughed, shrugging off his resignation, much as he shrugged off everything else. Surrendering willingly, I think he once called it. "And you are still a cynic."

"Yes. It is written, as you always said." After so many years our conversation was tentative, as if we'd forgotten our script. Our two lives had run parallel courses but the space between us was too vast now for seduction.

As I look down at the unopened letter in my hands, I wonder if he also noticed the beginning of spots on my hands. Not freckles, as on my face and arms, but spots that will soon intensify with age. But what does it matter now? I've grown so tired of memories that keep blurring the line between illusion and fact. In any event, there have been too many circumstances, more immediate and indisputable, that have redefined over the years my understanding of love.

Yes, this letter will be different from the others. It may resort to accusations of betrayal, denounce my cruelty and deceit. I'm surprised how nervous I am as I reach for the silver letter-opener he once gave me, the one he said I should reserve only for his letters.

The envelope contains a folded card, a reproduction of a watercolor of a small town. Low, square buildings which were once white have absorbed so much light from the surrounding earth and sea they appear to be pale orange and turquoise. A penned-in arrow points to the name of the town—Le Port de Mahdia—and "Where I was born." He's never mentioned his birthplace before. I assumed he was originally from Sousse, where he grew up. But then, over the last twenty years, there have been so many, many assumptions.

Figs

BEGINNINGS NEVER TELL ENOUGH. It may not be as simple as two strangers sitting on a park bench in Paris on a sunny afternoon in the spring of 1975 when a handsome young man asked a red-haired woman: "*Vous êtes au pair?*"

Since moving to Paris with my husband, Gilles, in January, I had taken our son, Jonathan, to the Bois de Boulogne several times a week. A large woodland reserve of gardens, man-made lakes and waterfalls, it was only a few blocks from the apartment Gilles had rented for us for the year he was on sabbatical. It included a children's amusement park, the Jardin d'Acclimatation, but this area didn't open until the first of May, and it was now only the beginning of April.

"When will it be May?" Jonathan kept asking. He relied on me to fill most of his waking hours, making me personally responsible for the upheaval the move to Paris had caused in his life. I tried to distract him by inventing previews of what we would eventually find there: life-size soldiers in red jackets with brass buttons, who came alive when you closed your eyes but froze again as soon as you opened them; birds with tails in the shape of lyres whose music was so soft only angels and children could hear it.

"What's a lyre?" he asked.

"A kind of harp."

"What's a harp?"

"An instrument angels play."

I told him about birds whose tails were so long that one feather, when used as a pen, contained all the stories of the world. And if he was very good and very patient, he would get to see the scarlet flamingo and the emerald cuckoo who laid red and green eggs for Christmas, and the giant rabbit who laid golden ones for Easter. There would be monkeys pivoting like trapeze artists on monkey bars so high in the sky, and deer and dolphins leaping so far beyond the Eiffel Tower, only children wearing special hats, like the one he wore, would be able to see them.

My predictions seldom fooled him. His four-year-old intuition had already figured out my need to create wonder, invent a space we could both retreat to when the real world became either too predictable or too unpredictable. If reality didn't always live up to the urgency of my task, if the long incubations of my imaginary red and green eggs—identical to the marble eggs his grandmother Legate used for darning—did not produce real scarlet flamingos and emerald cuckoos, my good intentions never disappointed him. Like most children, he intuitively understood the intricacies and rhythms of a parent's relatedness to the world and he had molded this knowledge into the simple configurations that make up a child's trust.

One afternoon, when I thought my inventiveness and undiscovered areas of the Bois were running out, we came across a cultivated garden that looked oddly out of place. The legend on the fence post indicated the garden was dedicated to the plants, trees and flowers of Shakespeare's plays. The French are always ready to honor genius and make it theirs. Several flowers and herbs listed were those my mother and my aunt Rose planted at the farm every spring.

Jonathan couldn't have cared less about Shakespeare or, for that matter, French and English gardens, but because he invariably got caught up in my enthusiasm he listened carefully as I pointed to Ophelia's rosemary which, my aunt Rose once told me, was grown for remembrance; pansies were for thoughts; and "fennel and rue are for you," I said as I tweaked Jonathan's nose. The rosemary and pansies had given me the impression I'd stumbled upon something familiar, something from home. When I was moved to tears by Cordelia's furrow weeds, nettles and cuckoo flowers, Jonathan instinctively understood that my sadness had little to do with weeds or flowers and he placed his hands in mine and whispered in my ear, "We'll go home soon, Mommy."

"I know, Jonathan," I whispered back. He listened even more carefully as I pointed to small buds peeking out from under evergreen boughs and acorn cups, barely large enough to acknowledge spring, and I told him they were little sprouting cowslip ears just like his. His bright-eyed vulnerability was beguiling but demanding at the same time.

April promised to be quite warm that year. Almost every afternoon, the students from the Université de Paris next to Boulogne poured into the park between classes, shedding winter clothes, singing "Let the Sun Shine In," everything imbued with anticipation. As when I first met Gilles that bright spring day five years earlier at the University of Toronto. For two weeks I had watched him as he sat by the glass enclosure at the end of the stacks in the fine arts section of the Robarts Library, meticulously taking notes on index cards. Disappointed on those days when he didn't show up, patiently waiting for him to make the first move on those days when he did.

Because I couldn't satisfactorily answer Jonathan's relentless questions about what the students might be doing, paired under coats and bushes, paying their own tribute to spring, I decided to take him to another park close by. It was too small and open to accommodate lovers between classes.

The benches facing the manicured flower beds in the center of Robert Schumann Square appealed mostly to elderly people, while the benches near the swings and sandboxes on the Square's perimeter attracted mostly women with children.

For a child living in an apartment in Paris, it was the closest thing to having a backyard and neighborhood friends. Within a few days, Jonathan had befriended a boy named Philippe. His mother, who introduced herself as Mme Noizet, was a formal woman who always brought a book with her. We never spoke at great length.

There were two types of women who accompanied children to the playground: mothers and au pairs. I thought I could easily tell them apart. The mothers were doting, while the au pairs were either exasperated or blasé. Most of the mothers, pristine and soignée, wore jeans or slacks neatly pressed, shirts crisp under classic cardigans, as if they spent most of their days getting dressed for someone else. The au pairs, on the other hand, more casual, even a little unkempt, gave the impression they spent most of their time taking their clothes off. Also for someone else.

Not that any of this was the case, but it was what I was thinking on that particular afternoon. About mothers and au pairs who came to the park so their children could play with other children, or people who came to watch others, ogling, interpreting everything they saw or heard as confirmation of their suspicions. Killing time in the guise of innocently sitting in a park. I was mulling this over when I realized a voice from the other end of the bench might be addressing me: "*Vous êtes au pair?*" it asked.

"*Pardon?*" I said, startled.

"*Vous êtes au pair?*" the voice repeated a third or fourth time.

"*Non. Non, je suis mère,*" I replied. "*Je suis mère.*" The young man shot a quick glance at the wedding ring on my left hand.

"Ah, too bad. I heard you speak English to the boy and I assumed you were an au pair from England."

"No, I'm a mother from Canada." I raised my shoulders and eyebrows to indicate the matter was out of my hands.

"Too bad," he repeated. "I was thinking selfishly. I hoped I found an occasion to practice my English."

"I'm afraid not. But your English is fine." He had a thick accent, his speech tentative, but he spoke passably well, certainly better than I spoke French.

"Oh, fine, *tout juste*. How do you say *tout juste?*"

"I'm not sure. I think you mean *barely*."

"*Bare?* As in naked?" he asked, confused.

"No." I laughed. "Not that kind of barely."

"I learn from books and tapes but there is little occasion to speak. Most people at the university speak not at all."

"You're a teacher?" I asked and immediately regretted it. I shouldn't be encouraging a conversation with a stranger.

"A student. Over there." He pointed toward the university buildings.

I gave a perfunctory nod then turned toward the sandbox where Jonathan was playing. My back, I hoped, would discourage further conversation.

"I study management," the voice said to the back of my head. "And you? What is a mother from Canada doing in a park in Paris? I've seen you sitting here before."

It annoyed me to think I had unwittingly been the object of someone else's scrutiny, but when I turned to register my disapproval, I was completely disarmed by his smile. A charmer, I concluded, and shook my head.

"I sometimes sit here between classes," he explained. "I was hoping you were not married."

"Well, I am. I'm here with my husband. And my son," I added to clarify any misconceptions he might have regarding my marital and maternal status.

"Your husband works in Paris?"

"No. Yes—he's doing research. Related to his work."

"What is this work?"

"Psychoanalysis. He's a psychiatrist, a teacher."

"*Oh! Un homme sérieux alors.*"

"*Oui, très sérieux,*" I answered too hastily, making light of what I most admired in Gilles. More focused than anyone I knew, he gave himself to projects with the concentration of the near-sighted while I kept losing my sights to shifting horizons. For the last few years, he'd been following the controversial course of psychoanalysis in France. A baroque character had developed an original if somewhat unorthodox approach to Freud and he wanted to see for himself what the fuss was about. His teaching schedule and practice in Toronto had been determining too much of his time, diverting him from a new area of study and research he wanted to pursue: the family complex in the making of the individual. The irony wasn't lost on either of us. "I can't find enough time to devote to family complexes what with all my family obligations and my patients' domestic problems." He laughed, but I failed to see the humor.

His love for me and Jonathan was never in doubt, but his work was certainly as important to him as his family. I never had any misgivings about this. It would be only a matter of time before I also figured out what I wanted to do once Jonathan went to school. In the meantime, I would enjoy Paris for a year.

It sounded so extravagant, Amelia Legate Gérard living in Paris. It was one of the many qualities I adored in my husband—the extravagance with which he could displace the most rigorous reserve.

"Jonathan and I will stay out of your hair," I promised when he first brought up the possibility of spending his sabbatical in France. "Maybe I'll work on my thesis, take advantage of the museums and libraries." After three years of sporadic course work toward a masters in art history, I was trying to jumpstart the incentive to get back to my thesis.

The young man had moved almost imperceptibly closer to me. He was no longer at the other end of the bench. I could detect a fragrance on him. Nothing as flowery or overpowering as aftershave or cologne, but a resinous soap or incense. His gaze never wavered from my face. He hadn't said or done anything offensive, yet I found his manner too direct. It implied familiarity. His outsized smile playing about the lines on each side of his nose above his short beard, his black eyes exposing me to scrutiny, drawing me in.

I could never pinpoint what set a few men apart from all the others, those I found attractive and those I didn't. When I first spotted Gilles in the library and sat across from him hoping he would notice me, it wasn't so much because he was handsome, although he was in a quiet sort of way, but because he projected confidence and trust. He always carried a briefcase bulging with books and I trusted men who trusted books. I assumed he was one of those fervent graduate students, pale and gaunt from spending too many hours in libraries and shuttered rooms. I relished the idea of a man in a shuttered room unraveling obstinate books with the patience of an alchemist, dreaming up solutions to the complexities of the world. His eyes slate gray because, I imagined, he used them too much; his wavy brown hair grown over the narrow band of white above his sweater at the back because he didn't have time or couldn't be bothered having it cut; the sleeves of his sweater and shirt too short for his long arms and frayed at the edges from too many hours at a desk. Precisely what an intellectual should look like, I told myself.

But this stranger sitting too close to me on a park bench unnerved me. He challenged how I should behave. I should have ignored him or asked him to leave, but each time I met his glance my determination vanished and my heart scurried about inside my chest. Nothing frenzied, not *un coup de foudre*, as the French call it, but a door gently closing and opening.

I stood up and began gathering my things. "We must be getting back. It's time to go home, Jonathan," I called to the sandbox. But Jonathan was too busy playing with Philippe to pay attention. I walked over. "We have to go now, Jonathan."

"Not now, Mommy, not now," he yelled in a voice meant to dismiss me.

"Yes. Let's go, Jonathan."

"No, Mommy, it's not time," he insisted, his interior clock confirming it was at least an hour earlier than when we usually left the park. "It's not time," he repeated, loud enough to attract attention.

Mme Noizet, who was sitting on the other side of the sandbox, left the bench where she had been reading. Was everything all right, she asked in French. "*Oui, oui, tout va bien,*" I replied.

"*Madame a des ennuis?*" the woman persisted.

I assumed she was referring to Jonathan. "*Non, non, pas du tout,*" I answered as pleasantly as I could to convey my appreciation. "*Merci quand même.*"

"*Parce que vous savez il faut se méfier de ces sales étrangers,*" she continued as she nodded toward the young man on the bench.

For a few seconds I thought I had misunderstood. *It is necessary to be wary of those filthy strangers.* The more I translated this to myself, the less I could believe it. It wasn't Jonathan's childish stubbornness that worried her, but my safety. Because I was speaking to a man sitting beside me who didn't look French. The woman not only assumed he was bothering me but that he presented some danger because he was a foreigner. A dirty one at that. A man depersonalized, interchangeable with all other people who were not French. As she stood there, her petty grandeur waiting, expecting me to agree, cold rage began to seep behind my eyes and into my temples. You stupid bitch, I wanted to shout. You stupid, bigoted bitch.

I tried to compose myself. "No," I answered as calmly as I could. "My son isn't ready to leave so I'll stay a while longer." This time I spoke English, pretending I'd misunderstood. Pretending this man's presence on the bench, his sitting too close to me, was perfectly normal. Then, before I could check myself, I added, "After all, I'm a filthy stranger myself."

It took a few seconds for my words to register. Then, with a contemptuous movement of the head meant to convey that I was a fool, and that perhaps all these dirty foreigners deserved each other after all, she simply said, "*Comme vous voudrez*," and walked away.

Flustered and angry, on the verge of tears, I struggled not to break down as I returned to the bench. I fixed my eyes straight ahead, aware of the young man's stare. When I turned to face him, he tossed his head back and laughed. He had either heard or guessed what happened and my outrage amused him.

"You are upset?" he asked. "She was afraid for you. Sitting in a park full of people in the middle of the day and speaking to a black man can be very dangerous."

Why was he dismissing this as if speaking to a stranger in a public place never presented any risk? "Speaking to a stranger in a park is stupid and I shouldn't be doing it, period." And calling himself black. "Why do you call yourself a black man?" I asked impatiently. He was starting to get on my nerves.

"In France an Arab is a black man, madame," he said with a mixture of cheerful resignation and rancor.

"Your skin isn't black." His complexion was olive at best and I couldn't understand why anyone would claim to be of a race or color different from his own. "Aren't things complicated enough as they are?"

"If my skin had been as white as yours, the woman would not have been so concerned for your safety. A white woman shouldn't be speaking to a Maghrébin."

"A what?" He must have been from a country I'd never heard of.

"Maghrébin. You've never heard of the Maghreb?" he said.

"No, I haven't."

"North African countries, Morocco, Algeria, Tunisia? For those of us who live there, the Maghreb is a source of pride but for some people it is a convenient way to group Arabs."

"But calling yourself black ..." I was still trying to figure out the threat this man represented to Mme Noizet, the dread on her face because she perceived him to be so different from herself. And the peculiar identity I suddenly assumed the moment I said, "After all, I'm a filthy stranger myself."

"Ah, madame, what difference does it make what color I call myself? If I don't, someone else will, so I do it first. To ... how do you say...." He made little side moves with his head.

"Dodge?" No, he wasn't the dodging type. "Deflect?"

"Deflect, yes, so you have a place to ..." He pushed forward with his arms as if he wanted to withdraw.

"Retreat?"

"Retreat. This is a good word. I am getting an English lesson after all."

Was it only lessons in another language he wanted from me? "You make racism sound like a boxing match."

"Similar, is it not? Is there no racism in Canada?"

"Oh, I'm sure there is. But I can't say I've experienced it first-hand." Which wasn't entirely true. There had been that scandal involving my mother's sister when I was very young. Rose and the man she had fallen for. My parents seldom mentioned race, language or social background, so it was difficult to gauge exactly why they considered some people to be different from us. Except perhaps for people who went to church. Most of my relatives were suspicious of anyone who did, which included just about everyone who lived around New Erie, the town closest to our farm in Southwestern Ontario.

"Did you say you were Algerian?" I asked.

"Tunisian. But some French people assume all Arabs are Algerians, so they are not very fond of me."

"What's wrong with Algerians?"

"Ah ... what's wrong with Algerians," he repeated and made a whistling sound between his teeth. "You presume something is wrong with Algerians."

"I meant what do the French think is wrong with

Algerians." Nothing I said came out right. I suspected he was younger than I was yet he made me feel backward and self-conscious.

"Where do I begin? The fight for Algerian independence was long and brutal. France was going through difficult times and it needed someone to blame. The French are not a forgiving people but the Algerians even less. When I arrived here two years ago, I had a room in a small hotel where Algerians live until they find more permanent loges."

"You mean lodgings?"

"Yes. Then I saw how it is to be afraid."

"Afraid of what?"

"Many things. Being arrested. They told me if you see the police, you look the other way and slowly cross the street. You never wear a scarf or a tie because it is too easy for the police to ..." He made a knotting and pulling gesture near his throat that reminded me of the fate of the live rabbits in the Paris butcher shop where I sometimes bought meat.

"They must exaggerate." I couldn't imagine the police going out of their way to arrest someone simply because he might be Algerian.

"I do not think so. They have their reasons. They saw and heard enough, especially after October '61. There is plenty of evidence to what really happened. And witnesses. The police haven't changed much in fourteen years."

"What happened in 1961?"

"They killed hundreds of Algerians."

"Who did? Where?" The idea of policemen going on a killing rampage was contrary to everything I knew. This was, after all, Paris, the most civilized city in the world.

"The police. Here, in Paris," he insisted, to emphasize I had misconstrued the most important fact.

"Why? What had they done?"

"Who?"

"The Algerians."

"The Algerians? Again you presume *they* were the ones who did something wrong." His pitch raised another octave. "So wrong they deserved to get killed?"

He was so indignant I felt I had to apologize. "I'm sorry," I stammered. "I don't know the circumstances. I was only trying to find out what the situation was."

"A *manifestation*. Not even. It was organized by Algerian workers but it did not take place. It did not have time. As the people came out of the *métro* at Concorde and the buses at Porte de Versailles on their way to the *manif*, they were met by the police."

"How do you know this? It's probably all propaganda."

"Ah, madame. The persons who were there have no reason to lie. A man I know was on one of those buses and they …" He made a striking signal with the edge of his hand and a cracking sound with his mouth.

"No … it's not possible. These things don't happen in countries like France or Canada."

"*Mais si, mais si,*" he repeated. "People were lying in blood, moaning. No one listened at the hospital when he told them he saw a policeman put unconscious people on a wagon and dump them into the Seine. They laughed at him. But bodies were found the next day as far downriver as Rouen."

"That's ridiculous. There would have been an inquiry." He imagined the French to be suspicious of him, I thought, but he was just as suspicious of them.

"Your innocence would be charming but it is too dangerous. There was an inquiry, *chère madame*. It was officially decided three Algerians died in a clash with the police when it was closer to three hundred. There are no inquiries, madame, when crimes are ordered by those in charge."

I didn't know how to react to events that had supposedly taken place fourteen years before, to people I knew nothing about. I tried to redirect the conversation. "What about you? Are you ever afraid?"

"Fear is no longer an emotion I can afford."

"Which means you used to be afraid?" I shouldn't have been prying, shouldn't have been showing so much interest.

"I am not sure, madame." He said nothing for a few seconds. "Yes, I will admit it, I was afraid when I left home. A little, certainly. There were rumors as I grew up. Confirmed by those who left Tunisia for a better life, but returned with unpleasant accounts of what it meant to be a stranger in France. Also rumors from Algeria about French troops killing and torturing people in Algiers. But I put up a brave front for my mother. I am good at putting up a brave front. Especially after discovering that some people consider themselves not only different from me but better. I learned very quickly how to conduct myself."

I nodded in agreement, as if I'd gone through the same experience. "It's a rude awakening, finding yourself in someone else's culture, not sure how to communicate." I still had the impression, as when I'd first arrived in Paris, that someone had shaken me from the slumber of belonging somewhere. I had never been to Paris, but the famous landmarks, the art nouveau decorations at the entrance of metro stations, the balconies and tall windows I'd seen in photographs, confirmed everything I expected as in a kind of déjà vu. Still, I couldn't get over the feeling that I had merely stepped into an animated daguerreotype and become a character in the fiction of that city. "What did you learn?" I asked.

He raised his thumb. "*Un*, if you are Arab, you make yourself invisible." He said this as if it were a given. He raised his index finger. "*Deux*, always expect the worst." He raised his middle finger. "*Trois*, depend on no one but yourself. And," he concluded, unfolding his ring finger, "focus on the important task at hand—an education. It leaves little time for intimidation or fear."

"I feel very intimidated here." Having to speak another

language required a talent for mimicry that I didn't have. Most French people who spoke English sounded like bad imitations of Maurice Chevalier yet they still came off as charming while my mouth refused to contort itself into anything remotely resembling a French accent. Tongue to the gum ridge behind the upper front teeth for the trilling "r" or the lolling "l."

I had taken several French courses over the years—high school, university. Then, after meeting Gilles, I took an intermediary and advanced Berlitz. Still I wasn't sure when to use the *passé composé* or the *imparfait*. One teacher had once said the imperfect was more appropriate to describe feelings, states of being. Which was quite fitting, I thought, since no verb could adequately express what I felt in a language that wasn't my own. And that appalling gender affliction, everything pigeonholed by *le* or *la*.

"You, intimidated?" He tripped on two or three syllables, his mouth trying to safeguard the French pronunciation. "You do not impress me as a woman who would be so easily *intimidée*. People in the Seizième are more tolerant," he said, referring to the arrondissement where the park was located. Through contacts at school, Gilles had leased a furnished apartment in the ritziest part of Paris from a French psychoanalyst, a Dr. Roussel, who was teaching in the United States for a year.

"So what did we just witness then?" I nodded toward Mme Noizet.

"They keep their distance, certainly. They don't want the smells of Arab cooking around them. Racism in the Seizième is more ..." He rubbed his thumb and index together, searching for the right word. "Refined." He pointed to the sandbox. "The woman is taking her son away. I'm afraid your boy has lost a friend."

"It doesn't matter. We should be going anyway." It was past the time we usually left the park. Still put out with Jonathan for not listening the first time, I walked to the sandbox and threatened to leave without him. I could revert to such tactics because he didn't believe them, but he knew they signaled the end of my patience. "Yes, yes, hold your horses, Mommy," he said, his voice weighed down with four-year-old forbearance.

"Hold your horses? What does this mean?" the man asked.

"Don't be impatient or get excited. At least, I think that's what it means." We laughed.

"I will walk with you," he offered as he helped gather Jonathan's toys.

"It's not necessary. We need to pick up a few things for dinner on our way home."

Roaming the food stalls within a few blocks of the apartment building had become part of my afternoon ritual, the displays as fascinating to me as they were to Jonathan: boxes of shaved ice heaped with shrimps; pyramids of tomatoes, their green stems all facing front; wreaths of watercress; green beans the size of grass arranged in woven patterns and decorated with daisies. How many crates had been packed in such a way and sent all over Paris? The cheese shop and the *charcuterie* with Parma ham sliced thin as pink chiffon.

"I have to pick up my money at the fruit and vegetable market, so I will walk with you," he insisted.

"You work there?"

He nodded. "I ... *décharge*, discharge produce and dairy from the trucks in the morning. Before classes."

"Unload," I corrected him. "You unload the trucks."

"Unload. You are a good teacher." He bent over to observe my face, a gleam of amusement crossing his.

In spite of my objections, he insisted on carrying the bag with the toys as we crossed Boulevard Lannes, his other hand firmly at my elbow while I held on to Jonathan.

Tunisia. Until a few weeks ago, I had never heard of it. In addition to the apartment we were renting, Dr. Roussel also owned a house in Tunisia. He'd written to Gilles to say he and his family had decided to see "l'Amérique" next summer and wanted to know if we would be interested in renting his house in Sidi Bou Saïd, either for the month of August, when everyone left Paris, or even for the entire summer if we preferred.

"Can you believe it?" Gilles had said. "We could spend all of August there."

"Why not longer?" The idea of staying in hot and polluted Paris the entire summer while Gilles did his research wasn't particularly appealing to me. "If you can't be there the whole time, Jonathan and I could fly over earlier and you could join us in August."

He obviously didn't take to the idea. He suggested we rent a car in late July, drive through France and Italy, then spend the month of August in Tunisia. "There's a ferry from Naples to La Goulette, next door to Sidi Bou Saïd," he said, spinning off names I'd never heard before.

"Can we afford it?" I'd asked, secretly planning that Jonathan and I would leave in June. I could make it happen if I waited it out. If I quietly made plans and presented them to Gilles as if they had been a mutual decision.

"Not exactly," he'd muttered as casually as he could, a sure sign we couldn't. "But it's such a great opportunity, how can we afford not to? We won't have any money left when we go home, but I think it's worth it, don't you?"

We never had much money but always managed somehow, thanks to Gilles. And Tunisia did have a romantic ring to it, although I knew nothing of that part of the world. The closest I'd ever come to anything Arabian was a book Rose had in her bedroom, *The Thousand and One Nights*, with one line I repeated, hopping to school during those months when Rose read me a different installment each day: "But morning overtook Scheherazade, and she lapsed into silence." The book always smelled of dried herbs and flowers and mothballs.

"My husband and I are thinking of going to Tunisia this summer," I said to the young man, whose shoulder kept brushing mine. "Someone offered us a house in Sidi Bou Saïd for a few months."

"You are renting *le docteur* Roussel's house?" the young man asked.

The unexpected reference to Roussel startled me. "Why, yes! How do you know Dr. Roussel?"

"We live in the same building," he said.

"You live in our building? I've never seen you there."

"I have seen you. I thought you were the au pair for the family who rented the doctor's apartment. I did not think you were the mother. I prayed you were not the mother." He emphasized *prayed*.

"I've never seen you." I blushed so intensely, my freckles probably all disappeared.

"So you don't think I should live in your building?" he asked.

"I wasn't thinking that at all. I just wondered how you knew the doctor." His defensiveness surprised me. It splintered the easy confidence he'd presented in the park.

"I know Mme Roussel, she is also from Tunisia. She found me the room on the top floor because it was close to my work and the university. Now that you people no longer have full-time maids, students as myself can rent the rooms at reasonable prices."

I assumed he was joking until I realized he had every reason to believe that Gilles and I were as well off as the Roussels. "I assure you my husband and I can't afford maids. We couldn't afford this apartment if my husband hadn't found it through the university and the doctor hadn't been desperate to rent it at the last minute." Why was I justifying where I lived? What business was it of his? The apartment wasn't even that luxurious. "Those dormer windows on the top floor used to be maids' rooms? I would have thought they belonged to the apartments on the floor below. They're very charming from outside."

"Yes, poverty is very charming from outside."

"Fearless *and* sarcastic," I teased.

"A realist, madame, a realist. Dormer windows? This is what they are called? From the verb *dormir?*"

"I guess so." A realist who was unrealistically handsome. And with a social conscience to boot.

He held my elbow as he directed me toward one of the shops. "I have to go in here." He pointed to where I usually bought most of my produce. "Those dormer windows are not much narrower than the rooms. Large enough for a bed, a table and a sink." He reached into an open box on a stall in front of the store. "They received crates of figs this morning. Do you like fresh figs?"

"I've never eaten them."

"You cannot be serious! How is this possible?" he exclaimed. "People have eaten them from the beginning of time. It should have been the defended fruit in the Garden of Eden."

"The what?"

"The defended fruit," he repeated. "*Le fruit défendu.*"

"Oh, forbidden. The forbidden fruit."

"For bitten?"

"Forbidden. With two *d*s."

"Yes, forbidden," he repeated stressing the *d*s, and we began to laugh.

I ignored the biblical references. He picked up several figs, and sliced them into quarters, leaving each quarter joined at the stem. "They are my favorite fruit. Do you know how they are pollinated?" he asked.

"I don't know anything about figs." How surreal to be standing on a street in Paris with a stranger giving me a botanical lesson on the pollination of a fresh fruit I'd never eaten before.

"They carry their flowers here." He pointed to a small opening with the tip of the knife. "Hundreds of flowers that can only be reached by tiny wasps who bury inside."

Burrow. He meant the wasps burrowed inside the fig. I took the four crescents from his hand and gave one to Jonathan, who grimaced as soon as he put it in his mouth but refrained from spitting it out when he saw the scowl on my face. "We only get dried figs in Canada but I don't eat them. I don't like them. But these are quite good. Very subtle."

"Dried figs lose the taste from the sun. They are good for cooking but it is not their true taste." He popped two of them into his mouth, one inside each cheek, his handsome face distorted for Jonathan's benefit. He slowly sucked in and made a gulping sound as he swallowed the two figs.

"Do it again," a delighted Jonathan demanded and the young man obliged.

He went inside to collect his pay and, although I could have walked away, I stayed. I needed to buy a few things for dinner. And I did enjoy his company. I should have been more prudent, but I felt that we had certain things in common: we were from vastly different backgrounds yet we were both foreigners in Paris. When he reappeared, carefully counting franc notes, folding them and putting them away, he advised me about the freshest vegetables and fruits I should buy, picking them over, placing each package in a mesh bag.

He recommended a particular butcher shop but I explained that we no longer went there since Jonathan had asked about the rabbits' little skinned bodies hanging by their furry white socks in the window. And especially after my husband informed me that the bright ribbons around the live rabbits' necks were for garrotting when someone wanted a particularly fresh one. We also avoided the shop with the sign in the shape of a horse's head, nor would I buy sausage after learning that the *andouillettes* I grilled for dinner one night were pig intestines stuffed with tripe. All of which had narrowed my choice of butchers considerably, I explained. The corners of his eyes fissured as he laughed. His hand always firmly at my elbow.

"Other than intestines and tripe, you enjoy Paris?" he asked. "The experience is good?"

"I guess so. I miss home." I hadn't realized how much until coming across Shakespeare's garden in the Bois de Boulogne.

"Will you be here long?"

"Another seven or eight months."

"Your son's name is Jonathan?" He pronounced it *jaune-a-tant*. Yellow-has-so-much.

"Jonathan. Yes."

"My name is Habib."

I found myself reluctant to tell him my name, for some reason. People who call each other by their first names occupy a particular space in each other's lives and this man would take too much room if I allowed him into mine. As long as he didn't know my first name, we could remain passing acquaintances. I thought that if I asked enough questions for the half-block left before we got to the apartment building, he wouldn't have time to ask. "Does Habib have a special meaning? In Arabic?"

"Friend. It means friend." He gave me another one of his grins.

"Really? Are you making this up?"

"Why would I make it up? I swear. It comes from the verb *ahabba*, to love. *Hob* means love, *habibi*, my love, and *habib*, friend."

How easily he relinquished his name and its meaning. He had undoubtedly shared this etymology before. "It must be a convenient name to pick up girls."

"Yes, so far it has worked well," he said without any embarrassment. "And you, you must have another name besides *maman*?"

"Mme Gérard," I blurted. It sounded so priggish and condescending I could hardly believe it had come out of my mouth.

The beginning of a smirk skimmed his face, a knowing smile. He must have understood what it meant to be a stranger in Paris, confronted with questions that demanded unequivocal answers, the skeptical rebuttals meant to remind you of who you are.

"And does Mme Gérard have any other name?" he asked resolutely. Nothing, apparently, strengthened his resolve more than aloofness.

I would have to tell him. "Amelia, but everyone calls me Amy." Why was I adding details? What difference did it make what everyone called me?

"Emmy? E-M-M-Y?" he asked.

"No, Amy, with an *A*. As in *amie*," I said facetiously.

"Ahh, as in *amie*. Friend. Are you making this up?" He beamed.

"Actually, that's not what it means. But the French pronunciation is similar." How witless and inane I sounded.

"*Amie. Amy,*" he repeated several times trying out the French and English pronunciations. "But the way you say it, it doesn't sound like *amie*. It sounds more like *aimée*." He chuckled as he opened the door of the apartment building with the exaggerated movements of a doorman stepping aside to admit an important person. "After you, Madame Loved One."

Jonathan ran to the elevator to push the button, shouting "Me, me, Mommy," as he always did, hoping he had miraculously grown the necessary inches that would allow him to reach it. Habib lifted him and indicated the button with the arrow pointing up. As the doors opened, he said the elevator didn't go to the fifth floor and, in any case, the people who lived up there, in the maids' dormers, which he pronounced door-*mère*, his tone insolent, were supposed to take the service stairs. He handed me the mesh bag of parcels and toys and a small paper bag which, he said, was a gift. "To the next time then, Madame Aimée." He nodded, shook hands with Jonathan and turned toward the door to the service stairs.

It was more than caution that warned me never to see him again. He was much too charming, this insistent young man whose name was Habib, which came from the word *habibi*, to love. Not to mention the discomfiting joy he aroused. And the wariness. I was a married woman and I couldn't let just any intruder into my life, certainly not a stranger with such a winning smile. There was too much intrigue behind that smile. I would have to change the time when Jonathan and I went to Robert Schumann Square or I would have to go back to the larger and more anonymous Bois de Boulogne. He would never find us there. Habib. Was that really his name? I peered inside the bag. It contained several green and dusty mauve figs. Perfect for a centerpiece for dinner later with Gilles.

Rose

UNTIL THE INCIDENT IN ROBERT SCHUMANN SQUARE, I hadn't paid much attention to newspaper items relating to North Africa or North Africans. But after I had met Habib in the park, something in *Le Monde* caught my eye almost every morning: France promised to offer workers from the Maghreb more opportunities for professional training; a young Tunisian living in Paris had killed himself a few hours after being told he would be extradited; during a visit to Algeria, President Giscard d'Estaing proclaimed Algeria the door to the Third World, and was given an Arabian horse named Assul, "messenger dressed in gold"; the next day, an Algerian father of five working in France was beaten to death by one French soldier while being held down by another. There were photographs of the soldiers, their eyes opaque, showing no emotion of any kind. I tried to imagine myself in the Algerian's place. Instead I found myself thinking of Rose.

Of all my aunts, Rose was the only one who had managed to escape the compound of farms my parents and several relatives owned around New Erie County. She returned after only a few months but, to my mind, that was less important than her having broken free from a circle of relatives as unyielding as the barbed-wire fences guarding their lands. Her escape made even more sensational because it involved a secret.

Rose had gone to work as a housekeeper for a widower with children, a man who may have been part French or even part Indian, and then she'd fallen for him. Face pressed against the iron grate that allowed air-flow between the second floor and the first, I listened to my mother and her sisters sitting around the kitchen table, castigating any woman who didn't have the plain good sense to stick to her kind.

I was not to worry my pretty little head or talk about it to anyone, my mother warned, especially not to my friend, Aisling Mooney. Reality was not a place Rose checked into often, it was implied, and there was no need for everyone to know that she spent most of her time in her room now, sewing up scraps into gaudy bedcovers. "All we need is for the Catholics to get a hold of this," my mother told her sisters, all of them rolling their eyes and shaking their heads, the air in the kitchen stilled by their thin-lipped silence.

My mother and her four sisters had appointed themselves the custodians of family secrets. Especially the one involving Rose and something about blood that didn't mix. So much blood that Rose had to be taken to the hospital in the middle of the night. A night drenched in such shame that it was decided Rose's judgment could never be trusted again. She would have to quit her job and live with one of her sisters. Since we were the only ones with a spare room she came to live with us. I couldn't wait to tell Aisling Mooney.

Rose did her best to stand up to her sisters but the discussions invariably escalated into everyone calling each other names, Rose shouting they were a bunch of narrow-minded bigots who wouldn't know what love was if it stared them in their two-faced faces. She would then retreat to her room in tears. It eventually became her house, her country, her universe.

I was the only one allowed free access to Rose's room. Whenever I wanted her to read to me from one of the five books she had exchanged for a quilt at one of the county fairs. Except for old copies of the *Farmer's Almanac* and a few seed catalogues, they were the only books we had in our house. It was only when I began reading them myself that I realized that Rose had adapted their language so I would better understand them. There was Virgil's *Aeneid*, *The War of the*

Worlds by H.G. Wells, *The Thousand and One Nights,* a *Complete Works of William Shakespeare,* and a sumptuous illustrated volume entitled *The Works of Geoffrey Chaucer,* which featured "A Treatise on the Astrolabe," written for his son. It explained how to build and use an instrument for measuring the heavens and for following the movements of the stars. I longed for one of my own.

"I want an astrolabe, Rose. Where can I get one?"

"What would you be wanting an astrolabe for?" she asked.

I thought the answer quite obvious. "To measure things that are far away," I said.

"Ah! First you have to learn to measure what's under your nose, child."

Several years later, in one of my art history classes, I came across the two illustrators' names: Edward Burne-Jones and William Morris. They had published the *Chaucer* through Morris's Kelmscott Press in 1896.

Rose's room became my refuge whenever I needed to reevaluate my experience of the world. When my brothers called me "Brillo top," or teased me about the cattle or hogs being loaded onto trucks on their way to the slaughterhouse. I had made the mistake of seeing them off once: I went up to the truck and peered between the slats to say goodbye. Their eyes were terrifying, so eloquent and defenseless. My mother tried to reassure me. They weren't afraid because they didn't know where they were going, she said. But that only made it worse, I cried. "Because we know, and they trust us." I never did get used to the idea of animals as part of the farm's efficiency, each one an implement inseparable from its utility so we could never let ourselves love them.

On those slaughterhouse days I swaddled myself in one of Rose's quilts, its protection molding itself to my body. "Crazy quilts," my mother and aunts called them, because they almost never sold at the county fair. Rose stacked them everywhere—bed, chair, her obsolete hope chest. "Crazy" because she didn't follow traditional patterns. The family's drab tatters of broadcloth and wool highlighted by bright, satiny selvages and borders, buttons and ribbons from the local notions store. Hearts and peculiar sayings padded with batting. "Love is not a subtle argument," one of them said, the saffron-colored letters meticulously stitched to a tomato-red background. "Crazy" because, although it was all happening under my nose, I still didn't understand what was going on, and I still wished I had an astrolabe that would tell me.

I often imagined Rose in love the way Gilles and I were in love shortly after we met. Or my parents. My mother greeting my father in a dress similar to the ones she still wore, except the prints would have been more distinct and lively then. Before their foliage, primroses and violets turned into parched sprays, the fabric worn thin. Most of it too thin for quilts, so Rose used the discarded dresses to stuff the raggedy Ann dolls she also made. Their small, geometric features as sharp as those of the women sitting around our kitchen table puffing on home-rolled cigarettes.

Gilles

WHEN I FIRST ANNOUNCED MY ENGAGEMENT to a French-Canadian fourteen years my senior, the most educated person my parents had ever met and a Catholic to boot, I heard my mother muttering to her sisters that she should never have let me play with that Mooney girl all those years. Aisling Mooney had been my best friend since first grade, when the teacher sat us side by side in the front row because our first names both began with A. Two unsuspecting girls in braids, unaware of the fact that we weren't supposed to like each other because she was Catholic and I wasn't.

Partly out of spite, but also partly because it wouldn't have mattered anyway, I neglected to tell my mother that Gilles had never been a practicing Catholic. No one could have persuaded her that a Catholic was worthy of one of her children, and no one, especially not my mother, could have dissuaded me from marrying Gilles. I had wanted his gentle face demanding my attention from the first time I spotted him in the library.

When he finally did notice me, my complexion radiant that day because of an allergy to my woolen sweater, he wrote something on a piece of paper and pushed it across the library table. "What are you doing and why?" the note asked.

Without lifting my eyes I scribbled on the reverse side "Preparing an essay because I have to."

"Do you want to go out for a bite?" he whispered, leaning across the table.

"To eat?" I whispered back.

He laughed so spontaneously and loudly that everyone

around us looked up. "Unless you have some other kind in mind," he said, not bothering to lower his voice again.

He asked the usual questions and I gave the usual answers. My major: art history, with a minor in literature. Fourth year. I was researching a paper for my Prehistory of Modern Art class, examining the new directions art took at the end of the nineteenth century when artists abandoned mythological and historical themes and looked closer to home for their subject matter. "I think art should hit you where you live," I said. "If the ideal is to be made real, art has to reach beyond the narrow field of fine arts. At least, this was William Morris's view," I added, to substantiate my statement. Prattling on because I wanted to impress him and because I was nervous. No, I wasn't sure what I would be doing after graduation. Maybe take a year off. I hoped that he could tell there was more than art history under all the red hair, and that he could see the curve of my breasts under the woolen sweater.

"Are you a graduate student?" I asked.

He hesitated. He later admitted he hated telling prospective dates about his profession. While most were fascinated at first, most also grew suspicious of a man who could detect in any twitch or slip of the tongue a potential or repressed obsession.

"No. An associate professor. A psychoanalyst, actually."

"A psychoanalyst? But you've been examining art books for more than a week. I assumed you were an art historian, or something." I felt my face turning scarlet.

"No, but I would *love* to be. I'm researching a paper for a conference on art and psychoanalysis." Analysis and art resembled each other, inasmuch as neither was constrained by facts and events, he said. Both relied on a complex interplay of perceptions, memories, desires, associations, anticipations. After a few minutes, he stopped and apologized. "I'm not very good at small talk."

"I don't need to be small-talked," I protested.

"I'm sorry, I didn't mean…"

"It's okay. I find it interesting."

But what I found interesting wasn't so much his psycho-analytical concepts as himself, Gilles Gérard. He had chosen a discipline and molded it to the core of his existence. I envied people who had no doubt that their interests mattered, to others as much as to themselves.

I did wonder what I was getting myself into the first time I went to his office at Trinity College and saw his walls lined with impressive-looking tomes, the gold lettering of their leather bindings another confirmation of his superior intellect. "Who reads St. Augustine?" I moaned, upon seeing thirteen volumes of *Confessions*.

A fugitive blush flitted across his face. I was to learn that he hated being pegged as a hopeless intellectual. "They were my father's. Left over from his seminary days. He couldn't bear to have them on his shelves and was going to throw them out."

"What for?"

"He didn't like Augustine's image of women. The dark, sinning, wicked soul, the negative other to his own exalted vision of himself as the converted and the faithful. My father couldn't stand that."

Gilles's father had been groomed for the priesthood since childhood, but shortly before being ordained he realized his faith was not as steadfast as it should have been. After much soul-searching and consulting ponderous dissertations written by men who should have provided him with better answers, he asked to be released. Unlike St. Augustine, who abandoned the women he seduced in his pursuit of divine love, he chose to return to his high school sweetheart, a woman named Jeanne-Marie.

Theirs was the most romantic story I had ever heard, their relationship carved out of conviction and revolt. It was the kind of certainty I longed for in my own life.

"So you don't believe in God?" I asked Gilles that day in his office to make sure there were no unbridgeable gaps between us.

"Oh, sure."

His answer surprised and disappointed me. "You do?"

"As the main character in a great piece of fiction, sure."

"I mean a God who judges and punishes."

"No. But it's irrelevant. My father always says we should live as if we'd have to answer to someone, whether there's a God or not. So it becomes irrelevant." Gilles seldom wasted time on stalemates.

"And if there's no one to answer to but us?"

"Then it should be good enough. We'll answer to each other, just the two of us."

By "us" I had meant people in general—friends, family, even strangers—but he had narrowed it down to him and me. We needed to answer to no one but each other. At the time, I believed this would be more than enough.

"Your eyelashes are like copper wire," he said as he pushed me against the leathery spines. Before kissing me, he turned around and locked the office door.

The Sitter

CONSISTENCY AND ROUTINE, I decided, would help authenticate Paris as our home. Every morning, while Gilles got Jonathan out of bed and helped him get washed and dressed, I walked to the neighborhood boulangerie rehearsing in my head what I would buy for breakfast once I got there. *Trois croissants* or *trois pains au chocolat, un bâtard* or *une baguette.* I hated spluttering when confronted with the sales-girl's measured patience. "*Oui? Madame désire?*" Hesitation transforming me into a mime or a court jester.

"I don't know why I bother, I should just speak English and let them sort it out," I complained to Gilles as I set the breakfast table. Crusty bread, milk whisked in a double boiler, its white foam poured over black coffee or chocolate: it was a ritual unlike anything required by the plain cereal and toast we usually ate in Toronto. Even the jar of Bonne Maman jam with its checkered lid summoned a certain refinement. Muffled sounds of a piano from the apartment above. "Mr. Frankl from Hungary," the concierge told me when she asked if his practicing bothered us.

"Not at all, we enjoy it." Sonatas blending with morning traffic, metronomic and circuitous, while a man in blue overalls swept the sidewalk—swish, pause, swish, whisking away any of the night's remaining shadows; children in uniforms, school bags strapped to their backs, shouting as they left the building with parents or au pairs. A mutiny of noises.

"It's a good opportunity to practice your French," Gilles said, scanning *Le Monde.* "Don't go settling for lesser options," he said as he absent-mindedly dunked his croissant in his bowl of coffee, a deplorable habit since Jonathan copied

43

everything his father did and invariably left a sludgy mess at the bottom of his hot chocolate.

"How does wanting to be myself and speak my own language translate into a lesser option?" I tried to catch his eye over *Le Monde*. Every morning I competed with "The World," confrontation being the most effective way of getting his attention.

"That's not what I'm saying—"

"But then women married to brilliant men must resort to lesser options all the time."

"That's not fair, Amy." He made a show of carefully folding his newspaper and placing it beside him. It would only be a few minutes before he tried to glance at it again.

"Forget it," I said. "Whatever I say, you'll hear something different." Much of psychoanalysis, I had learned, was based on the ability to hear something other than what was being said. The details of my insignificant life magnified into drama. It didn't take long after we were married for me to realize that Gilles expected me to go along with his preconceptions of what life in general should be. It was one of the conditions of a happy marriage and, I suspect, a successful therapy. Except Gilles wasn't my therapist, I wasn't his patient, and it surprised me sometimes that he wasn't more in tune to his own wife's needs. But then, I guess I wasn't that much in tune with them either.

"Aren't you working on your thesis?" he asked. "You couldn't wait to get here to begin your research."

I hadn't done any work at all on the thesis. There were, instead, too many walks to the park, too many stories to tell Jonathan, too many dinners to plan and prepare. My beautiful child a tyrant and an enchanter, not unlike his father. "I haven't found a sitter. I don't know if he's ready." I motioned toward Jonathan.

"He's ready, Amy. He'll be fine."

It was so easy for Gilles. Fluent in French. Spoke English with no detectable accent. His activities in Paris were associated with real events and substantial institutions: he visited the École freudienne de Paris; attended seminars, a hotbed of ideas for a new generation of intellectuals writing so extensively on psychoanalysis that it had become a major component of French culture; worked at the Bibliothèque Nationale on his cherished family complex. And there were the occasional lectures at some new, progressive university established on the outskirts of Paris after the student uprising in '68. "The times they are a-changin'," he would quote from his favorite Dylan song to confirm that the seventies were finally fulfilling the sixties' mandate. The new order challenging the old. Which was probably what I expected when I decided to major in art history, and when I fell in love with Gilles. I hadn't foreseen art history's inertness once I was no longer a student, or love's passivity when Gilles and I weren't together. My thesis on Art Nouveau, the blending of different styles—oriental, primitive, rococo— seemed hardly relevant compared to his professional concerns and timetable. I felt paralyzed and I couldn't figure out why. There was no understanding from which to move.

While reading *Le Monde*, I came across an excellent review of a controversial Quebec documentary, *Les Ordres*, recently released in France. According to the article, it dealt with the War Measures Act invoked after members of the Front de libération du Québec had kidnapped a British trade commissioner and a Quebec labor minister in 1970. Gilles and his family had been horrified by the draconian measures that allowed the police and soldiers to search, without warrants, the homes of those suspected of being nationalists and to arrest them without specific charges. My parents, on the other hand, had approved. As far as they were concerned, stepping on a few people's civil liberties was perfectly justifiable if it meant the protection of all "good, law-abiding citizens." I had the distinct impression that my parents' undue interest in this matter had come about mainly because of my marriage. It provided good fodder for arguments with Gilles, which they always lost since he could articulate his views infinitely better than they could, providing them with yet another excuse to remain aloof.

The film would be a good opportunity for a night out with Gilles, so I decided to ask the concierge, Madame Renée, if she could recommend a sitter for Jonathan, someone she would trust.

"*Vous connaissez l'Arabe qui habite là-haut?*" she asked.

"*Non,*" I replied, expecting that a sitter would be a woman.

"You don't know Monsieur Habib? He was asking about you the other day."

"Monsieur Habib? Ah, yes. I have met him. Well, briefly." Why and what was he asking about me? I wondered.

The Arab, Madame Renée explained, often sat for people in the building, especially for *le docteur* Roussel whose apartment monsieur and madame were now renting. A nice young man, considering. Always finding ways to make money, but reliable nonetheless.

Her insinuations didn't surprise me as much as Mme Noizet's but they irritated me just the same. Yes, I had been wary of him in the park, his friendliness and flirtation, but he was accumulating so many questionable traits he was turning into a caricature.

"I'm sure Monsieur Habib will be very trustworthy," I said, compelled to defend him although I knew perfectly well he needed no one to defend him, least of all me. "I'd appreciate it if you mentioned it to him." I hoped a message relayed by Madame Renée would convey appropriate impartiality.

The next day I found a note stuck in my mailbox.

Chère Madame Aimée,
It is a few weeks since I have seen you and Jonatan in the park. I
hope your health is good. Madame Renée tells me you need someone
to stay with Jonatan when you and your husband go out during the
night. This is a service I offer to parents in the building so I pray you
are not too timid to let me render this service. We will understand
one another very well, Jonatan et moi.

*I have neither telephone nor personal letter box but you can
leave a word in the box designated to the fifth floor.*
Votre fidèle ami,
Habib

I found the note reassuring. We weren't being reckless in
leaving Jonathan with a man who regularly sat for the
Roussels and who was highly recommended by Madame
Renée. Plus Jonathan had already met him. From now on I
would make sure to keep all conversations and contacts formal and restore a proper distance between us. If he were avail-
able next Friday, Gilles and I would take full advantage of the
evening and have dinner out as well. On Valentine's we'd gone
to L'Entrecôte, an inexpensive restaurant famous for the one
meal they served—a first course of a walnut salad followed by
frites and a steak *bleu* in a mustard and pepper sauce. "A reason-
ably priced meal, simple but done with style," Gilles had said.
Simplicity and style, these were two of the main sources of
Gilles's happiness when he wasn't at work.

On Friday evening, I stayed in the bedroom for several
minutes rearranging my hair after Gilles answered the door to
let Habib in.

"You've met Habib, haven't you?" Gilles asked as I entered
the living room. The same resinous scent as in the park per-
meated the room, Habib's black hair damp, freshly washed.
"Habib Bakri?"

"Yes. We met in Robert Schumann Square where Jonathan
plays. Briefly. He'd seen us in the building and recognized us."
Whatever I was trying to justify didn't need so much explanation. "How are you?" I asked, extending my hand.

"Habib is from Tunisia," Gilles said, his tone suggesting an
uncanny coincidence.

"Really?" Only one word, the first in a list of deceptions.

"I was just telling him we were planning to drive there this
summer." He turned to Habib. "My wife wants to spend the
whole summer in Sidi Bou Saïd. But I can only afford to be

away from my work for a month and I'm not sure it's wise to leave her there by herself with our son."

Habib considered Gilles's statement for a few seconds, then, puzzled, asked, "Why would it be not wise?"

"Is it safe? A Canadian woman and child on their own?"

A shadow crossed Habib's face. "At *le docteur* Roussel's house?" he asked, his tone verging on incredulity.

"Right, you know Dr. Roussel. My wife said you baby-sit for them."

"Yes, I do. Sidi Bou Saïd is a very civilized town, monsieur. There will be no danger for your wife and son there." Except for the imperturbable stare he fixed on Gilles, it was impossible to know what he was thinking. I suspected it was the stance he had described in the park, the one he adopted when confronted with people who considered themselves his superiors.

"I have no doubt that it's a civilized town," Gilles said impatiently. "I would have qualms leaving my wife and son in any town I wasn't familiar with. You know the Roussel house?"

"Yes, monsieur, I have been there many times."

"I understand a couple tends the house and garden?"

"Yes. M. and Mme Maalouk." Habib held his expressionless gaze on Gilles.

If Gilles continued with this line of questioning, he would dig a hole from which neither of us would be able to climb out with a modicum of dignity. It was time to leave. "We have to go, Gilles."

"Perhaps you can tell us more about it when we have more time?" Gilles asked. My heart sank. He might as well have handed him a blank invitation to drop in whenever he wanted.

"Nothing would please me more," Habib replied with a nod that threatened to develop into a bow. A gesture of contempt, I suspected.

"We should get going," I repeated. "A hug," I said to Jonathan, who was busily gathering books and presenting them to Habib. "You'll be able to practice your English," I said to Habib. "Madame Renée will be in all evening if you need help." Jonathan hardly noticed we were leaving.

"We will be fine, madame. Amuse yourself well."

I ignored his full-blown smile and averted my eyes as I shut the door. There was no point in reinforcing any suggestion of complicity.

"A nice man," Gilles said on our way to the metro. "Mild-mannered."

"Yes." Precisely, I thought and wondered what other versions of himself he might have tucked away and what it would take to reveal them. "I don't think we should use him to orchestrate our holiday, though."

"Who's using him to orchestrate our holiday?"

"You asked him for information on Tunisia."

"I wouldn't exactly call it orchestrating our holiday, Amy. We could use a few pointers. We don't know anything about that country and it's an excellent opportunity."

"I don't want to use him as an opportunity. It isn't right."

"What isn't right? What are you talking about?"

"Using the house of a rich Frenchman who probably inherited it from his colonizing family, and asking Habib to do our legwork for us. It's embarrassing. We don't need a guide."

"Whoa! Aren't we being a little presumptuous? For your information, the house belongs to Roussel's wife. She's Tunisian. Apparently it's been in her family for generations and she inherited it. What's with all the politics, suddenly?"

"It's not politics," I protested. I didn't have the right to think about politics. The word belonged to people with well-defined causes and opinions, people like Gilles's parents who came from Quebec and had inherited a long list of grievances. Or Habib who was made to feel like an inferior in France. "I don't want him breathing down our necks. I want to plan my own holiday."

"Fine, we'll plan our own holiday. Aren't you being a little paranoid about this?"

"No, not at all," I half whispered, as I brushed a lock of hair from my forehead and caught a whiff of resiny soap on my hand.

Within a few days, an avalanche of pamphlets, travel guides and maps began to invade our mailbox, and whatever didn't fit through the slot was left at our door. Posters. *La mer a une patrie et c'est la Tunisie! La Tunisie est la Méditerranée du coeur et le coeur de la Méditerranée!* History books. Nomadic tribes perched on ancient dromedaries filed into our lives disseminating bits and pieces of Tunisia's evolution—Getulians, Nubians, Berbers. *La Tunisie: Carrefour du monde antique.* Tunisia—the crossroads of ancient civilizations. It seemed impossible that a country the size of a pocket handkerchief tucked between Algeria and Libya could hold history going as far back as the Phoenicians, whose alphabet, scattered along the Mediterranean coast, gradually took on worldwide configurations.

"Did you realize Sidi Bou Saïd is only a short walk to Carthage?" I asked Gilles one evening as we studied the books and pamphlets scattered on his study floor. "I didn't know the ruins of Carthage still existed. I never thought of it as a real place."

"What did you think it was?"

"A setting for Virgil's *Aeneid*, I guess. 'As Aeneas stood marveling at the sights of this rich and sophisticated city, unable to speak or turn his eyes away.'" I ran to the study door and sashayed in, making a grand entrance. "'Into the temple came Dido, the queen who would hold him hostage to her charms.'"

Gilles chuckled. "You make a great Dido. Carthage will never be the same."

"I can't believe I still remember this stuff. What else do you know about the Carthaginians?"

"Not much."

"Which means you probably know a lot."

"Sophisticated people. Always at war with the Romans. Freud dreamed of a father modeled after Hannibal."

"Isn't he the guy who went around crushing people with herds of elephants?"

He smiled. I had, according to him, the most disconcerting habit of reducing complex situations to guileless one-liners. "He was the brains behind the battles. He shattered enemy lines with elephants the way World War II strategists did with tanks."

"And Freud wanted this guy for a father figure?" I didn't know much about Freud but the more I learned, the less I liked him.

"Sons want heroes for fathers and he didn't think his was capable of heroism. It's probably why he was always searching for strong father figures for his theories on social organization. So Carthage became a symbol. Just as it was for Aeneas."

"So Dido was only a distraction for Aeneas on his way to Rome? He gets to tell his tales of Troy, seduce the queen, then move on to his promised land while Dido abandons hers and kills herself?" It had taken at least two weeks after Rose read me that story to get over Dido committing suicide and killing her son just because Aeneas left her. Considering that she founded Carthage, I had assumed the beautiful princess from Tyre would be more resourceful. Having been given as much land as she could cover with the hide of an ox, she had shaved it into gauze-thin strips and lined them up end to end so they covered the best land overlooking the gulf, and there she built Carthage.

"Laying down Rome's foundation wasn't exactly a trivial event, Amy."

"Neither was Dido's founding of Carthage. But he's the hero and she comes off as a love-sick lunatic who has to die. I don't believe the founder of Carthage would have done this. It's just another ... guy thing."

"What guy thing?"

"Women dying over men. It's the basis of just about every

damn classic romance story ever written. Somebody should analyze that."

Again, he laughed and shook his head. "You are becoming political. I may be in big trouble here."

Gilles had rearranged the Roussel study almost identically to the ones at home and at school, his desk and chair facing the window, so he worked with his back to the door. Many of the books on Dr. Roussel's shelves were duplicates of Gilles's. A few littered the floor. He usually had several going at a time, reading one for a few hours, putting it down, picking up another. After a few days, he systematically replaced those he'd read in their alphabetical order.

Photographs of Tunisia, postcards and reproductions of paintings, most of them left by the Roussels, covered the wall to the left of Gilles's desk between the bookcase and the window. One of the postcards, dog-eared and yellowed, depicted a wood-cut by Albrecht Dürer, the German painter and engraver, of a dejected winged angel crouched by an unfinished building, resting her head on one hand. *Melancholia.* Gilles had pinned it beside a photograph of myself because it reminded him of me, he said. The angel and I both projecting glum inertia.

"I'm not melancholy," I objected. I hated the word. It sounded medieval. Victims of the four humors—phlegm, choler, blood and dark bile—roaming the land of the black sun. I was rather fond of this brooding angel with a flower wreath sitting askew on her head.

He had also pinned up several photographs he had taken of Jonathan and me. Recent ones—close-ups of a hand, a bare shoulder, part of a child's face—gave the impression that Jonathan and I were slipping out of frames. "Why don't you include more pictures of yourself with Jonathan?" I asked. "There's only one here and it's not even recent." It was one I'd taken a good three years before of him tossing an eight-month-old Jonathan in the air, in the split second before catching him, our son's face released by laughter and surprise.

"You never take pictures of me and Jonathan," Gilles said.

"I never think of it, actually. Jonathan is with me all day, I don't need to take pictures of him. Anyway, you're a better observer than I am."

"Oh, I don't know about that. I'm not with you all day and you don't take pictures of me."

"I never think of you as being that far away. I don't need a camera to see you."

"Oh? And I need one to see you? Here I thought I was taking pictures of you and Jonathan because I love you."

"And the photographs. You love the photographs."

He took his camera everywhere. He couldn't wait to have his films developed so he could discover the surprises that would have remained undetected had he not taken the pictures. It wasn't unlike therapy, he'd once said, in that you had to catch the moment.

"Did you see this one? Isn't it strange?" Gilles handed me a shot he'd taken at an amusement park a week before: the three of us standing in front of one of those convex mirrors that warp and distort reflections. He was standing behind me and Jonathan, camera to one eye, the three of us laughing at our undulated shapes. We could have been trapped under a distorting surface, like water, yet we appeared to be having such a good time. Why had Gilles taken this particular photograph? I wondered. What had he seen?

"Do you think you see the real me?" I blurted. I wasn't sure what I meant or if it had anything to do with the photograph. It might have had something to do with a sentence I'd read recently in a book I had seen on his desk. The author was the famous French feminist Julie Aubert, whose face on the back cover beamed with self-assurance at her invisible audience. "You should read it," Gilles suggested, but I had only glanced through it. I could understand Aubert's French only enough to confirm my linguistic and intellectual inadequacies. Except for the one sentence that had jumped out at me as I flipped through the pages. It circled in my head for days. "Freud," Aubert had written, "did not analyze women but representations of women."

"I think I see you pretty clearly," Gilles said. "But for the sake of argument, do you see the real me?" He must have done this with his patients all the time, throwing questions back to them, giving them the impression they were arriving at their own solutions.

"Oh sure. But I love you in spite of it."

"You think you're pretty smart, don't you?"

I was sitting across from him on the floor and he rolled over the books and pamphlets and clasped his arms around me. "If I told you I see your body for what it really is, would you hold it against me?" He nuzzled under my hair and ran his tongue behind my ear. It was always warm there, he said.

I tilted my head allowing his tongue to travel my neck. His hands slid under my blouse, across my breasts, to my waist, and unbuttoned my jeans. I pressed against his cupped hands as he pushed his fingers into my pubic hair. Currents still ran through me whenever he touched me there. I widened my legs and unzipped him.

"Is Jonathan asleep?" he asked.

"Yes."

"Let's go to bed…." His slackened mouth, unable to hold on to sentences, fastened itself to mine while his fingers moved past the wiry hair into hollows and folds of soft skin. I loved this. His entering me, sinking into me, filling out muscles, sliding together in one motion, the repetition of one motion, until we reached that split second when the world narrowed itself to the two of us, and we let ourselves fall until all sense of time and place disappeared.

Legs and spines sapped, we languished on the floor. "Moving to another city must trigger unusual sexual impulses," I giggled.

"Or maybe I just love you." He gave me a playful punch on the chin then kissed the non-existent bruise.

For the first two years after we met, our lovemaking had been so unrestrained Gilles often complained his body wouldn't hold out. I suspect we both felt relieved when it subsided, although neither one of us wanted to admit it. Neither one wanting to betray, I don't know what exactly: a loving marriage, a perfect sex life? I was grateful for this new surge. The City of Love triggering the same kind of curiosity about each other as when we first met, each body a lure for the other as it tried to reorient itself.

He reached under him and removed a book and a crumpled pamphlet that Habib had left. "These have been great. We should do something to thank him, have him over for a meal or a drink. He could probably use a home meal."

"I don't want to encourage him."

"Encourage him to what?"

I hesitated. "To leave more stuff." My ineptitude, when discussing Habib, astounded me.

Perhaps I would have invited him eventually if Gilles hadn't beaten me to it. If the two men hadn't been standing in the entrance hall of the apartment a few days later, Gilles sheepish because he knew how I felt about unexpected dinner guests. "I met Habib in the lobby and asked him up for a drink."

"Yes, we've been meaning to have you over. We're just about to eat, you can join us." I gave the two men a toothy smile, the kind meant to conceal what I really thought.

"I would be honored," Habib said.

"I hope you eat *choucroute*." I had made an Alsatian-inspired casserole of cabbage, sausage and left-over ham.

Habib paused. "*Choucroute?* This is made with pig?"

"With ham."

"Ham?"

"*Du jambon.*"

"Yes. I'm sorry but I do not eat pig," Habib said with an embarrassed grin.

I glowered at Gilles, partly in exasperation, partly in victory.

"Well," Gilles said as quickly and cheerfully as he could. "We can always have a drink. Wine, vermouth, Scotch?"

"I don't drink alcohol. Water would be fine."

"I'll have Scotch, a double," I said. "There are lemons in the fridge for Habib's water. Unless you object to lemons?" I asked Habib as Gilles made a quick exit to the kitchen.

"No, I do not object to lemons," Habib replied, his tone weighed down with restraint. He turned his back to me in the guise of paying attention to Jonathan. "*Bonjour, Jaune-a-tant, ça va?*"

"*Oui, ça va.*" Jonathan shyly handed him a book.

"Habib can't read to you now, Jonathan. He's visiting with Mommy and Daddy. I'll read to you later." I turned to Habib. "Is it for religious reasons?" I asked.

"Pardon?"

"The reason you don't eat pork or drink alcohol."

"Yes. Religious and cultural."

"Why, exactly?"

He studied me for several seconds trying to assess whether I was truly interested or merely facetious. "It is written in the Koran," he said finally.

The ease and familiarity he'd shown in the park had disappeared. I, on the other hand, felt relatively more in control. It was easier to hold his gaze and confront its suggestiveness on my own turf.

"Yes, I would guess it's written in the Koran, but why? My husband, whose family is Catholic, told me that up to a few decades ago Catholics couldn't eat meat on Fridays because at one point in history few people ate fish so the Church decided to help the fishermen by forbidding meat once a week. It was a practical decision yet it became church doctrine and, for centuries, eating meat on Friday was a sin. A mortal sin, which was a shame since fish became associated with eternal damnation, turned everybody off it when, in fact, it's better for you than meat." Why was I rambling? "I was wondering if there were similar reasons why Muslims can't eat pork or drink alcohol?"

"No. It is for health. Mohammed worried of the health of his followers."

"I see." I turned to Gilles, who was returning with the drinks. "Habib was saying he doesn't drink alcohol or eat pork because Mohammed didn't think it was healthy." My sarcasm was as palpable as the scent of ham and cabbage permeating the room.

"I see, well, to all our health then," Gilles said and lifted his glass of Scotch to Habib's glass of water but avoided looking in my direction. Avoiding each other's eyes in awkward situations was our shorthand to a mutual understanding. Otherwise we would have dissolved into a fit of giggles. "You're a religious person, are you?" Gilles asked.

"Not as religious as my mother wants me to be. She is a true Muslim but I am a lazy Muslim," Habib replied, dismissively. "Madame tells me you are a psychoanalyst?"

The quick redirection took Gilles by surprise. It appeared that Habib didn't want to expand on his religious standing. "Yes. Yes, that's right. Doing research at the moment," Gilles replied.

"It is interesting?" Habib asked.

"I suppose it is. Lots of interest in psychoanalysis in France at the moment."

The two men obviously didn't know what to say to each other; the pauses between their questions were interminable. I set myself a deadline. If no one spoke within the next ten seconds I would announce dinner and force Habib to leave.

"What about Tunisia? Any interest in psychoanalysis there?" Gilles asked before I had the chance to get to ten.

"I am not aware of it," said Habib. Another pause, until a

faint smile played around his mouth as he added, "We don't need it, we have Islam."

I wasn't sure how we were expected to react. Was he allowed to joke about his religion and were we allowed to laugh? I looked to Gilles but he either chose to ignore the ironic intent of Habib's remark or missed it entirely. "What happens to the mentally ill?" he asked, rather disingenuously.

"We make prophets out of them," Habib replied and broke into laughter made giddy from being held in too long. "Monsieur, we have mental hospitals like anybody else," he added with vindicated patience.

I couldn't blame him. I wanted to apologize, at least indirectly, for having been so rude earlier. "Your mother may think you're lazy, but from what you told me in the park, you work all the time."

"Physically I am not lazy. Spiritually, perhaps a little. I am not ... an example."

"Exemplary." I liked correcting a man with such incontestable self-assurance.

"Yes, exemplary. If I were religious, I would be a Sufi, but I am too much of the world."

"A Sufi. Interesting," Gilles exclaimed, sensing an opportunity for at least a few more minutes of conversation. "Sufism is based on a different interpretation of the Koran, isn't it?"

"The *principes* are from the Holy Koran, yes. Different groups developed different rules but they still follow the spiritual ... personality of Mohammed."

"Why do you like it?" I asked.

"Direct experience, madame. A Sufi believes that the teachings of the Prophet are ... how do you say ... *renforcés?*"

"Reinforced, strengthened."

"Reinforced through direct experience," Habib continued. "They believe this can conduct to perfection."

"Lead to perfection? Human perfection? That's rather

optimistic, isn't it?" I was starting to feel the full effect of my double Scotch.

Habib shrugged. "I am an optimist, madame."

"Would this be the kind of perfection based on deprivation? On the condition that people deny themselves everything enjoyable?" I asked.

"Deprivation?"

"Gilles, how do you say 'deprivation' in French?"

"*S'infliger des privations*," Gilles explained to Habib. I couldn't help but smile at Gilles's choice of the word "inflict." He got up and went into the kitchen to make more drinks.

"Sufis do not think this is privation. They exchange acquisitions of the world for certain other kinds." He was pronouncing most of his words in French. *Certain. Acquisition.* "But this is not experienced as *privation*."

"What other kinds of acquisitions? Can you give me an example?"

"Perception. A Sufi gives up acquisitions for a simpler life so he can have better perception." *Perception.*

"I see. An uncluttered life in exchange for better perception. What about you? How are your powers of perception?"

"I perceive quite well. Madame would be surprised."

No, madame would not be surprised at all. I was already aware of how little got past him. "Can you give an example?" I insisted.

"An example?"

"Yes. Of your powers of perception."

It was a little odd asking a guest I hardly knew to reach into thin air and produce tangible proof of his Sufic powers much as a magician would a bouquet of crepe flowers. He hesitated, then with the same mischief as before, he said, "Right now I perceive you are uncomfortable, *un peu gênée*, because you did not know your husband invited a stranger for dinner who doesn't eat pig or drink alcohol and you wish he would leave."

His candor caught me off guard and I responded with

spurious objections that sounded ludicrous. "Oh, no, no. Not at all. I really don't mind." I was mortified that I had been so transparent and so objectionable.

He smiled at me. "I also perceive a happy family," he added. He glanced around the apartment. "You have made changes."

"A few, nothing major. I wish I could have done more." I didn't care at all for the Louis-Something furniture: gilded commodes, fluted legs, a Gobelin-type tapestry over the dining-room sideboard. The pink velvet chairs and divan in the living room sat lower than normal furniture and I pictured women in towering, powdered wigs, wearing voluminous skirts with panniers jutting at the hips, trying to glide gracefully off the settee.

In an attempt to overcome the unhinged feeling of living in someone else's space, I had draped the back of one chair with a shawl my mother had given me when I was pregnant, and which I'd never worn. I also covered the velvet settee with Rose's wedding gift, a quilt depicting fat cupids aiming arrows at satin appliqué hearts. No scraps of old clothing had gone into the making of this quilt, Rose had bragged. The glossy new material, meant to wrap Gilles and me in its sensual texture, was also meant to offset the austerity of the marital bed my father and brothers had made for us. "Just because your father made your bed doesn't mean you have to lie in it," Rose had whispered in my ear.

I had replaced a few somber paintings with lively prints— Riopelle, Gilles's favorite, and Frankenthaler and Rothko, my favorites. I had also scattered oversized cushions here and there and covered the dining-room table with a crocheted tablecloth from my godmother.

"It is comfortable, *très sympa*," Habib said.

Gilles had returned with more drinks but wasn't saying much, his mind probably somewhere else as it often was when I was doing most of the talking. It frustrated me to no end that he could undercut my presence simply by not paying attention. He always denied he did this, so that even my frustration was invalidated. I tried to bring him back into the conversation. "It all sounds very mystical, this Sufism, doesn't it, Gilles? And a little joyless, don't you think?"

Before Gilles could respond, Habib jumped in. "Mystical? Perhaps. But joyless? I do not think so. Sidi Bou Saïd, where you are going, was founded because of its beauty. Abou Saïd Al Béji chose it as a place of meditation because of the extraordinary view over the gulf. Sufis search beauty. You will love it there. When you see it you will understand."

"Really?" Gilles said, suddenly very animated. "The person heading the philosophy department where I'm doing some of my research spent two years writing a book there. He was telling me just today what an inspirational place it is."

"It is, monsieur. Your *séjour* in Tunisia will be just as inspiring." He turned to me. "Monsieur tells me you're leaving in two weeks?"

"Yes, the three of us leave on June the fifteenth. The material you gave us has been very helpful. We both want to thank you." It was past dinnertime and I decided I might as well accommodate his dietary quirks. "Would you eat with us if I made you an omelet? A cheese omelet and a salad?"

"Certainly. It would please me very much."

"I want a cheese omelet too, Mommy. I don't want pig." From the moment Habib had entered the apartment Jonathan had settled beside him, working his way under Habib's arm, pushing books at him.

Gilles cleared his throat. "Habib was telling me he'll be working in Tunis for the summer. Since Tunis is next door to Sidi Bou Saïd, he offered to drop in on you and Jonathan after I leave, if he has time."

I couldn't believe my ears. "You asked Habib to check on me?"

"No, Amy. I did not ask him to check on you." He turned to Habib and smiled apologetically. "I said I was worried about leaving you and Jonathan there and he was kind enough to offer. Even if the house is perfectly safe, he can make sure you won't be bothered by anyone. For God's sake, Amy, don't be so rude."

"I am sorry, Habib, but my husband is forcing me to be rude, springing this on me now. I don't know how many times we've gone over this. I'm telling you, I'll be fine. The caretakers come every day, they'll even stay overnight if I want. And I have a friend from Canada coming in July."

"Aisling is coming for sure? When did you hear?" Gilles asked.

"I got her letter today."

"Great. I'll feel much better if she's there. But it doesn't prevent Habib from dropping in to make sure everything is okay if he happens to be around, right, Habib? There's safety in numbers."

"Clichés don't become you, Gilles." I turned to Habib, who was obviously amused by the squabbling. "My husband thinks I'm going to a barbaric country and I need protection."

"For Christ's sake, Amy."

"Not barbaric, madame. But Tunisian men don't always know how to act toward Western women. They can be very persistent."

So I've noticed, I wanted to add. "I'll be fine. My friend is joining me in July and I hear the house is very private. Under no circumstance do I expect you to check on me. I am an adult even if my husband tends to treat me like a child sometimes." I gave him a mechanical smile to convey that the reprimand wasn't directed at him so much as at Gilles. "I think we should eat now. It's almost Jonathan's bedtime."

They exasperated me, these men. I could hear them from the kitchen discussing the matter in French but couldn't make out what they were saying exactly. Discussing my obstinacy, no doubt. The subject of Habib checking on me in Tunisia didn't resurface during dinner but I had the distinct feeling I hadn't heard the last of it.

Children and Other Offerings

A DRIVE ACROSS FRANCE AND ITALY should create lasting impressions, but much of it was a blur of mountains, valleys, bodies of water and foreign names on a map. "If we miss the ferry in Naples we're screwed," Gilles said. "You have to make reservations weeks in advance to get on one of those things. I want plenty of time to settle you in when we get to Sidi Bou Saïd." There would be other opportunities to see more of France and Italy, he kept reassuring me, the promise that dazzled tourists always make. I couldn't imagine when that would be, as we hurtled through French and Italian landscapes singing along to the Temptations' "Papa Was a Rollin' Stone" on the radio.

On the first day, we stopped for a picnic of cheese, baguette, pears and wine, one of Gilles's favorite lunches. Then a late dinner of bouillabaisse at a restaurant overlooking the Paillon River dividing Old Nice from the modern part of town, a must according to our *Guide Bleu*. Jonathan ate nothing but spaghetti, which he pronounced "pasghetti," throughout Italy. We were typical tourists, but all those church spires projecting above the countryside were new to me. As was the pervasive smell of the sea in Genoa.

By the time we got to Florence, we were well ahead of schedule. We spent two nights and two days there and we must have seen every painting ever done of the Virgin Mary. I found them quite beautiful at first until they all began to meld into one insipid image.

"All that resignation and tenderness is sickening," I

complained to Gilles. I preferred paintings of women whose faces reflected their real lives more accurately. "This isn't how people see mothers."

"That's how they wanted to see them. You've said yourself men don't see women for who they truly are." He grinned as he always did when he thought he had scored one over me.

It was easy to fall under Italy's spell, and I wished that we could spend more time there. Gilles agreed we should visit Casa Guidi in Florence where Elizabeth Barrett Browning had lived with her husband. In a course on women's poetry six years earlier, I'd been so impressed that a woman would write about a subject as mundane as the apartment she lived in. The windows, I remembered, opened directly onto a beautiful church, a sidewalk's width across the street: "I heard last night a little child go singing 'neath Casa Guidi windows by the church. O bella Libertà, O bella!"

From Florence to Naples, the gnarled trunks of olive trees hobbling in every direction made the countryside look venerable. Leaves shimmering like silver cloth. We avoided Rome and followed the little towns along the Tyrrhenian Coast. Idle young men tending black-haired goats. Solemn women sitting in front of their houses as if waiting. We boarded the ferry in Naples at noon, the port frenzied and overcast with pollution. But within minutes at sea, the heavens opened and light swept down into a cauldron of clear and shimmering water and air.

"So, what do you think?" Gilles asked, his eyes sparkling with excitement.

"I can't quite believe we're doing this. Paris, Italy, Tunisia. It's surreal. I love it." And I loved Gilles for making it possible.

"Pretty amazing. We really must go back to Florence one day. Which was your favorite painting, of all the ones we saw?"

"My favorite painting? That's hard to say." I thought for a few moments. "I guess the one I loved best was the Martini at the Uffizi."

"Which one? There were several."

"The one where Gabriel interferes with Mary's reading to announce she's about to become the Mother of the Son of God, her book fallen by her side. Her down-in-the-mouth expression saying, 'I don't want any part of your cockamamie plan.' You know that Mary never picked up that book again, never finished it."

"Unusual painting since most women wouldn't have known how to read in Martini's time. With so many theorists writing on the maternal these days I'm surprised this painting hasn't come up."

"You should do a paper on it," I suggested.

"Why don't you? Maybe you need to change your thesis. You could work on all those madonnas."

"Nah ... it's the last thing I want to do in Tunisia. I'm going to spend the next couple of months lolling in the sun, thinking of you doing research in hot and polluted Paris." I ducked as he tried to swat me on the head.

Perched above the Mediterranean, one of many links in a chain of Tunis suburbs stretching along the northern shore, Sidi Bou Saïd curled around itself like a snail shell. Dr. Roussel had neglected to mention that the narrow, angled streets of the old town made it impossible to drive directly to the house. After half an hour of circling, Gilles finally asked a growing string of children following the car where we could park. With great confidence the children took charge, showed us where to leave the car, appropriated the luggage and Jonathan, and led the way to the Roussel house a few minutes' walk away.

Although we'd read that the town had long been a favored retreat for government officials and the conservative well-to-do, it had managed to escape the disfigurements of most summer havens and gaudy tourist resorts. It wound around cobbled streets hugging walls and white houses with blue shutters and balconies with filigreed grilles. Everything white and blue, the blue intensified by the whiteness all around, vibrating within its own particular light.

"I feel like an intruder," Gilles whispered. The children pressed a buzzer beside two studded doors and an eye peered through a small opening. After the eye and Gilles had exchanged a few words, the doors opened. The eye belonged to the caretaker, M. Maalouk, a stern man standing beside a broadly smiling woman, Mme Maalouk. A large tree with what appeared to be small green figs stooped over an elaborately tiled center courtyard. Potted plants had been grouped here and there.

It seemed inconceivable that the same people who owned the formal apartment in Paris also owned this house in Sidi Bou Saïd. Modest in size, white, cubic and domed, it sat high above the sea, and the only sound came from crests of waves breaking and sighing below. A neon chameleon moved like mercury along one of the walls.

Inside, each room bristled with light, the sharp line of the sun cutting across the floor, stripping the walls to a glare absorbed by rugs, flatweaves, geometric kilims, the furniture upholstered in brocades and stripes, the overall effect a mix of modern and rococo. I loved it. It lacked the formality of the apartment in Paris and the usual monotony that makes everyday living practical but bland. The entire house beamed in a luminous tranquility. I wondered if the rooms ever closed their eyes.

The founder that Habib had mentioned in Paris, Abou Saïd, had come to live in the area until his death in the thirteenth century and a town had grown around his tomb. I imagined the view from the terrace through the gaze of a visionary and understood why Abou Saïd had come and stayed. Freed from gravity, his heart and mind must have leapt then nested there. His days spent meditating or presiding over theological discussions and prayers or, with distracted tenderness, redressing injustices and performing miracles when necessary. In solitude, unconstrained by the presence or absence of others, unafraid of seclusion or silence, feeling no need of companionship or love, he moved closer to his idea of perfection.

Intense heat skimmed my face leaving salty impressions on my lips. "This may just be my promised land," I said to Gilles, not realizing it was the other way around: my idea of the promised land was shaping itself to this new space.

Aware that our time together here was short, we planned different activities for each day, but also reserved blocks of time for the solace of routine, much needed even when on holidays. If we stayed home in the morning, Gilles and Jonathan went to the beach before the sun got too hot. I also went a few times but since I burned so easily I usually watched from the terrace as they wound their way down. Gilles teaching Jonathan how to swim, a Tom Thumb frog in gilded waters from my bird's-eye view.

After sightseeing we usually dropped in at one of two cafés for pine nut tea in the late afternoon. Either to the mysterious Café des Nattes where Jonathan played with an old abacus on the counter for as long as he wanted, or to the spectacular terraces of Café Sidi Chabanne set into a cliff over the marina, below the shredded clouds over the Bay of Carthage. Jonathan always insisted we stop for a *bonbalouni* doughnut on our way home. He learned and retained the names of desserts the first time he saw them. They were his major discoveries wherever we went. In Paris it was the dessert carts, the mobile panorama of butter creams and petits fours. On Valentine's we let him select our desserts and to our delight he chose three white heart-shaped molds of creamy cheese and raspberry purée. He was so proud and pleased when I told him it was the best choice he could have made because it was like swallowing spoonfuls of silken heart.

In Tunisia, he didn't have to search very long since there

were sweet shops everywhere. I couldn't tell a *briovat* from a *sellou*, but after only a few visits in any one shop my four-year-old child could rhyme them off without any prompting as he pointed to the honeyed orange and red pyramids, his eyes anticipating their charged and sugary glow. As far as Gilles and I could tell, he was never disappointed.

Carthage, a twenty-minute walk from the house, was a bustling suburb of highways, airport, government houses and a few ruins. To perceive in those ruins the splendor of powerful and magnificent societies required more than a knowledge of history or a few tourist brochures. It required faith and imagination, easily summoned when one stood on Byrsa Hill on bright June mornings or afternoons, watching Cape Gammarth spool dunes into the sea.

I imagined that the ruins, a grid system of stone foundations, were pretty much as they must have been after the fire destroyed the original city more than two thousand years ago. Gilles pointed to a cistern extending beneath what he thought was once a courtyard. "Pretty fancy work." A necropolis, cut into the hillside, revealed several graves.

As we walked along Rue Hannibal, Gilles took my hand. "We are strolling through history," he said. He was having such a good time. "It's only a few minutes to the Tophet," he said to Jonathan, as if Jonathan would know, or cared, what a Tophet was.

It was the name given to an open-air area where Phoenicians and Carthaginians had offered children in sacrifice to the protecting gods of the city. When we got there, we discovered the area had been cordoned off by an American archaeological team in the process of excavating new sections of the field. We weren't allowed inside the cordoned areas but, when it became clear we wouldn't leave, one of the archaeologists walked over. An affable man, he explained that the work should have been completed by now, but the site had proven more difficult than anticipated.

The archaeological team was sifting through six to seven hundred years of burials for tombstones and pottery urns in which the Carthaginians buried the bones and ashes of sacrificed children, from newborns to four-year-olds. A few of the urns had been found whole but were so fragile a mere nudge could shatter them. Two workers were carefully packing them for a model of a burial site for a museum.

He showed us the contents of some of the pots: tiny bones, some in the shape of levers, some of wishbones, others sections of a small, collapsed pillar, the pieces scattered in the palm of the archaeologist's hand. "Are those vertebrae?" I asked.

"Seems like it," Gilles said.

I pointed to a mound of bones on the ground. "Isn't that a skull?"

"Can't be more than a year old," Gilles said.

"There's a hole in it. It must have been cracked."

"No," Gilles replied. "That would have been the anterior fontanelle. It hadn't closed yet."

The pulsations at the top of Jonathan's head when he was a baby had reminded me of rising water in a fountain and I'd been struck at how easily his small skull could have been emptied of its substance.

The archaeologist pointed to a row of tombstones outside the cordoned area. "There are so many we can't get at them all," he said. Stelae, he called them, each one bearing symbols, some so faint they were almost impossible to make out. He ran his finger along the outline of a figure resembling a paper doll with a circle head, two stick arms on either side of a triangular body. Tanit was the paper-doll goddess to which children were sacrificed to appease the gods in times of crisis such as bad weather or war, and to honor a religious belief that firstborns were best returned to the gods since they were naturally theirs by right. But there might have been economic and social factors too, the archaeologist explained.

The ruling class wanted to keep its wealth from being distributed among too many heirs. One stela depicting a priest carrying a frantic child to its sacrifice was going to the Bardo Museum in Tunis.

"I hate this," I whispered to Gilles. "I don't need to know this." No matter how long ago these sacrifices had been carried out, nothing could justify killing children, especially under some religious pretense that firstborns should be returned to the gods.

"It's history, Amy," he said. He picked a wild flower sprouting against one of the stelae and pushed the stem through a buttonhole of my blouse. "We can't avoid history." The red flower, plucked from an overgrown garden rooted in layers of earth and urns, from a long succession of bloodlines and bones, bobbed in agreement as it arched toward my heart.

We thanked the archaeologist and were about to leave when I noticed white shapes rising from a few of the excavated cross-sections inside the cordoned area. Perfect shapes of urns and one of a musical instrument, a small triangular harp. All of them too white and intact to have been in the earth for hundreds of years.

"What are those?" I asked.

"Sometimes we come across holes in the earth indicating that an artifact was also buried there. It might have been made of unfired clay or wood which rotted or dissolved over time, like that little harp over there, leaving a perfect mold in the earth around it. We pour plaster into the hole, let it dry, then dig around it and get a clear impression of the empty space."

They were so eerie, these ghostly imprints released after so many centuries, especially the little harp, which could have fallen from heaven. "Was one side of the harp carved in the shape of an animal?" I asked.

"Yes, a horse," the archaeologist replied. "The parents might have wanted the child to be accompanied by music as it traveled on its journey on a horse."

"Mommy, is that the harp you said I would see in the Bois de Boulogne?" Jonathan asked. "The one angels play?"

"Yes, Jonathan. I guess it is."

"But you said only angels and children could see them."

"That's why the archaeologist had to pour plaster into the mold. So we could see it too," I said, holding on to his hand, his pliable, four-year-old bones safely locked in mine.

The day before Gilles was to leave, he decided on one more trip, a drive to the ruins of a Roman amphitheater at El Jem. Though smaller than the Colosseum in Rome, according to Gilles's guidebook it was the most impressive Roman monument in Africa.

"What's an amphitheater?" Jonathan asked, disheartened at having to spend another day seeing sights.

"What's an amphitheater?" Gilles repeated because he also enjoyed listening to the stories I invented for Jonathan.

"It's where people held circuses in the old, old days."

"What kind of circus? What did they do?" Jonathan asked.

"All kinds of neat things." I couldn't very well tell him about Christians being thrown to the lions or Roman gladiators hacking each other to death. "Let's see. The Romans had races in gold chariots."

"What's chariots?"

"Little carriages pulled by horses. That's how people traveled in those days. But they also raced them. Like when you race your tricycle with your friends."

"I don't have friends."

"What a silly thing to say. Of course you have friends."

"I don't see them. They're in Canada."

"You'll see them again soon. And you'll be able to tell them about all the neat things you've seen here. You can tell them about a place where shiny black panthers used to pull gold chariots full of monkeys. And lions who carried rabbits in their paws and let them go when they were told, without even hurting them."

"Is that true, Daddy? Do lions do that?" Jonathan didn't seem as credulous of late and often checked the accuracy of my yarns with his father.

"Absolutely."

"What else, Mommy?"

"Elephants who could write the entire alphabet in the sand with their trunks."

Even Gilles couldn't help chuckling at this one.

The sight, as we approached, was spectacular but also spooky. The three semi-circular tiers that once held more than thirty thousand people were now rows of archways in different stages of deterioration against an unclouded sky.

The people who traveled by foot to El Jem centuries ago didn't come merely for animal tricks. At some point someone must have come up with the idea of teaming the writing elephant with another beast, perhaps one with a horn in the middle of its forehead. "A rhinoceros," someone in the stands might have whispered just before the rhinoceros rammed its horn into the belly of the unsuspecting elephant, and the crowd roared. They came to see dancing bears goaded into fighting buffaloes, taunted by men who shot arrows into them. They came to see lions in cages raised from the lower levels to the main area by pulleys manned by slaves. On opening day of the amphitheater of El Jem, five thousand lions had been slaughtered, their carcasses dumped into deep excavations along with human bodies.

A warm breeze sighed through the missing doors of the upper tiers and down my neck. I'd seen enough but Gilles wanted to take photographs. As he clicked away I imagined murmurs sifting through the absent crowd: "Cyprian to the lions." The inflationary spiral of expectations escalating into a roar: "*Bene lava!*" Wash yourself well in blood. The emperor disdainfully waving his handkerchief or raising his thumb to seal a gladiator's fate. A poet in the stands writing poems about love or how to pick up girls at the games.

As we drove away, the amphitheater's skeletal presence seemed as mysterious and indestructible as some indelible truth. "This place gives me the creeps," I said. "Whenever we come across something great we discover something sinister behind it. History is so depressing. I don't know why we bother visiting these places."

"History's here to stay, Amy. Whether we like it or not. You of all people should understand that."

I half expected him to launch into his "psychoanalysis is the outcome of history and the past is only a prefiguration of the future" speech again. "Why 'me of all people'?" I asked, feigning ignorance.

"An art history major? History is our map. That's where we come from. Genetic, personal, cultural. It's who we are. It's what makes civilization."

"Throwing people to lions isn't part of my civilization." Insignificant Amelia Legate Gérard, raised on a farm, wasn't about to be caught in someone else's peculiar idea of entertainment.

"Civilization doesn't begin at the Canadian border, Amy. Or on a certain day, at a certain time."

"But nobody ever learns, it's so discouraging."

"Someone at school calls it 'the ancient proliferation of errors.' But I think we do learn."

"Nothing ever changes. Except maybe to get worse."

"We have to believe in better possibilities."

From the day I'd met him I'd relied on Gilles for clarity and it still surprised me when he couldn't provide it. "I think we've exhausted all our possibilities," I said.

"We have to imagine new ones."

"I don't know.... Isn't that what Hitler did?"

"Jesus, you're in a mood today. Okay. So what if Hitler had

had a different vision? What if he'd wanted to do good instead of evil?"

"He thought he was doing good. He was mad, Gilles. Visions are easy when you're mad."

"That's why we have to consider all possibilities, including madness. We have to envision different outcomes in case we're ever faced with another Hitler."

I didn't care for his pronoun "we." It made me complicitous in someone else's lunacy. How effective would I have been against evil on Hitler's scale? Against gladiatorial combat or a society sacrificing firstborns? Gilles expected too much from the imagination. I wanted mine within boundaries I could control. I couldn't wait to get back to the beautiful house behind the studded door and the eight-foot fence. Tomorrow I would be alone with Jonathan, away from man-eating lions and Tophets, from concepts so worn by time there was nothing to relate to but reprehensible ghosts of little harps and children in the shape of wishbones.

"Amy…" Gilles hesitated. "Speaking of possibilities, I don't feel right leaving you here. I think you should reconsider and drive back with me to Paris."

I moaned. "I don't want to go over this again. Why does staying on my own upset you so much?"

"That's not what worries me. I'm afraid you'll sell the Roussel furniture on some crazy impulse." He was jokingly referring to my selling most of our furniture to two of his graduate students, who were newly married and renting our house on Palmerston Gardens in Toronto. Neither of us had planned on period furniture when we chose the durable dark tweed for the living room, and the sturdy, knobby legs for the walnut dining set, but the co-ordinated effect gave the overall impression of something between English Windsor and early Sears. It implied a compromise I couldn't wait to escape.

When the graduate couple commented on how much they liked it, I spontaneously asked if they would be interested in buying it. Except for the old Quebec pieces from Gilles's family, and the bedroom set my father and brothers made us as a wedding gift. They could pay for it each month with their rent so when they moved to their own place they would already have their furniture, I told them, avoiding the stunned expression on Gilles's face.

"I won't sell the Roussel furniture but I may steal it. I just love that stuff." Worn leather chairs next to an alcove done up in oriental reds. The kitchen with all its strange implements and five different ceramic tiles on walls, ceiling, floors. The bed in the main bedroom sat on a dais, the walls and a banquette covered with tapestries and cushions. The overall effect eclectic, foreign, as if entering into someone else's vision of how everyday life should be lived.

"For all we know it could be dangerous for a woman to be here alone. We may be tempting fate."

Neither one of us had ever admitted to believing in fate, although I could see how Gilles would have to, to a certain extent, what with all those psychoanalytical theories based on myths. How did these myths differ from destiny? I often wondered. "Don't think of it as tempting fate, just revising it a little," I said, trying to sound cheerful without being flippant.

"We have to consider all the possibilities. Things could go wrong."

"You just finished saying we have to imagine better possibilities. Of course things could go wrong. Things can always go wrong. It'll be different. Probably more than I ever dreamed. Chances are I'll run into problems. But we've been here almost three weeks and it's quiet and friendly, certainly friendlier than Paris. Everyone we talk to says it's perfectly safe. I have an eight-foot wall surrounding me, and the Maalouks said they would stay in the house if I wanted." I had no intention of having the Maalouks around but offered it as additional assurance. "Chafia is twenty feet away and Aisling will be here in a couple of weeks. I'm not going to take unnecessary risks. So why can't we see what happens, instead of worrying about what could happen? Just this once, I want to be responsible for my life."

"We're also responsible for him." He nodded toward Jonathan, who was busy scribbling and sketching on his Magic Pad, a writing tablet covered with a transparent sheet on which he traced with a small stick. Once he'd filled the tablet or wanted to erase something, he pulled up the top sheet and the tracings disappeared.

"I would never do anything to jeopardize Jonathan," I said.

"I know, I know. It's just … I'll miss you."

"No, you won't. You don't know I'm around half the time."

"That's not true."

"So stay then. You've said this was a great opportunity for us. Stay for the rest of the summer."

"I've committed myself to these conferences, I can't back out now." He'd been talking a lot lately about a paper he was writing on the influence of various disciplines on the discourse of psychoanalysis—philosophy, anthropology, social theory, feminism.

"Then go. You either stay or you go."

"It's not so simple."

"Actually it is, Gilles. It's that easy. Anyway, the change will do us both good."

"Have we reached that stage then?"

"What stage?"

"When being apart is better than being together?"

"It's only for a few weeks. I don't understand why you're so concerned about this."

"You've never traveled. Never on your own."

So this was it. He still thought of me as the innocent farm girl incapable of making my way in the world. He had tried to shield me ever since we'd met. Never letting me drive in the city unless it was absolutely necessary and even then he would meticulously trace the appropriate route on a map in case I got lost. He kept telling me I had no sense of direction. I couldn't help but wonder if his concern didn't mask something else.

"I have to do this, Gilles. Except for university, I've never done anything on my own. You're always talking about opportunities and this is the greatest one *I*'ve ever had. I can't keep living your life."

I could tell my remark about living his life hadn't gone over that well. "I thought this was *our* life," he said.

"Look, you want to be in Paris working on papers and conferences and I want to be here. Compromise would do neither one of us any good right now. So I stay and you go." The confidence in my voice sounded good. I hadn't been this assertive in a long time.

"I'll be worried sick."

"You won't. You'll be too busy."

"I'm not turning out to be such a great husband, am I? Or father. For all my highfalutin theories about fatherhood, I don't spend enough time with Jonathan."

I was not about to get into a discussion on any possible discrepancy between his work and his role as husband and father. I knew I was going to stay, whatever he said, but I didn't want to ruin our last night together. "You do in your own way. You're there when we need you, when it matters."

"I should be there all the time."

"Nobody can be there all the time. I wouldn't want you there all the time."

"We'll go back to the Bardo when I return. Maybe the desert."

"Sure, that would be great. Aisling will have gone by then and I'd rather go with you."

The one afternoon we'd spent at the Bardo Museum had been hardly enough time for us to skim its encyclopedic collections. A former palace, built over several centuries, it was surrounded by gardens filled with Punic stones and Roman mosaics, and housed dozens of collections—Punic, Islamic, Christian, Dougga—of bronze and marble figures, furniture, jewelry and coins dating from the first century BC. One of Gilles's favorite rooms was filled with intricate and brightly colored mosaics, geometric designs, floral patterns, scenes of daily life, faces, animals and mythological figures. The largest and most startling mosaic depicted Oceanus, a wild Neptune figure. In spite of the shells, lobster claws and weeds caught in his tangled hair and beard, it reminded me of Habib.

"It will be the first time since we've met that we'll be apart," Gilles said.

"I know. It's time."

"I'll miss you. And Jonathan," he repeated.

"We'll miss you too."

"I'll call Chafia as soon as I get to Paris." The Roussel house didn't have a telephone but the doctor had told us the woman next door didn't mind if we used hers for emergencies.

"Everything will be fine, Gilles." I moved closer to him.

We hardly slept that night, turning to each other again and again, sensing something was about to change. Each body caught in the grip of a turbulence where it could find no foothold.

Jonathan

THE NEXT MORNING, after an hour of uncertain goodbyes, I dragged myself back to bed, the seclusion I'd craved blossoming into panic. What had I done? What was I doing in this foreign place, in a house so overexposed to the sun that all resemblances of myself—daughter, student, wife, lover—had vanished? I was so exhausted I could barely tend to Jonathan.

"Mommy," he kept nudging me, "what's wrong?"

"Nothing's wrong, Jonathan. Mommy's just a little tired right now." My listlessness could barely form words. I had only been on my own a few hours and freedom was turning me into a basket case.

A few minutes later: "Don't you want to get up now, Mommy?"

"In a little while, Jonathan. Come up on the bed and keep me company. I'll tell you a story."

He always preferred the stories I made up and he knew how to initiate them. "Why do we see things when we close our eyes? When we open our eyes we only see what we see but when we close them we see things that aren't there. Is that a dream?"

"That's right, Jonathan. When we close our eyes and go to sleep, parts of ourselves change into different shapes and those are called dreams. What do you see when you close your eyes?"

"The dark."

"Yes, the dark behind our eyelids can be the darkest dark of all. That's why you need to put a big moon-faced moon in your sleep, especially if it's very deep. And do you know who the big moon-faced moon is?"

"No."

"It's you. The big moon-faced moon is you."

"The moonchild!" he exclaimed, making the connection to his favorite song on the album *In the Court of the Crimson King*.

"What else do you see?"

"Monsters."

"What kind of monsters?"

"Scary ones. Lions." He liked to fill his dreams with creatures that would have made Grimm proud.

"Really? But they're not scary lions because it's only you pretending to be a lion, remember? And you can't hurt yourself in your sleep. Nothing can. What about people? Do you see people, too?"

"Mmm, yes."

"Who?"

"Monsters."

"Oh, come on, Jonathan. Why would you want to put monsters in all your dreams? Don't you want to see nice people too? Friends? What about Grandma and Grandpa Legate? Mémé and Pépé Gérard?"

"Yaah … I guess …"

"So what do you all do in your dreams?"

"We sing and run. But sometimes we run too far and we get lost." He wasn't about to relinquish his flair for the morbid and the melodramatic.

"But you always find your way again because it's only a dream, remember? Remember what I once told you. When you go to sleep, always put your magic whistle under your pillow, the one Grandpa Legate made for you. If you get lost, you can play it. No matter how far you've gone, how deep or hollow your sleep is, Mommy and Daddy will hear the whistle and come and find you."

"What's hollow?"

"Hollow is a big dream-space. It's the kind of dream that is so big, you can put anything and anyone in it you want. When you wake up, you can say, 'Last night I was a teddy bear, an orange tree.' Anything. Even an elephant that can fly so high it turns into a cloud."

"Elephants can't turn into clouds," he giggled.

"Sure they can. You said when we close our eyes we can see or be anything. And nothing can hurt us."

"Do you want to get up now?"

"In a little while."

"Do you want to borrow my magic whistle? Daddy said I have to take good care of you."

I wished Gilles hadn't burdened him with the responsibility of taking care of his dysfunctional mother.

"And you are taking good care of me. Why don't you tell me a story?"

"About the lion at the circus?"

"Okay." I wondered what story he'd concocted in his head about lions and the amphitheater.

He studied his books and picked one with large shouting letters and pretended to read: "Once there was a lady who was very tired because she was a mommy and she was all alone with her child in a country far, far away. She was afraid so she sat down and played her magic whistle and she became a lion who heard the flute, so he ran away from the circus where they kill all the lions. He sat down beside her but he didn't hurt her because she was a good mommy who loved me very much and lions can't hurt mommies if they love their children in their dreams. And that's the end of the story."

It was amazing to me how much he had taken in, arranging the details of our last excursions to fit his story. Responding to the wailing sound of my unspoken fear, the fear of being alone, far away from home, for the first time in my life. "That was lovely, Jonathan. I feel much better. You know, don't you, that you're safe here. There are no lions here to hurt you."

"I know," he said, not very convincingly. Had I done anything to make him doubt this, or was he getting, for the first time, a glimpse of the world and its possibilities?

"Have I told you today that I love you very much?" Every day I made sure to ask him this. And every day he answered, "No, not today," in a voice meant to reprimand me because I'd left it too long or might be capable of forgetting.

I loved this child beyond anything or anyone. Nothing had connected me to another human being as much as giving birth to him. The discomfort of carrying him for nine months like a growing Sisyphean stone, but also the intimacy of him pressing against my stomach, testing my limits. Hearing for the first time the fetal heartbeat through the doctor's stethoscope, as if from some faraway place. The ongoing rumbling of the world.

When he was born I first noticed his hands. Wrinkled little hands reaching out, his fist unable to close on my finger. His devouring mouth, frantic, searching for my breast, his cry summoning, insisting I respond.

His helplessness terrified me at first, until I perceived, in his eyes, the irremediable: he was helpless and I was his lifeline. His contorted face a mirror in which my own vulnerability was exposed. His demands etching themselves within each and every one of my cells, changing the code that spelled out who I was, who I'd been until then.

"Well, I do love you, very very much, just like the mommy in your story." I wanted to fulfill his vision of my love for him. Reassure him that whoever else I was, besides being his mother, I would always be the magic whistle that would keep him safe from lions and sacrificial rituals. "Let's have some lunch, then we'll go to the beach, okay?"

"Yes, let's go swimming," Jonathan said as he gathered his books, satisfied that he had personally restored a measure of stability to his mother's life and kept his promise to his father.

Cicada Night

HE STOOD BEFORE ME, A DISHEVELED and thin apparition. I had received no news of him since leaving Paris, yet I wasn't all that surprised to see him. Perhaps I had known all along that one day I would hear two or three knocks, faint and hesitant, I would open the door and he would be standing there. I had not, however, expected him to fall into my arms.

"Habib. What are you doing here? You look exhausted."

"It was such a long voyage. I did not find rides easily this time." He made a movement with his hand and thumb indicating he'd been hitchhiking.

"You hitchhiked from Tunis?" It wasn't that far. I couldn't understand why he would have had trouble finding a ride.

"Pardon?"

"Hitchhike. *Du pouce.* From Tunis?" I repeated, indicating my thumb.

"No, no, from Paris."

"You hitchhiked from Paris?" I'd never heard of anyone hitching rides across continents before.

"From Paris to Marseille," he said. "I made arrangements to work on the ferry from Marseille to La Goulette but I missed it. Fortunately for me the ticket collector on the next ferry let me on after I explained what happened and I didn't have to pay. They render this service to Tunisians without money. From La Goulette I walked."

"Why would you hitchhike from Paris to Marseille? Why didn't you take a train?"

"A train costs money. *Le pouce* nothing." He seemed very proud of this.

"You had no money to come home?"

"A little. But I would not spend it on trains and ferries. I can get here for nothing. I do it every year. Both ways." My bewilderment apparently puzzled him.

Until then I had always seen him in heavier clothes, and he looked thin, almost gaunt, in a worn T-shirt and cotton pants. "Have you lost weight?" I asked.

He shrugged. "I might have lost a few kilos. I ate little since I left Paris. Or slept."

"When did you leave?" I was still trying to come to terms with how he'd managed to get to Sidi Bou Saïd.

"A week ago. It usually doesn't take so long but I missed my first ferry. Is M. Gérard still here?"

"No, he left three days ago."

"I tried to get here sooner."

"This is insane. I'll make you something to eat while you wash up." There was hardly any food in the house, but, hopefully, my compulsion to feed him would inspire some creative improvisation.

"Later. I will go swimming first. I have soap in my bag. Why don't you come?"

I was about to say that Jonathan was having a nap when he came bounding into the room, swimsuit and beach bag in hand. "I want to go swimming with Habib, Mommy." He was beside himself at the prospect of being with someone other than his brooding mother. "I want to go in the sea with Habib."

"You come also," Habib said. "You can guard him while I swim."

"Yes, Mommy, you come too," Jonathan yelled as he pulled me toward the door with one hand, clutching his beach bag with the other.

"How did you know where to find us?" I asked as we spiraled down to the sea.

"I've been here before."

"Yes, of course. I'd forgotten. Do you know the Roussels well?"

"Quite well, yes. They give me jobs. I baby-sit and run errands for them. I met Mme Roussel here, in Sidi Bou Saïd. She learned how difficult it was for me in Paris and she arranged to have a room in their building. She is a nice woman. She understands the difficulties of living in a country where you do not belong."

"She doesn't like Paris?"

"It is not her home. She is a modern woman but she is from a traditional family. A Muslim woman is not supposed to marry a man who is not a Muslim if she comes from a traditional family. There are consequences. She comes back every year. It is the only place where she feels comfortable, but she says she is now an exile in both places, Tunisia and France."

"I can see how it happens. No matter how wonderful a place is, you miss your country." I could well imagine how disorienting it must be for Mme Roussel to be living, and to know that she would go on living, in a culture that was not part of her memory. The uncanny feeling that she didn't quite belong, although her French, unlike mine, was probably flawless. It was overwhelming at times to hear Arabic spoken all around me and not to understand one word. Although speaking French was easier here than in Paris. In Paris, I had the impression that what mattered most was how I spoke, having to concentrate on the accuracy of every word. In Tunisia, I never worried about pronunciation or grammar. I didn't need to apologize for my hesitant French. When people learned I was Canadian they became more interested in what I had to say than how I said it. Since few people spoke English, my confidence grew more and more each day, people's eyes and smiles conveying understanding and encouragement.

"So, now that you've found us, I must ask you why? I thought I'd made it clear in Paris I didn't want anyone checking on me."

"I am not checking on you, Aimée." It was the first time he had addressed me without the formal *madame*. It pleased me but also made me uneasy.

"Your husband said it would be good to make a visit if I was in the … *voisinage*. You should not be angry. He worries about you."

"Oh, I know. He was very upset when he left. I don't know what it is with men, always having to rescue women. Rescue them from other men. Do you think that I'm so vulnerable?"

"Not at all. On the contrary."

"What is the contrary of vulnerable?"

"You have a—" His hands drew a space around him. "—barrier. I noticed this when I watched you in the park. I found it interesting."

"I would have thought a barrier would discourage most men."

"Some. Others see a challenge." He grinned.

"Yes. My husband always complains that we're such riddles, us women. Women and their secrets, he says. Very Freudian." Gilles must have been back in Paris now, already working on his family complex. The family as static as a dead frog, each person a means to an end. Gilles's research reminded me of something Picasso once claimed. In order to truly capture a dove in a painting you have to kill it first. I had, until recently, assumed that Gilles's research was, at least in part, propelled by his care and love for Jonathan and me. But I was beginning to wonder if it wasn't a need to isolate us so he could shape us into a better model of what a family should be. Why else would he expect a total stranger to check on us while he cocooned himself in Dr. Roussel's study?

"So you're not angry I came?" Habib asked.

"I guess not. I was getting lonely, actually. I haven't met many people and the slow pace around here needs getting used to." Since Gilles had left, each day had proceeded in a slow-motion repetition of the day before.

"You speak to no one?"

"In the shops. And Mme Maalouk. Her French is no better than mine so we get along. Her husband never speaks to me. He disapproves. A woman on her own and all that it entails, I guess. I see the woman next door occasionally. Chafia. Her daughter, Fatma, is a little older than Jonathan and they invite him to play with her and some of her friends in their pool. Her husband must travel a lot. He's away most of the week but he usually joins them on weekends. She told me she prefers staying at home to traveling."

I didn't mention the other woman who also lived there, a baby-sitter or a maid. Perhaps a friend. I'd seen the two women in the garden from the second story of the Roussel house, the friend wiping tears from Chafia's face with one hand, her other arm, long and brown, circling Chafia's waist.

I couldn't hear them from where I stood, nor would I have understood if I had, but I could see the impact the baby-sitter's words had on Chafia. They eased her sadness, consoled, appealed; finally, they extracted smiles. Two women framed within the garden walls, against flashes of blue sky and motionless foliage. I wondered what happened outside that frame when the women went inside. "I don't blame her for wanting to stay home, it's so beautiful here," I said.

Chafia's house was twice as large as the Roussels' and although I'd never been inside, the marble pool and patio alone were more imposing than anything I'd ever seen. "I don't know why you would want to live in Paris," I said to Habib. "If I belonged here I'd never want to go anywhere else."

"I don't live in Paris. I study there."

"Couldn't you study here?"

"For certain courses it is necessary to go away." Then, as if trying to convince himself, he repeated, "I had to go away for a few years. If you stay here and have no education or money, you become a fisherman or a waiter. Tunisia has generations of wait- ers working their way through a hierarchy of waiters. A nation of waiters serving tourists. It is not my destiny. Come, Jonathan, let's go in the water." He turned to me. "Are you coming?"

"Yes."

Long collar bones stretched into sharp landscapes below each shoulder as he lifted Jonathan and pretended to throw him into the water. In spite of the thinness of his body— stomach caved in, ribs a cage under taut skin—his legs were muscular and his arms strong, cutting through slivers of water as he swam away from us. He had undoubtedly developed his strength hauling all those crates around. He carried within him the shapes of his country, a geography where the elements spoke in light and shadow, vulnerability and determination.

Did he think he was catering to a tourist now, I wondered? I'd seen men his age waiting on tables in restaurants and hotels, black pants shiny with wear, their white shirts wilted. Most of them courteous but professionally distant. But also those who sent barely perceptible signals with their eyes, nods, smiles. Young men sauntering up and down the beach in the briefest swimsuits, a bottle of Fanta Orange swaying at their side; boys much too young to be flirting with middle-aged European and American women who slathered creams and oils inside their thighs and between their breasts. Or with middle-aged men. It didn't take me long to learn that a greeting or a smile should never be acknowledged, and to ignore such questions as "What's the matter, you don't like Tunisians?" Ploys to encourage conversation and more. There were the regulars who came back to the beach every day who had seen me with Gilles and Jonathan so, for the most part, they left me alone. If someone did approach me, insolent and persistent, I told him my husband was at the house and would be back soon. I often referred to Gilles when speaking to Jonathan, telling him in French that it was time to join Daddy, *viens, ton père nous attend,* and since he almost never paid attention to my French, he never contradicted me.

"You are dreaming," Habib's voice teased as he shook water from his hair over me.

Perhaps I was dreaming. The summer heat quivering above the water, the beautiful house I was living in, the town of Sidi Bou Saïd, all of it dissolving into the landscapes of novels, taking on a peculiar aura disengaged from reality. Habib and I characters in some familiar fable.

He vigorously dried off Jonathan with his towel. "You are getting too brown, my little man. You'll be mistaken for a Tunisian." Jonathan leaned against him while Habib combed his hair.

He stretched on his back, face to the sun, eyes closed.

"Will you come back to Tunisia when you finish school?" I asked.

"Of course. Why would I go anywhere else?"

"I don't know. Opportunities ..."

"I would never live anywhere else. Tunisia is my home. I was only a boy when we became a *république* in '57 but I remember the *fierté* ... of the Tunisian people. *Le peuple tunisien, c'est moi.* Tunisia needs educated men." He said all this with such conviction yet he never opened his eyes. It sounded rehearsed.

"What kind of job did you get for the summer?" He'd mentioned something in Paris but I'd forgotten. The aloofness of a few weeks ago so distant now.

"An export company. They have bought a computer and want to put their accounts on it. I will help them."

"You know about computers?"

"Not very much," he said, laughing. "But they don't know this and I will learn." After a pause he added, "I will come back to see you and Jonathan. It is very easy to get here by TGM."

Jonathan, obviously delighted at hearing this, turned to me to see if I approved.

"TGM? What's that?" I asked.

"The train from Tunis."

"It's not necessary, really. A friend from Canada is coming soon and Gilles is flying back in mid-August."

"It's not necessary but I will come back just the same," he said. His eyes opened and rested on me.

I knew, even then, that it was futile to argue. He stood up, his movements almost always decisive. "In the meantime, I have to shave off this beard. We have to go now, Jonathan," he said and extended a hand to help me up. He insisted on carrying everything—mats, towels—as he had done the first time we met in Paris, except this time he and Jonathan walked hand in hand.

He clearly intended to shave at the house and I didn't see why he shouldn't. M. Maalouk was watering the potted plants when we entered the courtyard, his usual contempt exacerbated by Habib's presence, until Habib said something to him in Arabic and he walked away muttering, shaking his head. It was the first time I had heard Habib speak Arabic. The scraping sound at the back of the throat made him sound more authoritative than when he spoke French or English.

"I'll fix you something to eat while you shave," I offered. But he wanted to go to a restaurant owned by friends.

"You and Jonathan will come too. They are good people." He almost never presented anything in the form of a question, his statements inescapable.

"But you have to eat something."

"My friends will give us dinner. A cold drink is all I want now."

I could hear him singing in Arabic above the running water, his voice high, exuberant. When he came out of the washroom I hardly recognized him: his hair was much shorter and his cheekbones and shaved chin carved where the beard had been. He looked unmasked, much younger than in Paris.

"I like it." It was exciting to be discovering him, the different aspects of him.

He grinned. "In Paris I hide behind my beard but in Tunisia I don't need to." He pressed the frosted glass of lemonade against his jaw.

The moment we walked into the restaurant a dozen people surrounded us, everyone hugging, grabbing Habib by the shoulders, standing back to confirm he was the same as last year, the same man they knew before he went away to a city that could change him irrevocably. The men called women and children from the kitchen, everyone shouting their delight. He introduced Jonathan and me. The women nodded shyly, a few of the men extended their hands, said a few words in Arabic or French and I reciprocated with a few words in French. How had he introduced us? As friends? Although one man smiled as if he suspected something more.

The people I assumed were the owners rushed us to a second-story terrace decked with flowers in blue pots. Within seconds, glasses of perfumed water appeared followed by large platters of olives, artichokes, fried fennel. This was followed by a spicy mix of roasted and mashed vegetables, *mechouia*, Habib explained, which we ate with chunks of bread. When a bowl of red paste was brought with platters heaped with couscous, Habib pointed to it and waved his fingers in a "no" sign to Jonathan. "The *harissa* is not for you, Jonathan."

"*Non, non, chtat'ha, chtat'ha,*" one of the men said as everyone laughed and Habib explained that it meant "food that makes you dance." For the entire meal he suggested what Jonathan should or should not have on his plate, and Jonathan, thrilled by the attention, heeded every word and ate foods he would never have touched otherwise.

"Tunisians are too proud of their sons," Habib said, "especially if they are blond." He often exchanged the adverb "too" for "very."

The dinner lasted over three hours, far past Jonathan's bedtime. We walked back in silence, the night thick with cicada chatter, a sleeping Jonathan slumped against Habib's shoulder, his strawberry-blond curls nestled at Habib's neck.

I knew Habib must be very tired and when we reached the house I offered him the guest room. It was inappropriate but what did it matter? Who would care?

"Thank you. It would be difficult to find a ride to Tunis tonight and it is true, I am very tired."

"I don't mind, really." I almost hoped that M. and Mme Maalouk would come around in the morning as I tried to imagine M. Maalouk's reaction.

Blood Oranges

WHEN I WOKE UP, HABIB HAD ALREADY gone out for fruit and bread and made coffee. He had also set the table, placed potted flowers from the patio at the center, and he was peeling oranges. The first time I bought blood oranges in Paris and saw their clotted veins, I threw them out thinking they had gone bad.

I hadn't slept this late in several days. "Did you sleep well?" I asked Habib.

"Very well. You must have been tired too."

I couldn't tell what was going through his mind, but I knew what was going through mine. He was moving in. Just when I thought there was no room for anyone else.

"Jonathan didn't disturb you?" I asked. "He often wakes up at night."

"He did wake me, yes, he wanted to use the *water*." He pronounced it *vateur*, as the French did. "Then he wanted to sleep in my bed."

"I'm sorry. He usually comes and sleeps with me if he wakes up. Where is he?"

"Next door with Madame Chafia. She came to say Monsieur Gérard had telephoned. He wants you to call him. She was surprised to see me here."

"I bet." A collusive smile. Gilles. He had been so quiet the one time I phoned him, somewhat preoccupied. When I complained about it, he said he was trying to accept the fact that I had chosen to stay in Tunisia instead of coming home with him. I had grown impatient and cut the conversation short.

"So what will you do today?" Habib asked. Juice ran down

his thumb inserted into the navel of a second orange he was peeling.

"I should go to the market."

"Yes, there is little to eat. I will take you. It's too late to go to the fishing boats today. Maybe tomorrow."

Tomorrow? "Don't you have a job to go to? Your family?" How strangely presumptuous he could be. Yet it was precisely this presumption that was creating an unspoken bond between us. He did it so effortlessly.

"My mother lives in Sousse. I will see her later. I don't start work until Monday. Today I am going to show you Sidi Bou Saïd." He scanned my face, uncertainty lingering in his eyes.

"What if I asked you to go? Wanted you to go now?" I heard myself saying, belligerence goaded by conflict and fear.

"Then I will go," he said in a barely audible voice and with an exaggerated shrug. "Do you want me to go?" His eyes steadied into mine.

Say yes. Say yes, I want you to go.

I should have resisted more. "No. Don't go today. Go tomorrow." My chest pounded. Inside me a door opened softly then slammed shut.

"You are certain?" he asked as he wiped his hands on a towel. Our eyes locked.

Oh, please, I wanted to shout. Don't give me another chance to change my mind or think it through. "Yes," I said and turned away. We stood for a long time without saying anything, our silence broken by the splash of water and children shouting next door. A bird kept squawking in the courtyard.

He handed me the plate with the peeled and sectioned orange. It was bitter but lively, refreshing. He placed large chunks of buttered bread drizzled with honey on a plate and poured two bowls full of coffee and warm milk. He'd made himself the host, my compliance an unspoken agreement.

"Should Jonathan come along?" I asked.

"No. Let him play until we get back. He needs to be with children, and you need time away from him."

Until then I probably would have told anyone else that I alone was responsible for Jonathan. But he was right. Jonathan was spending too much time trying to humor his mother. And I was spending too much time mothering. I needed a break.

"Tomorrow morning we'll go to the fishing boats," he reiterated. "We'll go early when the men come in with the night catch. Today we will go to the souk for lamb and eggs. I found cans of white beans in the cupboard and I will make a *malsouka*."

"I thought moussaka was Greek."

"A *mousse à quoi?*" he asked.

I started to giggle. "No, not a mousse. A moussaka. A casserole made with lamb and eggplant."

"This one is a pie made with beans. And lamb, eggs, cheese. It's for special occasions and I need to eat it."

"If you need to eat it, then you should. What's the special occasion?"

"Whatever we want it to be." He placed a hand on my neck under my hair and left it there, warm in its temporary shelter. My spine buzzed with indecipherable messages.

Everywhere we went people knew him, everyone exchanging pleasantries, sometimes in French but mostly in Arabic. As the merchants handed him packets of meat, cheese, eggs, Habib turned to me and informed me how much money to give them. As I struggled with millimes and dinars, he reached over and extracted the right amounts from my hand. I assumed he had no money and I asked if I should give him some so he could pay for the food himself but he said it wasn't necessary. At the bakery, after a short exchange, the baker disappeared and returned with sheets of gossamer-light pastry which he carefully rolled in thick, waxed paper.

As we walked through the souk from one shop to another I became aware of Habib propelling most of my moves: a graze on the back through the thinness of my dress, his hand lingering very lightly on my hip as we crossed the street. Off the main square near Café des Nattes we entered a narrow boutique packed with jewelry, rugs, incense burners, mosaics, perfumes. He asked me if I preferred the scent of ambergris or jasmine but before I could decide he bought the jasmine. And because he was short a dinar he asked me to make up the difference. He also asked me to buy something in a package, which I assumed was spice. He did this so casually, I didn't find it necessary to question it. Even if he had money, there would be no reason for him to pay for my food. After all, I had invited him to stay: he was my guest.

"What did I just buy?" I asked and pointed to the package.

"*Henné*," he said.

"Henna? Isn't it for hair?"

"It can be. Your hair attracts much attention."

"Does it? I hadn't noticed."

"Oh, yes. The men stare at it. And some women too."

I hadn't cut my hair since leaving Canada and humidity always caused it to gyre every which way. "It's getting too long. I should cut it."

"Oh, I don't think so. It is very ... *exotique*."

"Exotic? Me? In Tunisia? I don't think so."

"*Mais si*. Some Tunisian husbands would demand you cover it in public."

"Why? Most women don't cover their heads here." I'd seen a few wearing a white sheet draped loosely over their heads and clothes, but not many. I'd also seen two or three women covered in black from head to toe, veils over the bottom half of their face, their eyes heavily lined in black kohl—the only part of their face or body exposed, adorned, seductive. I couldn't help but resent a custom so onerous yet I also envied their private space, if only for a few seconds.

"Most women don't have red hair. It is ..." he searched for the word "... agitating."

"Agitating? My red hair excites men, you think?"

"I do not think, I—I know." He raised his eyebrows and chuckled.

"Well.... A good thing my husband isn't Tunisian, then. You weren't thinking of using that stuff on my hair, were you?"

"No. I was not thinking of using it on your hair, Aimée. As your husband I would not ask you to cover it either. It is too beautiful."

"Thank you. Nor would I ask you to cover yours."

"Mine?"

"Black hair can be very agitating." The sexual tension between us was still tempered enough to pass as simple teasing. "We should get back to Jonathan. He'll be furious I've kept you to myself all this time."

In view of an occasion made special because Habib wanted to make a special dish, the three of us contributed to the preparation of the pie. Jonathan, having been given the awesome responsibility of breaking six eggs without leaving a trace of shell behind, whisked the yolks and whites together, elated with his grown-up competence. While Habib added the eggs to the browned lamb, spices, onions, cheese and beans, I lined an earthenware dish with six sheets of oiled pastry. Habib poured the concoction into this, then sealed it with the remaining six sheets of pastry. An unappetizing mess, I thought, until the most exquisite aroma started to permeate the house. An hour later Habib extracted a gold and saffron bubble from the oven. We dined on the terrace, the warm air and sound of waves washing over us, the *malsouka* an undisputed success.

After dinner Habib announced a surprise. He set a cloth on the terrace table and poured hot water into a bowl in which he made a paste with the henna. So he could paint my hands and my feet, he said, and Jonathan shrieked with excitement. "Oh, Mommy! Daddy's going to be mad!"

"Why *my* hands and feet? Why not yours or Jonathan's?"

"It is mostly for women. It would not be right for Jonathan."

"What about you? Why don't you paint yours?"

"Yes, I am allowed to paint the tip of three fingers on my right hand. I will do it after I've done yours."

"Me too, Mommy. I want to paint mine too."

"Can't we paint a few of his toes?" I asked, not wanting Jonathan to feel left out.

"Yes, we will do some of your toes, Jonathan. Give me your feet." Jonathan placed one foot on Habib's knee and Habib tickled it with the painting stick.

"Is this some kind of ritual? Does it have a special meaning?" I asked.

"I will tell you later. We need to wrap your hands and feet." He made rolling motions with his hands. "To help the henna, *comment dit-on … prendre?*"

It took several seconds before I finally understood. "Take? You want the henna to take? To set. You mean it will stain my hands?"

"For a while, yes."

He avoided my eyes, at which point I began to suspect I might be the scapegoat of some questionable joke. "In that case I don't think we should do my feet *and* my hands," I half protested. "Why don't we do my feet?" Jonathan's caked and oversized toes stuck out like a sculpture that has lost its sense of proportion.

"In that case, we will do only your hands. But you'll have to remove your ring."

I'd never taken off my wedding band. When I hesitated he took my hand and gently pulled off the ring. "How long have you been married?" he asked.

"Over five years."

"It was instant love?"

"Yes. We married a few months after we met."

"It is always the best kind," he said as he reached behind my head, unclasped the gold chain I always wore and threaded the ring through it, the circle a cold interjection against my breastbone. He placed my fingers in the warm paste, pushed them to the first joint. "Leave them in for a while."

After several minutes I pulled my fingers from the henna and each one bore a brown-gold thimble. With the end of the stick he made crisscrossed patterns on the back and the palms of my hands. "I am not very original," he said, apologetically. "Women usually do this. Maybe you should wear the *mitaines.*" He pointed to the oven mitts by the stove. "To help it take."

"To make it last longer? Not bloody likely. Is this cosmetic or does it mean something? Tell me."

"It doesn't mean anything, it is a custom. It is done on the eve of an occasion."

"What occasion? Am I to be the victim of some weird rite?"

"I must explain later," he insisted. He dipped three fingers of his right hand—index, middle and ring—so they barely reached the first joints into the rest of the henna. "You are more indisposed than I am so I'll help Jonathan get ready for bed."

"We should take the henna off his feet. He'll stain the sheets."

"I want to see Mommy's hands when she gets the mud off," Jonathan complained as Habib removed the henna from his barely tinted toes.

"I'll come in and show you when you're in bed, Jonathan," I said.

I could hear them from the terrace, Habib teasing and Jonathan shrieking. What would Gilles think of another man helping his son brush his teeth and put on his pajamas, reading him bedtime stories? Flakes of dry henna fell onto my dress. Gretel leaving a trail to find her way home again.

I walked to within a few feet of the kitchen door and watched as he made tea with his left hand, his right hand with the painted fingers a bewildered bird flying gingerly among Moorish tiles, conical pots, carved hammers and whisks. I would have to ask him later where I could buy items like these to take back to Canada. To keep elements of this house, this town, this summer from disappearing forever.

He was using the elaborate silverware for special occasions, each little glass in its ornate holder. I wanted to touch him. Feel the weight of his flesh and bones, hear his blood coursing through him, my head pressed against his back.

He looked up and it struck me how his smile always cast a seductiveness on everything he was about to say or do.

"I made tea. Jonathan fell asleep in the middle of a story."

"He usually does. How am I going to hold a cup?" I raised my hands as if I were being held up. He poured the tea in a glass, walked over and put it to my mouth. It was too hot and smelled too strongly of mint. I turned my head. I would have given anything for a double Scotch. "On what special occasion do Tunisian women have their hands painted?" I asked.

"You will not be angry?"

"Come on, Habib. On what occasion?"

"There are several. An engagement, a pregnancy. But mostly on the eve of a marriage. Women assemble to paint the hands and feet of the bride the night before the wedding."

"They still do this?"

"Some modern women don't. But many do, yes."

"I'm a modern woman and I'm already married."

"Yes." He lowered his eyes but I didn't believe for a moment this sudden meekness and embarrassment.

"Why do men paint their three fingers?"

"It is symbolic. Men do it twice during their life. For circumcision and marriage." He put the glass of tea to my lips again but I found it too sweet and pushed it away.

"I think we should take it off now." Impatience welled inside me, my heart pounding.

"Yes, it is dry." He led me to the sink and broke off the caked paste, exposing my hands.

"Why do they do this if it's only a custom without meaning? Customs are performed for a reason."

"Yes," he said, his voice reserved.

"So? What is it?"

"To excite. Men find it…."

"Agitating? I should have guessed. The enjoyment of husbands. How long will this dye last?"

"A few days, depending on how well it has set."

"A few days? How many?"

"Maybe one week, maybe more."

"One week! This is so presumptuous. You are so presumptuous! I can't go around flaunting painted hands when everyone knows what it means. It's outrageous. I can't believe it." This time he'd gone too far. "You should have told me, asked me. We have to *communicate*, Habib. One week!" I would have to hide my branded hands each time I stepped out or when the Maalouks came around, or Chafia. "People will know."

"But we are communicating," he said with such earnestness I didn't know whether to be angry or shake sense into him.

"No, we're not. You assume we do but we don't." I turned on the faucet to wash my hands but before I could he pulled me to him, his stomach pressed hard against mine. "Let's not do this," I said, my voice unconvincing. He lifted my hair and kissed the side of my nape, much as Gilles did. I didn't move, didn't flinch. At least not outwardly.

"This frightens you?" he asked.

"No, it doesn't frighten me. But I have a husband. It will complicate things."

"It has nothing to do with your husband."

"That's ridiculous. I take my marriage seriously. I have a husband and I love him. This excludes any other man from kissing me." And from my bed, I should have added.

"I'm not talking about who you love. I'm talking about letting someone else love you for a little while."

"Oh, Habib, what a line. You're talking about taking me to bed is what you're doing."

"Well, yes. Partly. But only partly."

His forearms locked behind me forcing me close and I didn't try to break away. I wanted to stay where I was, my body molded to his. "If someone other than my husband tells me he loves me I'll be expected to love him back and I can't do that. Not even for a little while." I was so out of breath I could hardly speak.

"Nobody is asking you to," he insisted.

And I wondered what else was not being asked as his mouth explored mine. I thought of Gilles and how much he loved me, yet I wanted this man's lips spreading their wetness against mine. His hands cupped on each side of my face allowing me no room to move or change my mind. I was about to cross into infidelity, which I would never tolerate from Gilles, yet I didn't want any of this to stop. Didn't want to think about what was happening, couldn't have even if I'd wanted to.

And he knew. He led me to the bedroom holding my wrist. The shutters had been closed, the lamp shade in the corner covered with a thin silk scarf so that it radiated shadows throughout the room. He undressed himself slowly, deliberately, while I stood watching. When he made no attempt to undress me, I appealed to him for help. Instead, he took one of my hands and guided it to his penis. My engraved hand encasing, moving along his swollen penis. He was offering himself as the condition of our desire.

He asked me to undress while he stood watching, his lids so heavy he could hardly keep them open but he forced them to stay on me, permeating my body with new sensations, as if it had been retraced, like my hands. Even our love-making spoke a language I had never spoken or heard before. His caressing slow, gently leading me to that delirious place that begs for release. A place where I didn't have to think of the consequences of making love to a man who was not my husband.

Assara

IT WAS BARELY DAYLIGHT WHEN JONATHAN whispered in my ear. "Come on, Mommy. We're going to the fishing boats."

Habib stood in the doorway, leaning on the frame, giving the impression he'd been there for some time. "Your coffee is ready. We must go soon if we want to buy fish."

"Oh, Mommy, your hands!" Jonathan shouted. "Daddy will be very mad. You better wash them." A deep blush spread to my face from where the white sheet stopped above my breasts, brown henna stains everywhere. Thank God, Habib had woken before Jonathan.

"Go with Habib while I get ready, okay?" In the washroom I washed my hands for several minutes but the dye clung to every pore. I would have to wear a dress with pockets.

The morning spread out with the freshness of clean linen, crisp and bristling, as the three of us made our way to the harbor. Shutters rattled open. The sky unveiled itself to birds lilting everywhere, whole delegations of birds complaining. I felt light-headed and weightless, the night before still circling in my head, the early hour urging me to unfold my wings. What had I done? I should have been feeling remorse, but I could think of no name or excuse for what moved and circled so perfectly inside me.

"I love those," I said, pointing to a three-sided window covered with blue grilles, a kind of shallow sun porch jutting from the front of a house. Many houses had them, some made of metal, others of intricate wooden panels.

"The *moucharabieh*? They are typical of traditional houses in Sidi Bou Saïd."

"Is it true they were originally built to keep the women

from being seen from the street?" This was only a guess but it sounded plausible.

"Who told you this?" Habib asked, shaking his head. "They were built for privacy when the windows are open. To let in light and allow the air to circulate." He paused. "Not everything has to do with the confinement of women."

I ignored the remark. As a guest in a country I knew little about, I was hardly in a position to debate or defend the confinement of women or their rights. "They're very mysterious. As if they were hiding secrets."

"I am sure they hold many," Habib replied and grinned.

"How do you say 'secret' in Arabic?"

"There are many secrets in Arabic. I would say this kind is *assara*. It is secret, yet it is not, like a veil covering a beautiful woman's face. We know that she is beautiful even when her face is covered, so it is no secret."

"Do you think women should cover their faces?"

"No, no. May God protect us from this fanaticism. God can see beyond veils and disguises, so it is not necessary to hide from him and no one should have to wear a disguise for a man. If your face had been covered, I would never have met you."

"Precisely. But I'm not so sure you're making the right argument."

He reached into my dress pocket and held my hand. "Are we communicating now?" he asked.

"I suppose we're communicating now," I conceded.

The fishing boats, faded to silkscreen greens, reds, yellows, could have sailed from another time or history. Bloated nets quivered like magicians' bags behind some boats, while the hollows of others gleamed like metallic trophies from the night's catch. Jonathan insisted on a better view so Habib picked him up, waded in and handed him to one of the fishermen. No sooner had he seen the glassy-eyed, indolent sea creatures than he appealed to me for help. I waved to reassure him, remembering too late the henna on my hands. One of the fishermen cast a rapid glance toward Habib, said something in Arabic to the other men in the boat, and they all laughed. Our night's intimacy exposed.

They might have been making fun of me but I didn't care. I took off my sandals, hiked up my dress and waded in after Jonathan. Habib extended a hand, placed a protective arm around my shoulder, his gallantry a telltale sign of what already existed between us. Was this too public a mark of affection between a man and a woman in this country?

"Come, Jonathan, you choose our dinner," Habib said. "What about this one?" He picked up a squid and after a few seconds' hesitation Jonathan grasped it by one of the tentacles. "Look, Mommy, a monster!" he shouted, pleased with his boldness. "Are we going to eat it?"

"If Habib wants to cook it. Because I'm not."

"We will buy different kinds and make a fish stew." Habib handed Jonathan's plastic pail to one of the fishermen, pointed to fish parts too mangled or small to sell to commercial vendors, plus a variety of small shells. When the pail had been filled, Habib told me to give the fisherman a dinar, but it hardly seemed enough. I placed two dinars in hands chapped and scarred from years of exposure, hands driven by need. When I searched the fisherman's face I detected no reaction, no judgment. He simply stared past me.

Intrigued by the contents of his red pail, Jonathan wanted to know what would become of the shells, unaware each one housed a flabby little mollusk. We sat on the beach and with a pin Habib extracted an inert grub from a shell and ate it. Jonathan covered his face with his bronzed hands and made gagging sounds.

"These are very good, Jonathan, you must have one. What do you call them?" Habib asked me.

"I'm not sure. Periwinkles, I think. Don't force him to eat one if he doesn't want to."

My admonishment clearly annoyed him. "I would never

force anyone to do anything he didn't want, but Jonathan probably wants to try one, don't you?"

"No, I don't," Jonathan said as adamantly as his four-year-old resoluteness allowed. He moved closer as Habib extracted another grub from its shell. "What was it doing in there?" he asked.

"This is his house," Habib said. "They carry their house wherever they go." He offered me one.

Jonathan frowned with suspicion as I ate it. "It's good," I reassured him. It tasted salty.

"Doesn't the pin hurt them?" Jonathan asked.

"They're already dead," I lied. "Sure you don't want to try one?"

"No, thank you," he answered politely. But he watched as Habib probed, pierced and pulled the mollusks.

A boy carrying a basket of terra cotta oil lamps stopped before us. He and Habib exchanged a few words until Habib waved him away. "He says they are ancient, that the fishermen dragged them up in their nets, but they are probably still warm from the ovens. All of Tunisia's earth is slowly being exported through phony little oil lamps for tourists."

Waves of sunlight poured down, bouncing off the sand. "We should go," I said, "the sun is getting too strong for Jonathan." As we walked along the beach, Habib gathered pieces of flat, chalky bones. "What are they?" I asked.

"I don't know how you say it. We call them *biscuits de mer*."

"Sea biscuits?"

"They are bones from a *seiche*."

I had no idea what he meant.

"We put them in cages for birds to sharpen their beaks," he continued. "They will also soften the hardness on your feet."

"Oh yes, a cuttle bone. I don't have calluses on my feet."

"Of course you don't. I was speaking generally." Again he reached into my pocket and held my hand. For the next few minutes we walked without saying anything until Habib asked what I was thinking.

"I didn't call Gilles yesterday. He must be worried."

"Call him this afternoon."

More silence. Gilles had become an uncomfortable topic. As long as I didn't talk or think about him, I didn't have to question my recklessness.

"When did you say he was coming?" Habib asked.

"Mid-August. He needs a holiday. We want to go back to the Bardo. We also want to see some of those art deco houses in Tunis. Did you know there are four or five hundred of them?" I needed to speak of Gilles and myself as a couple. Seal our future together.

Habib's sudden reaction and antagonism startled me. "Art deco," he spat out, shaking his head. "What's the matter with you people?"

"What do you mean?"

"If you want to see Tunisia, visit people and souks. The sea, the desert."

"I am visiting the people, the sea and the souks. Anyway, what's to see in the desert except sand?" I added, mainly to alleviate his sudden mood change.

He didn't think it funny. "You will see better things in the desert than art deco houses."

"I'm sure the desert is wonderful but it doesn't mean art deco houses aren't wonderful too. They're extensions of the people who built them and live in them. They're important."

"Yes, wonderful, if you are rich enough to build extensions of yourself. Those houses were built by colonialists. Their clean lines were meant to be a … an … antidote to the bad taste of ornate Arabian style." He waved his hand, as if to dismiss what French colonialists thought of Moorish and Arabian architecture.

It was too hot to argue. I knew nothing about French colonialism in Tunisia, how to interpret the present from this perspective, or what position to take in such a discussion. "Habib, I'm sorry for the past. So much of it is dismal. I probably shouldn't be here either. But I'm learning a lot and if it means wanting to see art deco houses built by colonialists, then that's part of learning too. I don't know how to separate what one group of people did from what another group did. I don't know what I should be personally responsible for. But if being here is wrong, I want to find out for myself."

"It is not wrong, you being here. This is not wrong."

"Isn't it? I'm not so sure. After last night, I don't even know how to separate right from wrong. I don't know how to divide acts and people. You from me. Him from you." I pointed to Jonathan.

"I know you don't. This is what I love about you," he said.

"Love. I don't know how to divide that either." I couldn't say I loved him. I had to safeguard at least that much for Gilles. "Who gets what kind of love and how much. What does love mean to you, Habib? How do you know when you love?"

"I just know."

"How? Describe it."

He pondered this for a while. "It's like jumping on a scale on one side of the world and the other side balances. This is how I feel this morning."

"It's too late for us, Habib."

"There is no early or late for us. It just is."

"I don't see the world that way. There are issues to deal with, practical ones. What to tell Gilles when I phone him. I don't want to hurt him. I don't want to gamble my whole life away." I didn't add I loved Gilles, partly out of consideration, but also because I already suspected it was this very love that had led me to my betrayal. I had been happy with Gilles, at least at first when happiness progressed not so much from any one thing in particular as from the feeling that the world had shifted to its proper place, as Habib just said. But then I had felt so distilled by that very love and the world had shifted again.

"You tell nothing over the telephone. It is not the right circumstance. We will tell him later, when he's here."

I had no intention of mentioning anything over the telephone and I certainly had no intention of letting Habib discuss the matter with Gilles either. The two of them discussing me and our respective futures. Habib taking over, as he always did, and Gilles analyzing everything to death. "I don't want you saying anything to him," I said. "This is between me and my husband."

He said nothing for a while then leaned over and kissed me on the cheek. I wondered what Jonathan made of such intimacy between his mother and a virtual stranger. He placed his hand in Habib's and studied him. The three of us walked hand in hand, our gait clumsy.

As we neared the house a scent of jasmine, sweet and thick as when flowers are about to wilt, saturated the air. We stopped before a bush cascading over a wall. Habib broke off a stem, one of the few still bearing buds. "When women in love place these on their beds at night the flowers open."

"You're like my husband: you see sexual organs everywhere."

He shrugged. "They are such important organs, perhaps this is why God put them everywhere." His laughter exploded against my pointless remark.

"What is the word for sexuality in Arabic?" I asked.

"There is no such word in Arabic."

"Everything has a word to describe it." I thought of the clumsy descriptions in English for making love: *He knew her.* "Things are naked, unfinished, if they don't have a name."

"I disagree. Some things cannot be named. Last night, for example. There are no words for last night," he said as he braided twigs of jasmine together. "Making love is like poetry, so is it not better to find poetic words?" he asked.

"Why? To disguise what's taking place?"

"No. To make it more beautiful."

"I disagree. Some things are best described for what they are." I thought he was about to offer me the jasmine, but he put it behind his ear. "I often see Tunisian men wearing jasmine like that."

"Do you know why?"

"No."

"When a man wears jasmine behind his left ear, it means he is searching for a woman. When he wears jasmine behind his right ear, it means he has a woman and is no longer searching." He had placed his jasmine behind his right ear.

"Me too, Habib. I want one too," Jonathan insisted.

Habib wove a few sprigs together and secured them behind Jonathan's right ear. "He has a woman for the moment. He'll be searching for another soon enough."

"You think I should go to the desert?" I asked as we entered the gate of the house.

"Absolutely."

"Why?"

"It is the beginning of the world and it is the end of the world. It is very large and it is very small because to survive you must become its center. As when you love. It gives you a feeling of balance, a sense of the absolute. The illusion of crossing limits. Very soon there will be no more desert. Oh, it will be there but it will be full of tourists. It will lose its peace, its breathing space."

"What will happen to the people who live there when there are too many tourists?"

"They will have to carry their desert within, like us."

"I shouldn't go then."

"Why not?"

"I'll just be another tourist."

I could see him wrestling with this contradiction. "It would be a shame not to. Maybe for a few days. Jonathan, have you heard of the frog who never left his pond because the ocean was too much of a gamble?"

"No."

"The ocean frog came to visit the pond frog and invited him to visit him in the ocean. 'No,' said the pond frog. 'Not until you have described the ocean to me.' The ocean frog shook his head. 'I can't explain to you where I live, but let me take you there.'"

Aisling Mooney

I SENSED A CHANGE IN AISLING as soon as she entered the airport. Cropped hair, black jeans and T-shirt, face pared down from considerable weight loss, she exuded more confidence than usual. She held on to a knapsack with one hand and carried a book close to her chest with the other. As she walked toward me and I deciphered the name of the book, my heart sank. *Women, Resistance and Revolution.* I wouldn't be able to tell her anything about Habib.

We hadn't seen each other for a couple of years and I was so looking forward to this visit. We had written to each other regularly since she accepted a job in Vancouver teaching English literature at a junior college, but the long-distance friendship hadn't been the same.

Aisling Mooney, "pronounced *Ashling,*" she warned everyone she met, used to live on a farm down the road from ours.

"What does 'Aisling' mean?" I asked when we met.

"A vision," she said.

It was one of many reasons I wanted her for a friend.

Since there were no Catholic schools within walking distance, she attended New Erie Public School, the one I went to. It was perfectly all right for her to do so, she explained, because she had a guardian angel who protected her from the usual Protestant shenanigans. If her ingenuity was not wholly believable, I found it nonetheless impressive. I had four brothers, no sister, and could have used an angel of my own.

"So why can't I see your angel?" I asked her.

"Because it's invisible and you're not a Catholic."

"How do you know it's following you if it's invisible?"

She was probably used to people accepting her angelic pronunciations as a matter of faith and I could tell she hadn't anticipated so many questions. She pondered this for several seconds until her face lit up. "Because I can hear its wings."

"What makes you think you're hearing wings? Maybe it's the wind."

"Oh no! Angels' wings don't sound anything like the wind." Her determination was a challenge to my incredulity.

"What do they sound like then?" I sighed, my impatience goaded not so much by Aisling's suspect answers but by Catholicism's unrivaled advantage in the heavenly sphere. No wonder my parents thought Catholics were a gullible lot.

So I wasn't entirely surprised when Aisling said, "Leather. Their wings sound like leather striking the air."

The only sounds I vaguely associated with leather were of my father sharpening his razor on a strop hanging by the mirror in the bathroom every morning before he shaved, or a teacher's strap as it arched its way toward a boy's hand. My brothers often came home with welts on their palms, showing them off like badges of honor.

"Aren't wings made of feathers?" Not that I believed in feather wings any more than in leather ones, but even fabrication, my six-year-old mind reasoned, should yield to some convention and everyone knew that imaginary angels had imaginary wings made of imaginary feathers.

"No, no," Aisling had insisted. "Those are birds' wings. Angels' wings are made of leather."

If I begrudgingly admired my friend's resourcefulness, I also questioned how anyone could place so much faith in a religion that inspired such loophole logic. Maybe my parents were right after all: churchgoers had to keep lying to themselves. A peculiar claim coming from them, since I heard them fib all the time. Especially after Rose moved in with us and my mother thought it necessary to explain to everyone she met in town how poor Rose had to quit her job as a housekeeper because of an operation for the removal of a growth the size of an orange. I could tell no one believed her. They knew all about little white lies that concealed darker truths. Besides, Aisling's angel was not a real lie. As an Irish Catholic going to a public school, she simply needed to reinforce her defenses.

"Why aren't we Irish?" I asked my mother when I first met Aisling.

"Because we're Canadians of good English stock," she replied.

How boring, I thought. There were no heavenly creatures in the upbringing of a Canadian-of-good-English-stock. Nothing from the nether regions either, no vampires or demons. Except for the strange figure who began showing up in my dreams the year Rose moved in. It stood at the foot of my bed in a long black coat, motionless and staring. It disappeared only when I was awakened by my own screams. My mother or father, or sometimes Aunt Rose, rushing in, gathering me into their arms and rushing me to their rooms; my raggedy Ann and Andy placed on a dresser facing their bed because I couldn't leave them to the whims of the strange figure.

Since moving to Vancouver, Aisling had become, according to her letters, a most enthusiastic sinner. She drank, smoked pot and had collected a string of lovers. I so wanted to flaunt one of my own. Retrieve those afternoons when we hid in tall fields chewing on wheat grass, spying on brothers, dissecting topics charged with innuendo: the hard bodies of young farmhands, virginity, future husbands. By the time we were teenagers, Aisling had undergone a radical change of heart as far as Catholicism was concerned, and she vowed she would never marry if it meant having a dozen children and working like a slave as her mother did. As for myself, grateful, finally, for the absence of angelic or divine intervention in my own upbringing, I vowed I would marry but I would have only two children, a boy and a girl. We were plotting our escape from a succession of generations who never questioned how they lived, and so never saw any need to change.

Our mothers and their sisters must have suffered more than anyone we knew, their afflictions fiercely competitive. Who had the most difficult delivery. The most demanding husband. One year they vied for the largest tumor. My mother, having been operated on to remove a growth the size of a plum from an unmentionable part of her anatomy, held the record until the day, a few months later, when I ran home to report that Aisling's mother had had a tumor removed and hers was the size of a grapefruit.

It would be several years before Aisling and I came to recognize that people who talked incessantly about illness, hard times and lost love were doing so for a reason. Gilles, overhearing us discussing our mothers once, said he thought that people who no longer had passion or sexual desire in their lives replaced it with suffering. A libidinal investment, he called it. "Take the heart, for example. It doesn't enter into consciousness until it's either malfunctioning or broken. The pain is preferable to no feeling at all."

"Let's promise each other we'll never be without passion or have tumors the size of fruit," Aisling had quipped.

Aisling tried to distance herself from her family by moving to Vancouver, although she kept returning to New Erie for visits. My solution was to attend the University of Toronto and major in art history and criticism. In retrospect, I wonder whether our mothers were really as unhappy as we once imagined.

In the taxi from the Tunis airport, Aisling noticed the faint traces of color still on my hands. I'd given up trying to get the henna off, partly out of sentimentality, partly out of defiance. "What's this?" she asked, lifting one of my hands.

"A long story."

"We have two weeks."

"I'll tell you later." I didn't want the taxi driver to overhear in case he understood English. "How was your trip?"

"Fine. I had a few hours in Paris and phoned Gilles. He's very upset. He said you haven't written and the one time you phoned you sounded aloof, reluctant to say much."

Yes, he always filled my silence with his own fiction. "I have to use the neighbor's phone. It's not always convenient." I didn't think Gilles would be overly anxious. "He's probably assuming I'm going through one of my moods. He's been doing that a lot, lately."

"Maybe because you're giving him good reason to?"

"We may be going through a rough patch," I added.

"Are you now?" Depending on her target, Aisling's sarcasm could be funny but in this case I found it more annoying than anything else. I wondered if Gilles had said anything to her, if he suspected. "Where's Jonathan?" she asked.

"With Chafia. The neighbor with the phone. You'll have to meet her. She's neat."

Aisling was visibly impressed with Sidi Bou Saïd. As we walked to the house from where the taxi left us, she kept repeating she hadn't expected such luxury. "I must have imagined a Third World or something. But you have to be loaded to own a house like this *and* an apartment in Paris."

She had mentioned Marxism in her letters a few times, so I presumed the comments were meant mainly as criticism, in spite of my assertion that the house was quite modest by the town's standards. "Jesus," she said, with a hint of Irish brogue still, as she rubbernecked at the walls and ceiling in the living room. "If this house is modest, what are the others like?" She picked up a book from the coffee table: Frantz Fanon's *Studies in a Dying Colonialism*. "Are *you* reading this?" she asked, surprised.

It was Habib's book. He'd bought the French edition for me and the English translation for himself. We could each improve our respective foreign language while keeping up with political trends. "Yes," I said, without elaborating.

"Did you know Fanon was also a psychiatrist before he became a revolutionary?"

"Yes. Not much chance of Gilles becoming a radical though. He'd find Fanon's rhetoric excessive, and he certainly wouldn't approve of the violence." I was showing off. I wanted to prove Habib's good influence on me.

"At least you're keeping up with your reading," she said, suggesting nothing else I was doing quite met with her approval. "So. What have you done, Amy? What's the stuff on your hands and why is Gilles so upset?"

I had always admired her directness but now I found it invasive. I had hoped to ease into the whole Habib story over cool drinks. "It's a joke. We did it as a joke."

"Who's we?"

"Me and Habib."

"Who's Habib?"

"A man Gilles and I met in Paris."

"You painted your hands in Paris?" she asked in the same staccato grilling as when we were kids, her brow furrowed in exaggerated disapproval.

"No, here. He's from here. He's home for the summer. Fuck, Aisling, stop sounding like the Inquisition. Did you bring anything to drink?" I'd warned her there were no liquor stores in Sidi Bou, at least none that I knew of, and that she should bring a few bottles with her.

She fished into her knapsack and produced two bottles, one gin, one Scotch. "Why is he painting your hands?"

"A joke. I don't have tonic water, do you want Scotch?"

"Sure. I want to know why this guy is painting your hands."

"I'd forgotten what a terrier you can be. I'm having an affair. No big deal."

"No big deal?"

No one else could be so sanctimoniously condescending. "Come on, Aisling, you're always having affairs."

"*I'm* not married, for starters. Anyway, I don't have affairs anymore. Men are pigs."

"I see. *You're* no longer having affairs, so all men are pigs. What brought this about?"

"A long story," she said and started to laugh because she already knew what my response would be.

"We have two weeks," I said, picking up on a routine from when we were kids. After fierce rivalrous arguments, which happened regularly, we always resorted to humor as our arbitrator.

"You're having an affair with an Arab?"

"He's from Tunisia, yes."

"A Muslim?" Aisling howled in disbelief.

"A Tunisian who's an Arab who's a Muslim. So what?"

"Aren't Arabs supposed to be hard on women?"

"I don't know about all Arabs. This one isn't. At first I thought he was too nice, a little overbearing maybe, but it's his way of trying to please me." I wasn't entirely convinced of this argument. Habib was overbearing sometimes, but I needed to put him in the best light possible.

"It won't be so pleasant in a few months."

"I'll be gone by then. It's only a summer fling. I want to enjoy it while it lasts." I hadn't thought of it as a summer fling before but now that I'd named it, it became obvious that this was all it could ever be. It meant it would soon end.

"This isn't like you, Amy."

"What? Having an affair?"

"And being so careless. You can be impulsive at times, but even then you're never careless. Isn't it dangerous for a married woman to have an affair with a Muslim in an Arab country? Don't they stone people for this sort of thing?"

"Tunisia is modern, quite European actually. Jesus, Aisling, for someone who claims to have read all those revolutionary books, you don't sound too enlightened."

"What about all those organizations?"

"What organizations?"

"I don't know. The PLO or the FLN, or whatever those stupid names are. Algerians planting bombs in Paris. I read about it on the plane."

"Oh, Aisling, that's like saying the Irish all belong to the IRA. Tunisia has nothing to do with the FLN or the PLO. President Bourguiba doesn't support any of those organizations. Habib did mention some young Tunisians joining some group. More out of boredom and lack of jobs than conviction, he says. Anyway, this has nothing to do with me. Habib is political but he is not an extremist. And he is a pretty interesting guy," I added, trying to sound as suggestive as I could.

Aisling shook her head. "Jesus, Amy, how do you do it?"

"What?" I said, doing my best to sound innocent. I had my old Aisling back.

"Attract interesting guys. First Gilles, now this guy. I only attract schmucks. So what makes him so interesting? This place? Is he exotic? What?"

"I don't know. I fell for him the moment I met him in Paris." I hated the word *exotic*. It turned people into a parade. As if we couldn't be attracted to anyone from a different background without committing some major offense. "I guess he is different from me in many ways. But it doesn't matter. Where he comes from, the religion he belongs to, none of it matters. Actually, he's the one who thinks I'm *exotique*. He says it's my red hair. I just find him incredibly sexy."

"What about Gilles? He knows something's up."

"I know. I would never walk away from Gilles, not in a million years, and I know this thing with Habib is not permanent. It's crazy. I have no idea why I'm jeopardizing my marriage for this." I had no doubt Habib and I would part eventually, but not just yet. Come August, I would walk away, confident he would leave no more of a trace than a flock of migratory birds flying overhead at the end of a warm summer.

I thought I knew what I was doing, assuming that my life

and the lives of those around me were safely within my control. Poor Gilles. I seldom thought of him anymore except in relation to myself. Worried only about whether he would forgive me if he found out. Not once asking myself if I would even have the right to ask.

"The weird thing is, it was Gilles who sent Habib to check on me and Jonathan," I said, trying to shift the blame.

"I doubt this is what he had in mind, Amy." She exhaled to emphasize the seriousness of the situation. "I hope Muslims aren't as complicated as Catholics when it comes to sex."

"He isn't. Not at all. The other day, after we'd made love three or four times in a row and we were feeling rather giddy, he compared himself to Mohammed. Mohammed's love for Allah was so great, he said, that it thrived on sexual pleasure and several wives, whereas Jesus's fervor burned so low that women and sexual pleasure would only smother it."

"I can certainly relate to that. So he's religious?"

"I don't think so. More of a cultural thing, maybe. He said once he admired the Sufis."

Aisling had probably never heard of Sufis, but if she had she obviously preferred to press on to more immediate and intimate matters. "So what attracts you to this guy? Is it the sex?"

"Maybe. He's attractive. But then so is Gilles, so it can't only be sex." I tried to weigh factors I couldn't quite grasp. "I know I love Gilles, our life together, his intelligence and generosity. The thing is, I don't particularly feel that good when I'm with him. I don't like the person I become when he's around. I'm unsure about everything I do when I'm with Gilles. But not with Habib."

"Because it's new, Amy. It's new and forbidden. Take it from a Catholic."

I'd gone over this so many times in the last two weeks. With Gilles, everything I did or said had to be justified, if not to him then to myself. "I don't know. Habib's expectations are different. No, that's not it. There are no expectations with Habib. With Gilles, I feel a sense of loss. As if by marrying him I'd left something of myself behind. I can't quite put my finger on it. It's not like that with Habib. Our time together is what's important."

Aisling got up and poured two more Scotches. "I think people would call this love, Amy. Has he said he loves you?"

"All the time, but he probably says it to every second woman he meets. I have no illusions about that, but it doesn't bother me. It would bother me if Gilles went around telling women he loved them, but not if Habib did. What's important is *I* like how *I* feel when I'm with him. There are no expectations, only this enthusiasm, this energy."

"Gilles has all kinds of energy."

"I suppose. But Jonathan and I get mislaid in it somehow."

"He worships you and Jonathan. Even his work is about family ..."

I couldn't bear listening to anyone describe Gilles's work as if it had anything to do with Jonathan and me. I lifted my hand and interrupted her. "You mean some abstract notion of family. You think hunting down clues about family constructs, whatever that means, is about us? Right now he's in Paris working on theories, while his wife is fucking her head off. His theories are so far removed from who we really are that I can't see us in them anymore. We've become case studies. Objective reality, he calls it. And even if he were here, his mind would be somewhere else. He doesn't see me anymore. The only time I can hold on to him is when we're making love. As soon as it's over he's thinking of something else. Something more important."

"Okay, calm down, Amy."

"At least when Habib and I are together, he gives the impression this is what matters. It absorbs him."

"Because it's new, Amy. I know you. This will drive you crazy in no time, if it hasn't already."

"It won't have time to drive me crazy. I'll be gone in six weeks."

"You keep saying that but it doesn't work that way. What are you going to tell Gilles?"

"Do I have to tell him anything?" I hoped I could find an exit that would allow me my secret, my *assara*.

"You're not the best liar in the world. If he suspects and confronts you, you'll end up spilling out everything."

"Oh, I know. I may have really screwed things up. The strange thing is, I don't want to change anything right now. I don't want to give up Habib to go back to Gilles and I don't want to give up Gilles to stay with Habib. I can't think it through."

"Your hormones are doing most of your thinking right now, honey. It will be decided when Gilles finds out. And it will be messy. Are you ready for that?"

"No. I don't want him to find out. I should end it with Habib now. I have to." How was I going to store away these last few weeks and pretend they never happened? I didn't want to think about it just now. "What about you? Why have you suddenly concluded men are all pigs?"

"The usual. Affair gone bad. So watch yourself."

"What happened?"

She pulled down the corners of her mouth in feigned indifference. "Mr. Right moved in, stayed six months, walked out."

"For no reason? Without saying anything?"

"He was upset because I got pregnant. A few days after I told him, I came home from work and all his things and half of mine were gone. The bastard never discussed it. Just picked up and took off."

"Oh, Aisling. I'm so sorry. Christ, that's terrible."

"Yah. Fatherhood didn't appeal to him, I guess."

"What did you do? What happened to the baby?"

"An abortion. I couldn't go through the whole child thing alone. Anyway, it's done and over with."

"What kind of man was this? Weren't there signs?"

"Of course. But I didn't let myself see them until he'd gone. Women in love never do. I'm mad at myself mostly."

"Why?"

"For misjudging him. For misjudging my own judgment."

"Your judgment has nothing to do with this jerk." I wanted to absolve her of blame for her bad judgment as I expected her to do with me.

"But it wasn't the first time, you know? I keep picking the same jerk in a different suit. Well, different jeans. I thought I was good at sizing up people, but men have me stumped."

"Did you have trouble finding someone to do the abortion?"

"Nah…Practically everyone at school has had one. Expensive though."

"Abortion is legal here. Isn't that weird? I mean, I don't think women are all that liberated."

"I wanted this baby. Maybe that's why it didn't work, I wanted it too badly. Maybe I scared the poor bastard away."

"Poor bastard, my ass. Don't you go feeling sorry for him. Should you speak to someone about this? Someone impartial?"

"Impartiality is the last thing I need right now, Amy. It's you I want to speak to." She took my hands into hers. "I've missed you. I'm glad you invited me, I needed to get away." She studied the dark red lines etched inside my palms.

"Are you going to be okay?" I asked.

"Sure. Getting rid of guilt is the one valuable thing Catholicism taught me. So, when am I going to meet this guy of yours?"

"I asked him to give us a day or two. He'll show up, sooner or later. I better pick up your godchild from next door. He's such a great kid, so grown up."

"How is he handling having another man competing for his mother's affection? Doesn't it confuse him?"

"He never asks about it. He asks when Gilles is coming back but he adores Habib. And Habib adores him. He would make a great father."

"Jonathan already has a father, Amy."

"I didn't mean it like that."

When I picked up Jonathan from Chafia's, she invited us to come back for a swim and dinner the next day. Her husband wouldn't be there, and we would have a *fête* to celebrate the presence of two Canadian women in Sidi Bou Saïd.

Turn a Blind Eye

CHAFIA ALWAYS DRESSED AS IF SHE'D just stepped out of a French or Italian boutique, her sense of style casual and confident. I would never have thought of pairing various garments, colors and accessories the way she did and even if I had I could never have carried it off.

The *fête* began uncomfortably since Chafia spoke only Arabic and French, Aisling spoke neither, and I had to translate, as best I could, every word either one of them said. It got more confusing when Wassila, the baby-sitter, joined us. Apparently, Wassila spoke a mixture of Arabic and Berber. Since Chafia didn't want to exclude her, she also translated everything Wassila said. Aisling's English was translated into my version of French, then into Arabic or Berber, and vice versa. Our conversation must have resembled the parlor game in which a message is whispered to each person sitting in a circle until it reaches the end, when the message is revealed and it is completely different from what it was supposed to be. At least that's what I imagined it to be.

Chafia had suggested we come early enough for a swim before dinner. I'd already told Aisling that the grounds were as spectacular as any *Homes and Gardens* picture. The pool could have been lifted from Roman times, the floor and walls made of small mosaics, the arched entrance of the poolhouse supported by columns. It was her private *hammam*, Chafia said. The poolhouse consisted of a large open space with lounging chairs adjoining a steam room and shower. I would have been quite happy to nest there months at a time.

Fatma and Jonathan joined us in the pool until Wassila

took them in to get ready for dinner. After a while we gave up on conversation and concentrated on swimming. When we grew tired we floated on our backs, the only sound a trickle entering the pool, delicate as a thread, until the children returned to remind us they were hungry.

I was surprised, and relieved, when Wassila returned with glasses and two bottles of white wine. "I didn't think Muslims drank alcohol," I said in English to Aisling, then in French to Chafia.

Chafia said something in Arabic to Wassila and they both laughed. "Some of us drink a little wine now and then," she added in French.

We tried polite conversation. Questions about Canada and Canadian winters. Canadian men. What did my husband do? Why did he have to go back to Paris? Chafia's husband's work often took him to Milan, she said, then turned to Wassila, added something in Arabic and the two women laughed but didn't elaborate. Aisling and I were not to be privy to what they had just said. Did Aisling and I have jobs? I explained about Aisling's teaching position. Aisling mentioned the serenity of Sidi Bou Saïd, I spoke of the presence of history everywhere. We sounded like self-conscious tourists afraid of saying the wrong thing. Chafia repeated every word to Wassila and it was somewhat bewildering having to wait for Wassila's prolonged and animated answers. It was going to be a long evening.

Undoubtedly because we were running out of topics and because her recent abortion was still so prominent in her mind, Aisling blurted out, "I hear that abortion is legal here. You know it's still illegal in Canada."

I translated.

"Wassila and I are of different opinions as to abortion," Chafia said. They conferred a while longer, then Chafia asked if Wassila could tell us a story about her mother. "She was very independent in her own way."

"Yes, might as well," I replied. I had the impression that whatever we were about to hear had been told many times, but it would at least hold everyone's attention until the food arrived.

As Wassila began to relate her mother's story, Chafia's voice joined hers in French and I joined Chafia's in English. The confusion of earlier on disappeared, each voice entering an echo chamber, each echo translating itself into its own language and interpretation.

"As legend would have it, my mother was considered a very beautiful woman," Wassila began, "but like most beautiful women, she was always described in words that were not herself. They said her forehead was like the new moon; her eyes were as piercing as a deer's; cheeks as red as anemones; lips of carnelian; teeth, a row of pearls set in coral; her bosom, a fountain; her belly, a bowl of ointment. Sometimes they described her as a splendid fish swimming in a limpid pool; other times as a morsel of luscious fat in a bowl of milk soup.

"In the beginning her parents were delighted their daughter should attract such comparisons, for what parents do not want a daughter with sugared lips and eyebrows arched in bent bows? They expected and planned a brilliant marriage. But when the time came for suitors to call upon the young beauty, a strange thing occurred: they came once or twice, but never returned. This happened over and over again. Each time the parents thought they had made a perfect match, it fell through.

"Her parents were baffled but their daughter was not. She could only experience herself as the person she was and knew she could never live up to all her likenesses. Beautiful as she was, she knew she could only be a disappointment to the men when they discovered that her radiance was not as bright as the sun's, and could not make everything around her invisible.

"After a few years, the young men stopped calling altogether. In her sorrow, my mother began to sing and discovered a talent she hadn't known she possessed: she had an extraordinary voice. It soared so clear and high that people could hear it from village to village. It could split the night in two, so people who were awakened from the first half often returned to a restless sleep as they fell into the second half.

"As custom would have it, my mother's parents resisted their daughter's wish to develop her talent. It was dishonorable for a young woman to display herself in public as a singer. But after she had passed the age when it became clear she would never marry, they said she could go and do as she pleased because they had to consider their other daughters and could no longer afford to keep her. She left the village armed with only her determination and the sound of her voice.

"She could play the tambourine, but to earn a living as a singer, she also needed at least one accompanist, or, preferably, two. Women musicians were out of the question; few women were taught to play and none would have been allowed to travel without the protection of a man. So she hired two male accompanists. One played reed pipes and the other played a lute and a lyre. Most important, both were blind. If they were to play for a woman, it was crucial they not see her and be tempted by her womanly charms.

"It was difficult for her at first, traveling with two blind men. Looking into blind eyes is like looking into an empty mirror. You never know who you are. But my mother got used to it after a while and everything went well. The sounds the three extracted from their instruments were very different from one another but in such harmony the entire universe sang along with them. Water and whales, trees and wind, sun and stars, the hoofs of horses in the night, all joined and produced a music that came from the depths.

"People came from great distances to hear them. Although they had never heard the songs before, they realized they had, in fact, been murmuring each and every one of them for generations. They hadn't known until now that these were the stories they had wanted to hear all along, the missing stories holding all the other missing stories. Echoes within echoes.

"The more they listened the bolder their requests became. They asked for songs about the number seven because it held more truth than any other number. A story could only be accurate when told in seven tongues. A life couldn't be fulfilled unless it acquainted itself with the seven gods of happiness and traveled seven depths. A city always had to sit on seven hills and behold the seven wonders of the world. A holy man must avoid all seven deadly sins. Every couple who wanted to bear seven sons and seven daughters had to make love every seventh night.

"They also asked for songs about beautiful brides who only awaken to their husbands' demands, never to their own desires, which would cause them to abandon their husbands and children.

"They asked if children should be put through the test of poetry and courage by racing untamed horses.

"They asked why only boys are given horses with wings."

At this point Chafia suggested we pause to allow her to get the food and more wine. She lit candles and incense in little oil lamps. While the women and children ate, Wassila's story continued.

"No serious problems arose for many months. But as fate would have it, both accompanists fell in love with my mother's voice. Who knows what images unfold in a blind man's eyes, what dreams run through landscapes black as China ink? Since she had existed only through their listening, they could read her most intimate thoughts. Such knowledge can only lead to love.

"They came into her tent at night and cried at her feet, which put her at a great disadvantage, since the dark completely disoriented her, though for the two blind men it was no inconvenience at all.

"To have fired the men would have meant the end of my

mother's means of earning a living. The men's music, once so spirited, came out in pitiful mews and sighs. Something had to be done. In any event, they weren't unattractive men and she was flattered by their attention. She was delighted they had fallen in love with her best feature, her voice, and not with all those other comparisons of herself. She couldn't help but feel honored.

"After lengthy consideration she let one of the blind men into her bed and found the experience not entirely unpleasant. A few weeks later, when the other musician threatened to leave or kill himself, she let him into her bed as well. And so, the two men became her husbands.

"Everything was going well until my mother discovered she was pregnant. 'The world outside is much too vast and complicated,' she would tell the seed growing inside her. 'You don't want to be born, you should leave while there is still time.' Of course, the baby stayed and grew, which made my mother more unhappy. 'Why do you stay cooped up in the dark with eyes closed? Why don't you just come out and face the world. Leave.' She would give her stomach little jabs. But the child stayed and kept silent. Until, one day, when my mother pleaded more ardently than before, she heard a voice inside her cry out, 'Mother, there is no other world but here.'

"When I was born, the two men agreed they were both my fathers and all four of us lived quite happily for many years. Until I decided it really was time for me to leave."

None of us said anything for the longest while, not wanting to break the enchanting spell of Wassila's words. After one or two minutes, there came a sound from over the wall, on the Roussels' side. One of the women shifted in her seat. We became aware of the silence. Aisling was the first one to speak. "Have you considered writing this down, Wassila? It's such a wonderful story, it should be published."

"I don't think she would," Chafia said.

Sensing we were discussing her, Wassila wanted to know

what we were saying. Chafia told her, listened, smiled, then translated.

"Wassila knows how to write but she seldom does. Women, she says, have inherited mainly exclamation marks and periods at the end of sentences. Writing locks events inside one place and inside one time, when in fact memory of those events is always changing. A timeless story will lose itself if it is fixed in words and is never allowed to flourish. But enough about words. It is time to talk about something else."

Wassila opened her eyes unnaturally wide as if to hypnotize us all and, satisfied that her message had been delivered and understood, got up and went inside. She put a record on and I could hear a plaintive male voice singing to equally plaintive instruments. When she returned, she sang along, also in a nasal lament, but higher and clearer. I wondered if she had inherited her mother's voice.

Jonathan and Fatma had fallen asleep on two lounge chairs and Wassila covered them with blankets. Chafia added another empty bottle to those already lined up against the wall and opened more wine, giggling.

"I must ask you something, Chafia," I said. "A friend of mine was telling me there's no word in Arabic for sexuality. Is this true?" I would never have asked if I'd been sober.

"No, no! This is what men want you to believe," she said. "They make up vulgar words to describe sexuality so women won't use them, so sexuality and language will remain their exclusive domains." She spoke a few words in Arabic and Wassila gasped and the two of them almost choked on their wine. I assumed she had just uttered a litany of forbidden epithets, but she wouldn't repeat or translate them.

"Before my husband had so much business in Milan," Chafia giggled again, "he insisted we follow the instructions in an erotic manual. A different position for every day of the month. Every position carried a name that had nothing to do with making love. On Monday we did 'the camel's hump.' On Tuesday, 'the blacksmith's position.' Wednesday, 'Archimedes' vise.'"

The four of us became more hysterical as Chafia listed postures and names, our faces streaming with tears. Until suddenly, from beyond the garden wall, a voice shouted in Arabic. Chafia cautioned us to be quiet but none of us could stifle our laughter. The voice, more forceful this time, shouted again, and I realized it came from the Roussel side of the wall. It was the voice of M. Maalouk.

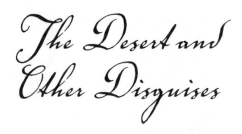

The Desert and Other Disguises

A WEEK INTO AISLING'S VISIT, Habib suggested we all go
to the desert. His brother, Mustapha, a tour guide, would take
us as long as we went on a weekend with a day at each end.
Four days wouldn't give us much time, but we would at least
get an impression of the Sahara, Habib said.

"What about your work?" I asked. "It's only been two weeks
since you started."

"I will make arrangements to work extra hours in the
evenings. It is no problem."

"I'll pay the expenses," Aisling offered, much to my relief. I
had already spent most of the money Gilles had left me and
I wasn't sure how I'd make it to mid-August. "I'll pay for the
trip but I hope your brother doesn't assume I'll sleep with
him," she warned Habib.

"My brother is married," Habib answered quietly.

"I didn't think it mattered around here," she shot back,
pleased to have finally registered her disapproval.

"Oh, it does. It matters very much." He gave her one of his
seductive smiles.

Aisling liked Habib from the moment they met. "What's
not to like?" she said. He moved so easily into another's life,
casually taking everything and everyone in his stride. It
touched her how well he took care of Jonathan and me. "Why
can't I meet this kind of man in the real world?" she wondered.
Nothing she had experienced in the last week was quite real
to her. "And pretty easy on the eyes. Jesus, Amy, I wouldn't
want to be in your shoes when it comes time to choose."

We left at sunrise on a Friday morning in a Land Rover painted camouflage brown and green, a strange choice considering the lack of vegetation in the desert. Habib made a headdress for Jonathan, a black-and-white kerchief held in place with a twisted cord, which instantly transformed him into a young Lawrence of Arabia.

We stopped in a few towns along the coast, visited medinas, souks, kasbahs, mosques, their histories related in Mustapha's sightseeing spiel of broken English. In Sousse we went to the beach, the morning groggy with sun and tenderness. Habib told us he would own a summer house and a fishing boat there one day or, if not in Sousse, in Mahdia. "No matter how successful or unsuccessful, I will come back to my fishing boat and be assured of something to eat."

In Kairouan we bought pastry stuffed with dates. Mustapha offered to drive to the amphitheater in El Jem but I didn't particularly want to see it again. After short visits in Sfax and Gabes we decided to drive directly to Matmata, where we would have an early dinner and spend the night. Mustapha said it would be fun to stay in one of the troglodytic caves. Many of them had been converted into hostels. "Not the kind you see in Canada," Habib warned as if these dwellings existed anywhere else. He complained that tourism had ruined the local way of life in Matmata. Aisling and I, feeling like accomplices, looked at one another and rolled our eyes.

Matmata's landscape was as moon-like as the moon. The surrounding hills, large circular craters, which turned out to be the troglodytic caves, square white houses flanking them, all gave the impression of a village secluded from normal geography.

By late afternoon, as we drew near to where we'd planned to spend the night, a man stopped us. He told us the area was off limits because an American film crew was using it as a set for a movie. As Mustapha tried to pull his tour-guide strings and talk the guard into letting us through, Jonathan cried out, "Look, Mommy!" Beyond the cordoned-off area, strange-looking creatures milled about. The desert had suddenly spawned a profusion of mutants.

"What is happening?" Mustapha asked the guard.

"They're filming inside," he said as he pointed toward the entrance to one of the caves.

"Any famous people in it?" Aisling asked.

"An English actor who's supposed to be famous." The guard pointed to a gray-haired man in a brown burnoose covered in dust.

"It's Alec Guinness!" Aisling shouted.

"Why are they wearing such weird costumes?" I asked.

"They're supposed to be from other planets," the guard said.

Mustapha, visibly annoyed and mumbling something in Arabic under his breath, drove to an elevation nearby for a better view of the set. The afternoon sun had begun to fade, and Jonathan sat on a blanket on top of the Land Rover. "Are they ghosts, Mommy?" he kept asking, my explanations barely adequate since the figures did resemble ghosts from a disfiguring hell: faces oozing out of shape; bird-ogres; human bodies with elephant trunks or reptilian skin; men with oversized heads and bulging eyes dressed in formal wear and carrying jazz instruments; dwarves whose faces were blacked out except for solitary, unblinking, electric eyes; leathery heads and predatory teeth; a robot-man in gold-plated armor followed by a three-foot-tall robot, a space-age Don Quixote and Sancho Panza.

In wanting to capture the hostile atmosphere of the future or some other imaginary time, Hollywood had come to the ancient town of Matmata. For more than an hour, suspended in some interplanetary space between reality and illusion, spellbound and disconnected from evolution as we knew it, we watched surreal creatures roam about the movie set.

Mustapha knew of another troglodytic complex opened to tourists a few kilometers away, but, he warned, it was more primitive than the first. I couldn't imagine how that could possibly be until we got there. There was no electricity or running water. Stacked bricks covered with grimy rugs served as beds. Jonathan, still hyper from the movie set and the idea of sleeping in a cave, ran about like a little out-of-control robot.

We ate our supper of goat cheese, bread, olives and bottled water outside, the sun sinking inside a bell-jar sky. When it came time to retire, out of propriety or discretion in front of his brother, Habib suggested he share his cell with Mustapha. In my damp and cold cave, I craved the warmth of his sleeping body, and experienced his absence as an ache for the first time.

Because of my allergies to wool and dust, the old carpets quickly filled my lungs. I could hardly breathe, let alone sleep. I went outside and sat on the ground, my back to the ice-cold wall.

Within a few seconds Aisling followed me. "Can't sleep?"

"No. I feel I've landed on a different planet." The sky and air glittered. The sky in brightness, the air in darkness. "My old life feels so far away. It's as if I were in some time warp where Gilles has disappeared."

"Yes. We might as well have landed on a different planet, everything here is so fucking weird." She craned her neck to the stars and a cyclops moon casting a pall on the caves.

"When I was a girl, Rose had a book with an illustration of an astrolabe in it. Apparently astronomers in the Middle Ages used it to measure star elevations and distances between points of light and constellations. This place looks like it belongs to another planet. No wonder Hollywood comes here to make films about the future," I said.

Aisling decided to go along with my digressions. "Hard to imagine an instrument invented to measure light from stars extinguished millions of years before," she said.

"I could use one of those instruments about now," I said.

I remembered reading how navigators also used the astrolabe to determine distances between destinations. Sometimes, after too many months at sea, when the seasons began to re-occur, they realized they were lost and most of them went mad. They drifted until the promised land faded against the watery shroud. Visions of long-haired sea horses gradually replacing the constellations in the sight vane of their astrolabe. "I can't figure out where this thing with Habib is going. I think I'm going mad, Aisling."

"You're not going mad. You should get some sleep," she said gently.

"I've really screwed up."

"Yah, you've screwed up," she sighed. "It's all very romantic and thrilling now, but these are the seventies, Amy. No tall, handsome stranger on an Arabian horse is going to rescue you because you got a little bored with married life."

I felt like telling her that her assessment was way out of line. Instead, I waited for a few seconds and said, "Actually, he's not that tall."

Titters. "No, I guess he isn't, but he is charming. And handsome."

"He thinks he's tall but by our standards he really isn't. Christ, it's cold. Who would have thought the desert could get so cold." I leaned against her for warmth. "I'm so glad you're here."

"I just want to make sure that you realize there's nothing permanent here. You know that, don't you? Habib is not going to ask you to stay in Tunisia."

"I know. He never said he would."

"Suppose he did, which he won't, and for some insane reason you accepted, how long do you think it would last? How long before you got fed up with this place? The rules are too different here, Amy."

"I don't want to stay. But it doesn't make it easier."

"Then why are you risking everything you have? You could

lose Habib *and* Gilles. And you could lose Jonathan. Are you prepared to gamble Jonathan?"

"I'm not gambling Jonathan," I objected, but I knew she was right. It was an insane and dangerous game I was playing and the stakes could be my child. And I wasn't even playing honorably—cheating on a husband I still loved and didn't want to lose. "It's as if I had these two really different men wired to different parts of my brain and they keep short-circuiting each other. None of it makes sense."

"You were always the reasonable one when we were growing up," Aisling said. "You were always punching holes in my angels."

"Your S & M angels."

"Why S & M?"

"Didn't they have leather wings?" We laughed. "And you made me want to believe in them," I said.

"But you never did. And I admired you for being the sensible one. Now you want to be swept away by this guy, so you won't have to make a conscious decision and assume the responsibility. If you want to leave Gilles, leave him because the marriage doesn't work, not because you've met someone else."

She was right, of course. What I needed was a dose of Gilles's objective reality. We continued talking through the night, but avoided the one subject looming over me: my indecisiveness. We both knew that it could only lead, as far as my future was concerned, to a vicious circle of unreasonable possibilities and reasonable impossibilities.

In the early morning, as the sun rose, we ate a breakfast of oranges and dates. I craved a large mug of hot coffee and steaming milk. And toast. Cool night sweat clung to everything we touched. We later drove through arid foothills, gorges and escarpments, through the bottom of a valley, all of which had once been laid bare by tides.

"Yes," Mustapha said in a rehearsed and official spiel.

"This area was once a Garden of Eden filled with grazing antelopes and gazelles until torrential rains drove the trees and mountains back into the earth. It was a punishment from God," he added.

"Punishment for what?" I foolishly asked.

"For adultery," Mustapha said with a straight face and glanced over to Habib, who made a point of ignoring him.

We drove over rolling terrain for almost an hour, the heat rising, our spines jarring against worn seats, when suddenly the land levelled and the desert opened on us like a mouth. I'd been expecting it, but still it surprised me. Habib said he'd made this trip at least a dozen times and he could never get used to it. The sand softly brushing against the sun and the windshield, defying gravity.

As it got hotter, long, glistening arms of water opened as if to embrace us, then closed again as soon as we drove through. When I turned to look back, the water had disappeared leaving only the tracks of the vehicle. "It is the desert's memory," Mustapha explained. "Images left from violent rainstorms thousands of years ago." Nobody contradicted him because we all knew that the desert's magic relied on our willingness to be pawns to its legends. In any case, who were we to question him? He and Habib knew everything about the desert. The only things I'd ever seen that were even remotely like mirages were the small puddles along Canadian highways on dry summer afternoons—wet blotches that always disappeared before I could reach them.

People riding by on camels waved and we waved back, the camels slow, their movements complicated and eurhythmic, their giant eyelids and lashes conveying stories of patience and survival. A man, kneeling beside one of the camels, was going through the motions he would have made washing his hands.

"What is he doing?" Aisling asked.

"Cleansing himself for prayers," Habib said.

"But there's no water," Jonathan shouted.

"He makes the motions. The motions and imagining water is as purifying," Habib said to a skeptical Jonathan.

By mid-morning, the sun spilled from every corner of the sky and I wished I could imagine something other than the stifling air inside the closed vehicle. I suggested we stop and Mustapha searched for a sand dune that would provide at least a little shade while we drank our bottled water. But as soon as we opened the doors, we stepped from an oven into an inferno. Sand, dried weeds, particles, unsteady in their shimmering, all caught within a steady electric chant.

We stood around trying to decide what to do next, too hot in the sun yet reluctant to get back into the Land Rover, when we saw a large speck quivering in the distance.

"Is it a man?" Aisling asked as the speck moved toward us.

"I think so. Where did he come from?" I said. There were no tents, no structures, no camels, no vehicles other than ours. "Maybe he's lost. We should see if he needs help."

"He is not lost," Mustapha said.

Jackets draped over our heads, we watched as the quivering stain against the sky approached. He appeared to be carrying something above one shoulder. A tray balanced on one hand, the sun bouncing off a silver pot and small glasses tinkling as they knocked against each other. Glass on glass, sounds of a river. Finally, when he was near enough, a man in his late twenties or early thirties exchanged a few words with Habib and Mustapha, his voice a rasp against the dry air.

"He has brought us tea," Habib said. The man nodded several times toward Aisling and me. "He welcomes you and invites you to pour the tea if you wish."

"It is an honor," Mustapha quickly added.

The silver handle felt too hot as I poured the mint liquid over pine nuts at the bottom of each glass, the gurgling sound of water magnified in the heat. We lifted glasses in a toast, sipped, and stood around nodding and smiling. Even Jonathan must have perceived the uniqueness of such an encounter and drank without complaining although he hated the sweetness of mint tea.

When we finished, Aisling asked Mustapha if she should place a few coins on the tray and he said it would be appreciated. The three men exchanged a few more words, the young man bowed, turned and walked away carrying his tray above his shoulder, all of us following him with our eyes until the sun blinded us and we could no longer see him.

As we drove away we could see a caravan of camels and people in the distance, balanced along the horizon, beyond where the man had gone. "He must have been with that caravan," I said.

"No, he wasn't. He's always here. What you're seeing now is a mirage," Mustapha said.

"But I can see it too. How do you know it's a mirage?" Aisling asked.

Mustapha smiled. "You learn to tell the difference."

"Jesus. You're not going to tell us the guy with the tea was a mirage, are you?" she said.

"No, I think the tea was real," Mustapha replied.

"What are mirages anyway? Aren't they hallucinations brought on when people spend too much time in the sun?" Aisling asked. She said she always assumed that travelers, feeling vulnerable and lonely before the desert emptiness, simply imagined something other than the emptiness.

"No. They are real." Perhaps because he had heard this question from tourists so many times, Mustapha had memorized the explanation for mirages. In his tour-guide patter, he relayed with confidence what he'd learned about light rays descending from the sky, bending as they struck layers of air rising from the desert floor. It was from this refraction that images from other places appeared. He stopped so we could get out, and made us crouch close to the sand until the mirage disappeared. By shifting position or perspective, we could make the image reappear or disappear at will. As we shifted to one side, the buoyed caravan vaporized into bleached parchness. When we shifted back the caravan reemerged.

"Is it possible to take pictures of mirages?" Aisling asked.

"It is possible," Mustapha said. "The image exists, but the mirage is usually too far away. You would need a special camera."

"Photographs of light rays or illusions," Aisling pondered as she tried to wrap her mind around notions of doubles and seeing without necessarily seeing.

"It is even possible to take photographs of upside-down mirages," Mustapha continued, encouraged by his audience's reaction. "When light rays from treetops fall at an angle and bend upward, the tops of the trees appear to be coming out of the sand and their trunks growing toward heaven." He had seen entire oases turned on their heads, mirroring themselves on the surface of a pond, he said. "It often happens at sea. This is why sailors sometimes watch the sky to see if there are approaching vessels."

Aisling remembered an experiment in one of our science lab classes when we would place a pencil in a glass of water. Because of the light passing through the different densities— air, glass, water—the pencil always looked broken.

The goal for the day was Chott-el-Jerid, the "devastated lake" where Habib and Mustapha told Jonathan he would see water as red as lamb's blood and as green as a Canadian Christmas tree, all from the same lake. By now, even Aisling and I were ready to believe anything.

Chott-el-Jerid might also have been a mirage. I'd expected water, but instead a colored crust spread as far as the eye could see. "The water runs under the surface," Mustapha explained. During the rainy season, an immense dip in the Saharan floor filled with water; in the summer the surface water evaporated.

He pointed to trenches on each side of a makeshift road running across the so-called lake, and as he'd promised the water in the trenches ran from blood red to coho salmon pink on one side and from midnight blue to Christmas green on the other. "Because of the minerals." I was as astonished as Jonathan had been with the fake mutants on the movie set.

A man had set up a rickety table piled high with flowery, faded pink forms. At first glance they appeared fragile, yet they were hard as ice. Sand whipped up by the wind in the shape of roses and preserved under dunes, their crystal petals symmetrically arranged, Mustapha explained. A desert rose. I bought two, one for myself and one for my aunt.

Mustapha insisted we see one more sight before driving to the next town and our hotel. He called it "an attraction," a term that only served to emphasize our tourist status. Within a few minutes we came upon what he called an *aïoun*, a well whose water had seeped to the surface and created a pond where a flock of long-legged, flame-colored birds waded. Flamingos. Blobs of color on tall stems. Some still as statues, others plunging their heads underwater.

"What are they doing?" Jonathan wanted to know.

"They sift food through little combs along the edge of their bills," Mustapha told him. We watched in awe as each shimmering flamingo tottered in a blood-red pool, on a pencil leg broken by the refraction.

The desert was unlike anything I'd ever known or seen. I'd come across pictures of it in magazines but it was beyond any book or film, beyond any memory. It bore no geographical information other than sand and wind, no resting place other than the horizon, which the eyes kept chasing. As Habib had said, the desert was elsewhere.

By mid-afternoon the unrelenting assault of sun and sand had left everyone grimy and exhausted. To my relief and Aisling's, Mustapha suggested a hotel with comfortable beds and showers in Tozeur, an oasis being developed for tourists.

The lobby of our hotel had a bar, and as soon as we'd

registered, Aisling and I ordered glasses of white wine. Mustapha offered to take Jonathan for a camel ride while we rested before dinner. After we finished our wine, Aisling said she needed a rest, and Habib took me by the wrist and led me to his room.

At dinner, Jonathan fussed and wouldn't eat. His face and arms were sunburned and he felt feverish to the touch. I took him back to our room, applied lotion to his face, tucked him in and lay down beside him on his bed, inventing stories about everything we'd seen in the last two days, until he finally fell asleep.

I must have dozed too, blanketed in sand and heat, until I heard someone calling my name. I half expected the voice to speak to me of love and it took all my will to pull myself from across some great distance. It was Aisling. "Amy, wake up. It's Jonathan. He's sick."

I sat up, bewildered, an overpowering vomit smell permeating the room. "What's wrong?" Aisling was trying to comfort Jonathan but he was crying and kept asking for me.

When I turned on the light by the side of the bed, my heart leaped. I hardly recognized him because of his swollen eyes and face. His forehead was burning, his breathing abnormal. Panic spread from inside my chest into my arms and legs and I realized I was shaking. "We have to get a doctor. Oh, God. Where are we going to find a doctor?"

"I'll get Habib," Aisling said, rushing out of the room.

I carried Jonathan to the washroom to get him out of his soiled clothes. Thank God we were staying in a half-decent hotel. I tried to comfort him but he kept screaming he wanted to go home.

"We have to find a doctor or take him to a hospital," I cried out as Habib entered the room.

"Mustapha will find a doctor," he said, trying to stay calm although he too was clearly concerned when he saw Jonathan's face. "He knows his way around here."

"Here? We're not going to find a doctor here! There's nothing in this Godforsaken place!" I shouted. "We have to get back to a city. Oh God, Gilles warned me about this. He warned me about exposing Jonathan like this."

Mustapha tried to soothe me. They would find a doctor faster in Tozeur than if they drove all the way back to Tunis. He'd barely gotten the words out when I lashed out: "In Tozeur? But we have to find a real doctor. We can't have some primitive guy from a fake oasis in the middle of nowhere looking after Jonathan."

Habib frowned. "What did you say?" he asked.

There was no time for niceties. I was frantic. I wanted a doctor I could speak to and who would understand me. "I don't want one of your marabouts or whatever you call them. I want a medical doctor, a real one."

Everyone stared at me in disbelief until Habib pivoted toward the door without saying anything and Mustapha followed.

"Jesus, that was uncalled for," Aisling hissed. "He is nice enough to go out in the middle of nowhere at two in the morning for your son and you treat him like a fucking lackey."

"Jonathan is ill. You're not a mother, you wouldn't understand," I shot back. I didn't need Aisling lecturing me on the etiquette of relationships just then.

"Mother or not, it doesn't take a genius to see you haven't been exactly a model mother lately. You should have been thinking less about getting into the sack with Habib and more about your son."

"I don't neglect my son and the rest is none of your damn business." If nothing else I was a good mother, I was sure of that. "I have to wash him down with cold water. I have to get his temperature down."

The only water from the bathroom faucet trickled out lukewarm. I turned to Aisling and suggested she make herself useful and find someone who could provide us with some ice. A few moments later she returned with the night watchman, each of them carrying buckets of water with a few cubes floating in each one. "Jesus, this is all the ice they have," Aisling said.

"I'm cold, Mommy," Jonathan kept crying out. He was shivering and heaving but there was nothing left in his stomach to bring up.

"We have to get your fever down, Jonathan, so you don't get sicker."

"I want to go home now, Mommy," he repeated.

"I know, sweetheart, I know. We'll go home tomorrow but first we have to make you better. Okay?"

The man stood around helplessly, making me more nervous and irritated. I asked if he could get us cold bottled water but as soon as Jonathan drank it he brought it up again. Gilles had lectured me several times on the dangers of dehydration in children and Jonathan's skin was hot and dry, his heart pounding.

Less than an hour after the men had left, I heard a vehicle come to a stop outside the hotel. When Habib and Mustapha entered the room with a man who spoke in a distinct New York accent, carrying a medical bag, I almost dissolved from sheer relief.

"You found an American doctor?" I asked Habib.

"Yes," he said, his tone icy. "Since you didn't want a witch doctor we went to the film company." The light in his eyes had disappeared, his gaze as steady as two black stones.

The doctor confirmed Jonathan had had too much sun and was suffering from heat exhaustion. He'd already treated several cases on the movie set but with a child it could be more risky.

"We want to avoid seizures," he said. He gave Jonathan an injection, waited several minutes, then took out a bottle of liquid and propped Jonathan against his arm. "Can you drink some of this, buddy? This is what athletes drink when they need to get strong." While Jonathan took small sips the doctor explained it would be preferable to administer fluids intravenously. "We should take him back to the medical trailer with the supplies," he suggested. "You got good and sunburned, buddy. We'll have to put something on that beautiful face."

"As long as I can stay with him," I said.

"Certainly. You and your husband can come along."

My husband. Habib didn't react but he dressed Jonathan in clean clothes and carried him to the Land Rover. After several questions from the doctor, it finally became clear Habib was not Jonathan's father. Everyone fell silent.

After the intravenous had been administered and Jonathan had fallen asleep, Habib and I went outside the trailer. We stood in silence, sipping on barely warm instant coffee, until I summoned what little courage I had left and placed a hand on Habib's arm. "I'm sorry about last night. I was frantic and said stupid things. I don't know what got into me."

"Yes. It is revealing what a woman says when she is frantic." He studied my face as he'd done so many times except now it carried suspicion and distrust, the threat of exposure. There were no smiles to draw me in.

"The doctor was right to mistake you for Jonathan's father. You couldn't have done more for him if you were." I hoped for some kind of conciliatory gesture or, at the very least, a few words of forgiveness, but none came.

He gave a derisive little laugh instead. "No. He was wrong. I am not his father. A son needs his true father. No other man can take his place."

"You don't think you could be a father to Jonathan?" I asked, not knowing why I pursued this line of questioning.

"*Non*, Aimée," he said, his voice honed with impatience. "I am not Jonathan's father. You understand this? Jonathan belongs to his father and I will have my own sons. And they will be Tunisians. Arabs. They will be proud of their doctors and their marabouts."

"I don't know how to convince you how sorry I am. Sometimes I'm too impulsive, I do things or say things I regret."

"I know you are sorry but it does not erase what you said. You think Tunisians are primitive. We are crude snapshots taken by tourists before they return to their civilized countries. This is all there is between us. An impulsive affair with a foreigner."

"That's not true. I've never thought of you this way and you know it. I'm the one who's the foreigner here. Don't turn this around. I'm not the only guilty one."

"We are both guilty. At least we have this in common. In everything else we are too different, Aimée."

"A little. Culturally. This is normal, isn't it?"

"More than a little," he said, holding his stare. Then, conceding the obvious, "Aimée, we do not come from the same world." His tone was gentler now but it was also meant to keep me at a distance and in my place. "We have nothing in common."

Nothing in common. We'd never talked about commonality. Feeling estranged in Paris, we had turned to one another without preconception. I wanted to tell him how much this meant to me, how much he meant to me. Chafia, Wassila. The desert. Carthage. People and places anchored in my heart. I didn't pretend to understand his country, his culture, but this had never been an issue when we were together.

Suddenly, the sun had risen and the coolness of the night was gone. How quickly everything reversed itself here. I needed to sleep. Shut my eyes and have the last few days dissipate like the cold night air.

In Sidi Bou Saïd I had told Aisling I felt better about myself when I was with Habib than when I was with Gilles. Was this what our affair had been, an exercise in self-appreciation? Was everything we'd experienced together in the last few weeks as ephemeral as a mirage? How had I let myself drift so far off course? The burned face of my child castigating me. What vanity had led to this?

"You're right," I said finally. "We have nothing in common. The doctor said we could leave after Jonathan's intravenous and after he's had a rest. We'll drive straight back."

Later that evening, the five of us must have looked like a startled band of grimy drifters as we entered the gate to the house in Sidi Bou Saïd and saw Gilles standing there.

The Magic Writing Pad

As soon as Jonathan saw his father, he let go of Habib's hand and ran to Gilles. "Daddy, I went for a camel ride and we saw movie monsters and the doctor said I was very sick."

Gilles inspected his son's face. "The doctor? What doctor?"

"He takes care of movie people and he made me better. I was very sick, Daddy, I almost died."

I felt like cuffing his cherubic little head. "He didn't almost die. He got a bit too much sun."

"I can see that. What's going on?" he asked. It took a lot to visibly upset Gilles but I could tell he could hardly control himself, his anger. "I've been waiting here three days." He spotted my wedding band on the chain around my neck, his scowl reaching into the pit of my stomach.

"You must have arrived just after we left." Since I hadn't returned his calls I couldn't very well reproach him for not warning me he was coming sooner than planned. "We decided to go to the desert before Aisling left. Mustapha and Habib took us." I must have sounded ludicrous.

Gilles nodded a perfunctory greeting toward Aisling and the two men. Habib mumbled something about retrieving some of his things. Which he'd left in my bedroom, I realized, horrified. Everyone stood around mute as dummies waiting for him to return. When he did, he kissed me on both cheeks, then left with Mustapha. I couldn't think what else he could have done, but I wished it had been vastly different.

Jonathan prattled on about real monsters, red and green water, camels who disappeared—pouf—into thin air. But after a few minutes, sensing he couldn't hold his father's attention, he asked if he could go to Chafia's to show Fatma his sunburn, and Aisling offered to take him.

I had never seen Gilles so utterly defeated. It pained me to see him in such distress, unshaven, hair longer than usual, but it also annoyed me that his anguish held sway over mine.

He could hardly look at me, let alone speak. It would be up to me to initiate the inevitable. "We might as well talk about it now."

"You've been sleeping with Habib." His statement was so indisputable there seemed no point in denying it.

"Yes."

"Why?"

I was supposed to explain *why*? "I wanted to, I guess."

"You wanted to?" he shouted. "That's it? Because you wanted to? You'll have to do better than that. I've been here three days thinking, trying to understand. Come on, Amy, I need to understand."

I had never heard him shout before, at least not in anger. Nothing I could say would mollify him. He expected logic, cause and effect. "I don't know how to explain. I don't understand myself."

His eyes darted about. I imagined his thoughts scurrying, searching for a pattern he would recognize, the kind the mind needs to protect itself. "Weren't we happy?" he asked, with a desperate tone to his voice.

"Yes," I whispered when, in fact, I wanted to scream that I couldn't stand our endless little measures of happiness any longer. Oh, we were happy. Day in and day out happy. Just once I needed to experience the exhilaration that comes when nothing is fixed. Every moment in flux. The state that sharpens all senses as when we had first met.

"For someone who always has some smart-ass reply you're not doing too well," he spat out.

I could only offer more confusion. "I want you to know I've

never stopped loving you." Though I meant it, it sounded duplicitous. "It sounds crazy, I know, but I do love you. I didn't go to Habib because I'd fallen out of love with you." It surprised me that there should be any question of this.

He stared, bewildered, then snickered. "I believe you, actually. Not that it clarifies anything. I love you, too, but it's not enough for you, is it? It's never been enough."

"It's not enough, it's too much, I don't know." How could I justify a craving as overwhelming and irrational as the one that had taken over my life these last few weeks? Gilles was the one who knew how to speak of such things. He was the one who understood the vocabulary of unfulfilled needs, filed them under pathologies, obsessions, perversions, kept them at a safe patient-and-doctor distance. But his ego was so bruised, I was willing to go along with whatever he wanted to hear.

"Are you paying him to sleep with you?" he asked.

Our eyes collided. "What? What did you say?" I couldn't believe my ears.

"Are you paying him?" he said, pausing after each word.

"Why would I need to pay anyone to sleep with me?"

"He has no money."

"Neither do I. At least he has a job. I don't even have that."

"He didn't have any money in Paris. I gave him some before we left so he wouldn't have to hitchhike all the way here."

I said nothing about Habib hitchhiking and wondered why he hadn't mentioned anything about Gilles giving him money. Had he been too embarrassed or, more likely, had he wanted to save it? Telling Gilles would only confirm his suspicions. "We never discussed money."

"Why not? You knew him well enough to sleep with him but not well enough to discuss money?" he jeered. "This may come as a surprise to you but I can't afford to support another man so he can sleep with my wife."

"But you gave him money to check on me. Why did you ask him to check on me? Why don't you analyze that?"

"I was worried about you, for Christ's sake."

"I don't want you to worry about me."

He wasn't listening. I guess it was easier to think of another man sleeping with his wife for profit rather than a mutual attraction. "I have little money left. I don't know how I'll finish my sabbatical," he said.

"I don't give Habib money and he doesn't give me any either. I was barely managing until Aisling got here. She's been paying for everything. So I'm hardly in a position to pay for sex. If Habib needed money so badly, he would have done better somewhere else."

A week after our first night together, Habib had apologized for not having enough money to pay for anything we bought. He gave me an anniversary card. It read, *"Pour notre anniversaire, je vous offre un solitaire. Moi."* The reasons I felt better with one man than with the other were becoming abundantly clear. Gilles's condescending attitude always managed to make me feel like shit.

"I suppose a few days of reckless passion with a stranger is livelier than the love of a husband," he said, having stumbled on the one clue that made sense to him. "Women would rather give their love to men who are obsessed with them than to men who just love them."

"Nobody's obsessed with anybody. You're inventing something that doesn't exist." He was so good at fabricating proof. And now he wanted me to be like one of those patients he so often complained about, even scoffed at: women addicted to romance, wrecking everybody's lives. "That numbing obsession that tries to pass itself off as custodian of the heart," he called it.

How big is the heart? I had once asked him. The size of a fist, he had responded.

I wanted to hit him, shake him. "Gilles, listen to me. I'm not one of your patients. I'm not obsessed, I made a mistake. I'm not the first wife to have made a mistake."

No sooner had I uttered the words than I wanted to retrieve them. Surely the mistake lay in the pain I was causing Gilles, not in sleeping with Habib. I didn't want to brand this as a mistake, not yet. "What we have to do now is figure out if any of this can be fixed," I said.

He sucked in deeply, trying to catch his breath. "It's not that simple. I have to understand what happened here."

He would, if I let him, dissect and sift through every moment I had spent with Habib until there would be nothing left but a sediment I couldn't hold on to. "Maybe it's not that complicated. Maybe I just wanted to sleep with him ..."

He sniggered. "Guess I underestimated him. I hadn't expected him to be so treacherous."

"He's not treacherous. He is charming and I let myself be charmed. He is manipulative but I played a part in it too. He's no more of a villain than either one of us."

He bridled with annoyance. "You might as well know...." He hesitated.

I waited. "What?"

"If you leave, I won't let you have Jonathan. I'll make sure Jonathan stays with me. I won't leave him here."

My stomach somersaulted. He must have been concocting all sorts of scenarios these last three days. Aisling was right. Children were the ones who always got misplaced in their parents' excesses. Mine was culminating in a showdown involving Jonathan.

"Why would I stay here?"

"Because if you are planning on staying, Jonathan comes with me. I'll fight you. I have good grounds."

Grounds? Had he gone this far? I tried to catch his eye. "Gilles, I'm not staying in Tunisia." Nobody wants me to stay in Tunisia, I wanted to add.

"What the hell do you want then?" I could see him desperately trying to collect his fragmented thoughts, fitting answers to questions, questions to answers. But none of the pieces matched. My affair would not yield to his conjectures, the reasoning of lovers inaccessible to outsiders. I suspect this was more painful for him than anything else.

A sudden sound, a wailing almost, startled me as he cried out and brought his fist down on the coffee table. I'd never seen this side of him, his frustration, the defeat and rage threatening to reel out of control.

"Okay. One thing at a time," I said, hoping my affected composure would calm him. "First, the world doesn't come to an end because a wife sleeps with another man. We're not going to get a divorce right now, tonight."

"No, not right now. But in the meantime, what?"

I had to come up with something plausible, fill in the gaps with something other than his fury. "Aisling came all the way here because I asked her to. We should allow her to finish her holiday. She only has a few days left. Can we be civil for at least this long?"

"Who else besides Aisling knows? Does Chafia know?"

"Is this really the issue here?" A futile question since I imagined being seen as a cuckolded husband was as tangible a fear as any.

"So we stay here until Aisling leaves. Then what?" he asked.

"Then I'll leave if you want me to. I'll go back to Paris, and you can stay here. You need a rest. It's up to you."

"Convenient for you, isn't it? If we stay, we pretend nothing's happened."

"Nobody is asking you to pretend. Something did happen and we'll have to deal with it. I told you, it was a mistake. It's over." I searched his eyes but saw little more than distress. "It would be good for you to stay. You've been on sabbatical for seven months and all you've done is work. We could try to figure things out from here. Or I'll leave, if you want."

"Because you assume we can figure things out? It's not only up to you. I'm never going to forget this."

"No, it's not only up to me." Suddenly, I'd had enough. I was willing to shoulder all the blame but I wouldn't be held hostage to his self-pity. "It's up to you too. If what I've done is too much for you to handle, you decide what you want to do. But since you brought it up, I want you to know I will never, ever, give up Jonathan. If you don't want me here or in Paris, I'll go back to Canada and I'll take him with me. You hardly ever spend any time with him so don't try to come off as the aggrieved and devoted father. You try to take Jonathan and I'll fight you every way I can. As his mother I'll probably win."

"I love Jonathan as much as you do."

"Oh God, Gilles, I know you do. I don't want to fight over Jonathan because of some stupid mistake I made, or because of your pride and some outdated, carved-in-stone rule on fidelity. I don't.... Oh, fuck it. I've had it up to here with men misunderstanding everything I do or say."

I did ask myself just then if the marriage wasn't over. There were so many facets of each other we hadn't been able to hold on to—the little idiosyncrasies people fall in love with, which either disappear or flourish into major sources of irritation. Gilles's unerring intelligence, which I trusted so implicitly when we first met, was imposing itself on every aspect of our lives. And I doubted he would ever see me again as the woman he first met. The past was being peeled back leaving only faint traces of who we once were, as on Jonathan's Magic Pad. "Maybe we should get to know each other again," I ventured. God knows, we had nothing to lose.

"We'll see what happens after Aisling leaves." He was beginning to relent. "I better go to Chafia's and get them."

On the surface, August proceeded relatively uneventfully. Gilles never brought up Habib. We resumed our visits to archaeological sites, museums, cafés. Conversation, strained at first, gradually stretched into late-evening chats on the terrace. Gilles spoke about articles he planned to write once he returned to Canada and about his disappointment with the psychoanalytical scene in Paris. The seminars and conferences had worn him down. He had gone to Paris for new ideas but found mostly old ones in disguise.

I told him about the desert and the lake with the thick crust. Mirages. "They're real, you know. Refracted images of real scenes happening somewhere else."

"Illusions are always refractions of reality happening somewhere else," he said. I suspected he would have liked to see the desert too, but I had spoiled it for him.

Jonathan continued to ask when Habib was coming back, until our evasiveness made it clear it was best to forget him.

I also tried to forget. Convinced myself that those few weeks had been but an aberration. A hand would soon sweep over the entire affair, much as when a breeze sweeps across the desert. But I didn't carry within me this kind of amnesia. Every night I dreamed of him the way a small tree clinging to the edge of the desert must dream of all the water locked under the sand.

One Sweet Letter from You

RESOLVED TO GET SOME WORK DONE on my thesis during the remaining four months in Paris, I suggested to Gilles we find a school for Jonathan and he readily agreed. French schools, we concluded, after looking into several, were too institutional and stolid for a child not quite five years old, so we enrolled him at the bilingual and multi-denominational Marymount Academy run by American nuns for children of foreigners based in Paris. The first time we went there, we could hear, from the front parlor, the Beatles' "Let It Be," a sure sign it was the right place and the right time for me to let go of Jonathan.

The school bus picked up the children at predetermined points throughout the city, the closest one to us only two blocks from the apartment. Jonathan enthusiastically took to the idea of boarding a bus to school, pulling on my hand as he led the way and as I tried to keep up with him.

I registered for two courses in eighteenth- and nineteenth-century art at the Louvre, although my heart wasn't in it. I chased every distraction I could think of. I remembered a record Gilles and I often played back home—Dizzy Gillespie's "Night in Tunisia"—and I went hunting for a copy. Played it loud enough to drown out the piano upstairs. Mr. Frankl's sonatas and études had nothing to do with me. Gillespie's "Tunisia" was one place in which I could disappear. I filled my days with "Night in Tunisia."

I detoured by Robert Schumann Square on my way home from Jonathan's bus. One afternoon I stopped and sat on the bench where Habib and I met, surprised to find other people there—other mothers with children, loud voices, traffic noises. I resented all of them. I wanted to be alone and hear *"Vous êtes au pair?"* from the other end of the bench.

I wandered the streets. Gigantic movie billboards of lovers kissing loomed up and down the Champs-Elysées, impervious to the hustle and bustle around them.

At the Musée Rodin, I stood before Rodin's *Kiss*. Lovers entwined in an awkward embrace. I sat in the museum's garden rereading *Madame Bovary* and *Anna Karenina*. Women driven to killing themselves and abandoning their children. Intelligent women didn't act like this, didn't think like this. Bovary and Karenina's obsessions had nothing to do with me. Yet I desperately needed to see Habib again. Circumstances had changed.

In a gallery window near Trocadéro, a sculpture of a heart made of barbed wire kept everyone at bay. How large is the human heart? The size of a pounding fist shredding the cavity inside my chest. I hated being in my own skin.

Everything we had experienced together held him. When I picked up Jonathan after school we stopped at the fruit and vegetable store and bought figs. September figs, plumper and darker than spring ones. The sound of my footsteps echoing his as I walked to the apartment, his hand at my elbow or on my shoulder. Once inside the apartment I cut the figs in the shape of a flower as he had done. Probed its ripening with my tongue until my mouth became his. I saw, spoke, felt him from within: Habib. I yearned to retrieve everything we'd known together, everything we'd touched or seen. For what were lovers but the repetitions of their gestures? One embrace, one kiss.

Until it finally happened. What I'd been waiting for. What I had willed: a letter, his handwriting.

My dearest Aimée,
Since I left you in Sidi Bou Saïd I think only of you and the last
night in Tozeur when Jonatan was ill. You tried to repair the things
you said but I was too proud to listen. I know how worried you were
and I could only think of myself. I regret this and leaving you to
explain by yourself to your husband. I should have stayed with you.
I am a coward. I beg your forgiveness.

Tunis is empty. It is the desert without charm. Even Sidi Bou
Saïd has lost its sunlight and I can no longer go there. Everything
covered by clouds even in blue skies. I remember you telling Jonatan
that clouds were elephants who had gone to heaven and when I
think of this I smile. Only memories of you can make me smile.
I work and the days pass and I think only of the tenderness in us
which resides in me still and will not leave. What have I become for
you? What did this short time together mean to you? Can you write
to me and tell me?

My courses in Paris start in October and I must stay here to
make as much money as I can before I return. To what, I ask?
Incertitude. Solitude. Étouffement. How will I rid myself of these
feelings? I have no right to ask but will you write to me? Will you
tell me if your feelings are similar to mine?

Aimée, I know this was not supposed to happen but I must see
you again, hold you in my arms. We must meet to speak of this. I
assure you I am sincere. These are not flowers I throw you. Please
write. I can no longer support the silence between us.
Your faithful Habib

P.S. I stole a photograph of you from the bedroom when I left
and keep it with me always. I have included one of myself so you
will not forget who I am. And a poem I have adapted from Rumi.

When I eat or work
Or visit friends, you are
inside me the arc
Of light as when I sit
under stars. If I walk and you are not with me
I don't know where I am.
H.

I found the poem a little over the top but moving just the same. The letter *H* at the end a sigh, as if the bearer had run out of breath or patience. The photograph shocked me a little. He looked different from the man I'd carried in my head these last few weeks, too much like Omar Sharif. I rushed out to buy another record: It featured Gillespie playing "One Sweet Letter from You." I listening to it for hours.

My behavior, like Habib's poem, was certainly over the top. It seemed perfectly normal. A desperate desire to believe that everything will turn out for the best can rewrite normal behavior like no other emotional state.

One afternoon I heard the stammering of Mr. Frankl's piano coming through the ceiling from the apartment upstairs. A note here, another there, one hand, then two, until the piano began to beat out its own improvisations of Gillespie's music. A duet. I'd never met Mr. Frankl—never even seen him—but he was trying to communicate something to me, I was sure of it.

That afternoon, as I went out to pick up Jonathan, I stuck a note in Mr. Frankl's mailbox. "Could you play something by Robert Schumann?" the note asked, and I signed it "the woman downstairs." I didn't know Schumann's music any more than I knew Mr. Frankl, but I'd read somewhere that Schumann was a romantic and I'd met my lover in a park with his name. The next morning a sequence of pulsations and rhythms came crashing from above. Whatever passage Mr. Frankl was playing sounded delirious and mad. I was delirious and mad.

I wrote to Habib almost every day, letters couched in laments and reproaches. Why wasn't he hurrying back? If he loved me, as he said, how could he bear to stay away?

Every day I waited for the postman. Carried his letters close to my body. Took them to Robert Schumann Square, pored over them while sitting on our bench.

It was mid-September. Habib had written he would be arriving in early October, depending on how much money he could save. He so seldom sent news of himself, his declarations the legends of heartache, his language too formal and elusive to bridge the vast geography between us. I wanted to know more about him, his job, what he did in his free time. Something tangible, a tightrope to balance the void I walked across each day.

"Who are those letters from?" a voice asked from the other end of the bench. It wasn't the right voice and it didn't speak the right words. It was an old man I'd seen sitting there several times in the last few weeks.

"Just letters." Go away, I said to myself.

"No, no. Not 'just letters.' A woman doesn't reread the same letters over and over unless they're from someone special, a lover."

He was probably in his seventies or early eighties. His face was kind but careworn, and in spite of the warm weather he wore a dark woolen suit and vest, a watch chain across his chest. Round glasses rimmed in black.

"Actually yes, they are from my lover," I admitted coyly. What difference did it make if this stranger knew? If the whole world knew.

"Ah, lovers. What luxury. The expectation in a lover's eyes, the parted lips. I would give anything to live those moments one more time," he said.

"What's stopping you?" I asked, ignoring the obvious.

"Age, *ma belle*. The incompatibility of passion and age. Fate is cruel."

"Can't people still feel passionate when they're old?" I asked, out of courtesy more than curiosity.

"Yes, of course they can, very passionate. This is the ultimate cruelty since age no longer has the luxury of a beautiful body. Or the stamina. We are left to our fantasies of what once was. Or we become passionate about other things."

"What other things?"

"Ideas. We can be passionate about ideas although they also

require stamina. Artificial things require the least. The kind money can buy." He chuckled. "Why is your lover writing to you? Is he away? Have you quarreled?"

"He's in Tunisia for the summer. He won't be here for another month." It was odd, speaking openly about Habib, fitting him into normal life.

"Ah, Tunisia. A beautiful country. Have you been there?"

"I spent the summer there. It's very beautiful."

"You miss him?"

"Yes. I leave for Canada in December. We won't have much time to spend together."

"You are Canadian?"

"Yes."

"And circumstances do not allow you to stay here beyond December or for him to go to Canada?" He kept reaching under his glasses with a handkerchief, dabbing his eyes.

He was getting too personal. "Do you have allergies?" I asked.

"No. Old age." He smiled, a tender, knowing smile. "How can he bear to stay away from such loveliness?"

I moved my head and shoulder in some kind of beats-me gesture. "He has to earn money for school. He's a graduate student. And poor."

"Tunisia. An Arab?"

"Yes."

"Arab, student and poor. For a man with so many strikes against him, he must have something very special to have captivated you."

"So, you're a racist?"

"Oh, not particularly. Too old even for that. Age is a great leveler and I can no longer bring myself to hate. Not even an Arab and this is quite something for a *pied-noir*."

At first I thought he'd said *peignoir* but it couldn't be right. "A what?" I asked.

"*Pied-noir*," he repeated. "A French person of European

descent born in Algeria. We are branded as *pieds-noirs* even after we move to Paris. No, I am not so much racist as envious of your Arab friend. Envy always leads to indignation." He smiled at his own witticism.

His gentleness, his meekness, invited solicitude. I placed a hand over his. Faint tremors, bones deformed with arthritis under flimsy skin startled me. He might have been an attractive man once, certainly elegant and gracious, but age had divested him of any power. How did one get to be so old? "I'm sure you've had your share of romance," I said, my voice teasing and flirtatious, but too patronizing. Was it possible to speak to the very old without condescension?

"Yes, I did. Twice. Married twice," he said.

"You were in love both times?"

"Of course, of course."

"Are you still married?" I asked.

"Yes, yes. My second wife is still with me, yes. She's angry with me today." One corner of his mouth raised, sardonically.

"Why?"

"Because I won't buy her a fur coat. Imagine, thinking of fur coats in this heat." Again he dabbed his eyes and forehead with his monogrammed handkerchief.

"Do you still feel passionate about her?" I asked.

"I love her, definitely. But passion? Old eyes, old skin don't reflect too well the glow of passionate embrace." He chortled and held on to my hand, his own a trembling animal on alert.

"I'm sure she's very beautiful." I imagined a woman made stately by age and propriety.

"Yes, yes, this is true. She was a great beauty and still is. Yes. The love of my life. *Pleine d'ardeur*. Like you, I imagine. Prepared to do anything to be with me, anything. I was very proud of it." He leaned closer and whispered, "It broke up my first marriage."

"It did?" I whispered back. "Do you ever regret it?"

"I don't regret being with my second wife, no. I regret what it did to my children. I had two children with my first wife. My second wife didn't want any. We lived for each other, which required all my free time so I almost never saw the children." He frowned. Perhaps the equation was no longer as equitable. "Couldn't be helped, I suppose," he said, his voice resolute. He sat quietly for a while, possibly reassessing the past, when, suddenly, he turned to me. "To what lengths would you go to be with your lover?" he asked.

"I don't know. I've never thought of it."

"Think of it now. To what lengths?"

"Well ... I'm not sure. I wouldn't break up my marriage. I definitely wouldn't leave my child."

"But you want to be with him, with the man who writes you those letters?"

"Yes, of course."

"More than anything else?"

I hesitated. "No, not anything...." My voice trailed, undecided, until my curiosity prompted a change of mind. "Well, I suppose...."

"And he is a young lover? Your age?"

"About my age, yes."

"Then I have a proposition for you. I want to see, one last time, the body of a beautiful woman caught in the vise of passion."

I'd heard what he said but it sounded so peculiar and outrageous that I needed to confirm it. "Pardon? You want to see me make love?"

"No, no. Not make love. This would be too indiscreet. I want to see once more through the eyes of a young man. I want to see you without your clothes on."

"You're crazy!" I cried out, part of me recoiling at the thought of parading naked in front of an old man, another part of me finding the idea so incongruous I lifted both hands to my eyes to block the image.

"You are offended?" he asked.

"I should be. But I find it more funny than offensive."

His face was so weighed down by lines, his skull tight as a helmet sprouting wispy white hairs. His eyes so cloudy behind his glasses, I couldn't help but wonder what they could possibly see beyond shadows. How could those old eyes receive the same images as Habib, whose eyes were so clear and bright?

"Now I should be offended," he said. "You think I'm a ridiculous old man."

"No, I don't. Really. I was trying to visualize ... your suggestion and found it rather funny." Would he want me walking, or lying on a bed, sitting with my legs apart?

"Should you agree to do this I will give you enough money to bring your lover back immediately, plus enough to pay his school fees for this year. And all his books. It will more than make up for the time and money he will lose by coming back early."

"You're asking me to prostitute myself."

"Am I? Is this what you call it? It is unfortunate. Would you do it for nothing then? Out of kindness for an old man?"

"No, I wouldn't. Kindness can be prostitution too."

"Especially kindness," he added. "It's a matter of semantics, you see. But if this is the word you want to use, then, yes, we would be prostituting ourselves. Myself, you, your lover, all three of us, in the same *chaloupe*, as you English say."

"I'm not inclined to do it at all, not for money or kindness. And I'm not English, I'm Canadian," I reminded him, although I failed to see the relevance of citizenship to taking off my clothes for a man almost three times my age.

"You're not inclined but you are not saying no? You are not shutting the door?"

"Yes, I am shutting the door."

"Ah, I am disappointed." He laced his fingers into mine. "Can nothing persuade you?"

"I don't think so."

"Could we not get beyond semantics?" he appealed, glimmering behind his glasses. "You want to see your lover and I want to see you through the eyes of your lover. Nothing else. I wouldn't try anything else. It would be too humiliating."

"But it would be humiliating for me to do it."

"*Et alors?*" he said, as if he were stating the obvious. "We will both be humiliated but we will both have what we want. What is so bad about this?"

It was crucial that Habib return as soon as possible. As for humiliation, mine and the old man's, it was merely an affinity between two people afflicted by longing and, possibly, by fear of what lay ahead. His old eyes, in craving the body of a young woman, would grant me what I craved—my lover. His eyes held my future. Would humiliation seem so important when I got to be his age?

As I said, "Yes, I'll do it," I imagined the lurching of an old and somnolent heart. "Where do you want this to take place?" I asked, trying to sound casual in spite of the pounding in my chest. Not only was I nervous but, strangely enough, I was beside myself with excitement.

"There's a small hotel across the park." He motioned toward Boulevard Lannes. "We could go there."

"When?"

"Now if you wish."

"I would like to stop by the post office first so we can telegraph the money to my friend."

"Certainly. But I would not tell him how you got it."

"I don't intend to."

"I have dreamed of a moment like this for a long time."

"Nothing is as wonderful as when it is dreamed," I warned him. "Will there be a mirror in the room, do you think?"

His eyebrows arched in surprise. "I would think so. Would you want one?"

"Oh yes, I've got to see this," I said.

"We will make sure there is, then." He smiled, almost

imperceptibly, as if he had confirmed what he already suspected.

Four days later, I found a note under my door. In it, Habib thanked me for the telegram and the money and informed me he was waiting in his room on the fifth floor.

Brancusi's Kiss

THE NEXT MONTH UNFOLDED MUCH as any clandestine affair does: stolen moments; fingers that fit too deeply into the ridges of another's spine, each cell of each body frantic as a crowd.

Habib hadn't exaggerated when he said his room was not much wider than the window. We sat in the middle of his single bed, the rickety spring and mattress as steady as an old barge on a rough sea. "This bed is awful. It's so bad for your back. Why don't you keep the mattress on the floor?" I asked.

"There would be no room to walk around."

How could anyone live like this day in and day out? Especially after the desert and Sidi Bou Saïd.

While the October rain drummed its sleepless chatter on the slate roof, I tried to learn as much about him as I could. His father had died when Habib was nine and since then he and his family had lived pretty much in poverty. His mother was ill with what he referred to as *la maladie du sucre*, which I assumed was diabetes. It was clear that he felt responsible for her and for his two brothers and a sister, in spite of the fact that Mustapha owned his own touring business and was thinking of buying another Land Rover and expanding. Their other brother occasionally got work as a journalist for the weekly newspaper, *Jeune Afrique*. His sister was much younger and still in school. In spite of having boasted that poverty was his pride, it was clear that most of his decisions for the future were made with his family's financial security in mind. It was no accident that he had chosen to study management.

Since Islam played such a prominent role in all aspects of Arabic life, I wanted to know the extent it affected his. "Do you consider yourself a Muslim?" I asked.

He was untangling and brushing my hair. "Of course. Do you not consider yourself a Christian?"

"I never think of it. I'm not very good at the whole abnegation and obedience thing." An understatement, to say the least.

"Muslims don't obey, they surrender. We surrender willingly."

"You don't strike me as the type who surrenders that easily."

He laughed. "This is true. To this I surrender also. You believe in nothing?" he asked.

"Oh, I must believe in something." My mind scrambled, anticipating the next question.

"What, exactly?"

Nothing I could say would be as lofty as willing surrender. "Creativity moves me more than religion."

"This is why you studied art?"

"Probably. An impulsive decision, actually."

He continued brushing my hair, putting it up in a French twist, piling it on top of my head, as I told him about my very first day in Toronto, how the rain and the city's indifference had stifled the exhilaration I'd felt the night before, when I left New Erie. I hadn't been ready for so many anonymous faces.

To kill time before an appointment with a course advisor at the university, I had planned on dropping into the Art Gallery of Ontario. I had never been to an art gallery before. I wandered in and out of rooms, amazed at the inexhaustible subjects and styles, until I found myself in an open area surrounded by large canvases with nothing on them but color. No shapes or lines, each canvas covered in either bright or deep tones, some smooth as churned butter, others scarred in deep gouges. I'd never seen anything like them. I learned later that this kind of art was known as color field painting, but at the time I had no idea what to make of it or what the canvases might represent. The longer I stood there, the more they reverberated, until the band I'd carried around my chest all morning began to loosen.

For an hour I went back and forth between the paintings, their surfaces urging me to remember something I might have forgotten: the fields around New Erie in the morning when they were slowly expanded by early light, or shadows the color of eggplant in late fall.

Did my parents ever have time to notice any of these marvels, I wondered? Did they ever perceive in the farm anything but acres to be plowed and harvested? If they did notice, did they ever speak about it to each other?

"Imagination playing tricks on us," my mother might have jeered, sensing the dangers in altering, even slightly, everyday reality. They, of all people, couldn't afford such luxury. She might have stepped away from the window then, afraid if she stayed there too long she would never again see the world as before, never recover the sure and competent way of doing things.

It was then, I told Habib, that I decided I would learn all I could about this strange occupation of making art. When I walked out of the gallery, the sun was shining and I felt exhilarated at the idea of starting my new life. "It was like walking into a clearing," I told Habib.

"A clearing? What is it?" he asked.

I couldn't think of the right word in French. "A clearing," I repeated, gesticulating with my arms to indicate a large space. He still didn't understand. He reached down beside the bed and retrieved a French and English dictionary. "Clearing," he repeated, his eyes following his finger down the page. "Here it is. *Évacuation.*"

"No, no, not evacuation." Again I made a sweeping gesture with my arms.

"This is what it says, *une décharge du ventre*. Clearing the bowels. Ohh," he said, pretending to be shocked.

"No, no. Clearing of a space, like a forest."

"Ah, clearing of a forest, here it is. *Une éclaircie*." He leaned over and kissed me. "But this is how I feel when I go into the desert," he said, stating the obvious. He beamed at the existence of our shared knowledge.

"There's this sculptor who used to live in Paris whose studio I often visit. His name is Brancusi. He's dead now, but the city moved his house into the Museum of Modern Art at Trocadéro. He once claimed there were no mysteries to his sculptures, but if you looked at them long enough, until you really saw them, you moved closer to God. I prefer to think that if you look at them long enough, you move closer to human beings."

"Then I would like to see these sculptures," Habib said.

There were two sculptures in particular I wanted him to see. Made of polished marble, they were astonishingly simple. The oval form of *The Newborn* had been segmented just enough to suggest the screaming, gaping mouth of an infant. The other, *The Beginning of the World*, also named *Sculpture for the Blind*, was simply an egg shape.

"What do you think?" I asked Habib a few days later, as we stood before the two marble pieces.

"They are very beautiful. It would be wonderful if life could be so perfect and so simple."

"Everything is simple in the beginning," I said. "That's why Brancusi used an egg to represent the birth and death cycle."

"Yes, birth and death are simple. But what happens in between? This is more difficult, do you not think?" He walked to a solid block of stone with a few chiseled lines, one of them delineating the joined forms of a man and a woman, her round belly pressed against the man's flat stomach, Brancusi's version of *The Kiss*. "I like this one better," he said.

"Why?" His reaction disappointed me. I wanted him to be as enthusiastic about *The Newborn* and *The Beginning of the World* as I was.

"This is what makes your life and death cycle worthwhile. These lovers are us, Aimée." He gently pushed his hip into mine.

"But the other two are more accomplished pieces," I protested. To me, their marble surfaces were subtler, more fluid than the rough limestone of *The Kiss*.

"You only think this because you are a mother," he said dismissively. "They have too much ... style."

"Too stylized? I don't think they're too stylized. What about this one? I suppose you prefer this one too." I pointed to a piece called *King of Kings*, a rough totem made of forms from an old wine press depicting an impudent Oedipus with hollowed eyes. "You find this one more interesting?"

He studied it for several minutes. "It is amusing," he said, then turned his attention again to *The Kiss*. "There is something sacred in these two lovers who have become one for eternity."

"That is so depressing," I sighed.

"But why?"

"People stuck together forever? So they can never be anything else but lovers? Never apart, always one, never two or three." Three. I visualized the forming skull of the baby I was carrying.

"You are too cynical."

"Am I?" For some peculiar reason I thought showing Habib the sculptures would provide an opportunity to tell him I was pregnant. I'd been wrestling with this for a month. But perhaps it was better not to tell him. What could he do about it? He expected me to be gone in another month and, much as he bemoaned the fact, my staying longer would only confuse him. He had no money and he was busy with his studies, and his plans for his future. His own family. I had no permanent place in his life, certainly not in Tunisia. Nor did he have a place in mine. Even if he wanted me to stay I would only be stepping into another version of domesticity while he struggled to keep alive some notion of something more sublime. More important, I didn't want to leave Gilles or lose Jonathan. My place was with them in Canada.

In spite of an ever-growing panic made worse by early pregnancy nausea, I tried to maintain a semblance of normality with Gilles. I needed time. After I phoned Aisling, she sent me money for an abortion but I wasn't convinced that was what I wanted. I did make sure to always be there for Jonathan, walked him to and from school. My time with him and Gilles was always segregated from my time with Habib.

Gilles suspected something wasn't right but said little, until one evening when he tried to kiss me and I spontaneously pushed him away. "Habib is back, isn't he?" he asked.

I feigned disinterest. "Yes, I see him around."

"He's back in your life. You're sleeping with him again. I can smell him on you, for Christ's sake."

I saw no way out. A denial would only lead to lies and recriminations. "Yes. I see him." I had to admit at least this much.

I anticipated a scene and was surprised when none came. "Fine," he said with composed indifference. "I guess you've made your decision." In Sidi Bou Saïd, my unfaithfulness had preyed on his mind, he said, but now it was simply taking too much of his time. He could no longer be sidetracked by my lies and my recklessness. He needed to concentrate on his work.

I felt too numb and nauseous to speak. There would be consequences and I would face them willingly—if only I knew what they would be. Fear kept me from mentioning Jonathan.

After a few minutes' silence, he asked, "Have you considered the source of this behavior?"

I hated this dispassionate, professional stance. "What do you mean?" I tried to sound as impassive as he.

"I'm curious to know if you have any inkling as to why you destroyed your marriage and your family by taking up with someone you have absolutely nothing in common with."

"How do you know what Habib and I have in common?"

"I see. You're telling me that you're fucking this guy because of everything the two of you have in common? Is that what you're saying?"

Right now we have more in common than you could possibly imagine, I was tempted to say. "He doesn't make me feel like an inept neurotic, for starters."

"So you feel like an inept neurotic. Can't say I'm surprised."

"Only because you treat me like one," I yelled as he left the room. I didn't know if I was fuming because of his double-edged questioning or because he'd walked out and retreated to his study, as he always did.

Nothing in common. The same words Habib used in Matmata the night Jonathan got ill. The same words I'd heard as a girl. Rose's defiant reply, "I wouldn't want a man who had anything in common with this screwed-up family."

Except this wasn't the case with Gilles and me. Not entirely. I couldn't let him walk away. Not out of the room, or out of my life. An argument would be more tolerable than his indifference. I followed him to his study.

"Maybe I'm just promiscuous," I challenged.

"No, that's not it." He sat very still behind his desk, head down. "I don't know why you're doing this, Amy. Whatever it is, I hope, for your sake, it will have all been worth it."

I waited for more. I couldn't think of a way to initiate what would lead to the inevitable admission. "So what do you think it is then?"

"I don't know. You've always had this talent for attracting people. The problem is, it's a talent that soon exhausts itself on a one-man audience. I see it all the time in my practice, people going from one person to the next." He looked up. His eyes had gone dead. He had cut himself loose. Slowly, without any menace in his voice, he said, "I'm not waiting until December to leave, Amy. I'll have things wrapped up in a week or so. I'm taking Jonathan with me. You can do whatever you want."

His dispassionate manner, the finality in his voice, was more frightening than if he'd gone into a rage. There would be no negotiating this time.

He had said once that it was very lucky that he'd found me in the library that day, because otherwise he would have had to look for me all his life. I had loved that. And now I was about to lose him. Still, I could not, once again, claim I'd made a mistake and follow it with remorse, as I'd done in Sidi Bou Saïd. I turned around, leaving him staring into the empty door frame.

The first days of November could not have been more dismal. Thinly sunlit days and cold drizzle reflecting the state I was in.

Jonathan kept asking how many days before Christmas, when we would be going to Grandma and Grandpa Legate's. I would have given anything to be at the farm, walking in the rain, getting dry and warm by the stone fireplace. My father and brothers were probably still sawing and cording the wood from the trees they'd felled earlier. Rose would have started to preserve her minced meat for her Christmas pies. Gilles hadn't said anything about whether he intended to live in our house, with Jonathan, when we got back. Or anything about where he expected me to go.

Walking Jonathan to and from the school bus each day became my sole purpose. I was careful not to leave him alone with Gilles, in case they both disappeared. Habib often contrived to meet us, he and Jonathan delighted as lost friends that fate had thrown together again. They would walk hand in hand, Habib's free arm around my shoulders, his attention too carefree and public. The walls of my secret eroding, becoming too thin.

A few days after the confrontation with Gilles, as I waited for Jonathan at the bus stop, Habib and another Tunisian student, Zine, joined me. They were headed for a café in the neighborhood and insisted Jonathan and I come along.

"Tunisia is invading the Seizième Arrondissement," he said, "and we need a Canadian for support." Zine stood by smiling while Habib pushed my hair from my face as he did when we were alone. He was putting on a show for his friend.

Jonathan, ready to follow Habib anywhere, spontaneously took his hand as soon as he got off the bus. I followed, a little dazed, feeling as exposed as the denuded trees, the cool air particularly sharp for that time of day. At the café I ordered hot chocolate for Jonathan and tea for myself.

Being a Tunisian student in Paris made for animated discussions, every topic earnest with political and philosophical import, the two men taking turns refuting what the other said. Habib complained, loudly enough for several people around us to hear, about the difficulties of being a foreigner in a country like France. He couldn't wait to go home and put his education to good use.

Zine didn't think it was all that bad being a foreigner. He considered it an opportunity, he said.

"For us or for the French?" Habib asked.

"For us, but also for the French. They need us to see themselves better, their narrow mentalities, their prejudices."

Habib jeered. "It is not my responsibility to teach the French about their narrow mentalities."

"France now has the largest foreign population in its history," Zine offered as justification for his position.

Habib moaned at Zine's gullibility.

"One day it may be possible to have double citizenship...." Zine insisted.

Habib redoubled his moans. "For other Europeans perhaps,

never for Arabs. They will identify you as Muslim in your passport the way the Nazis did the Jews."

"You are too cynical," Zine told Habib, then turned to me. "What about you?" he asked. "Are you going back to Canada?"

"Oh, yes. Soon."

"You don't want to stay longer?" he asked.

"No. I miss home." I avoided looking at Habib.

"What about you, Jonathan? Do you think you would like to live here? Or in Tunisia?" he asked.

"No," Jonathan said, with a child's firmness.

"Why not?" Zine asked.

"I want to go home."

"But why?" Habib insisted. "What do you miss most?"

Jonathan thought for a few moments. "Christmas," he said. "I want Christmas at Grandma and Grandpa's because Santa Claus doesn't know I'm here. There's lots of snow there for his sled."

"You miss the snow? Then if you came to Tunisia, I would fill your garden with almond trees. Thousands of almond trees."

"Why?" Jonathan asked and gave me a quizzical glance. He wasn't about to exchange a white Christmas at his grandparents' for any number of almond trees.

"A Tunisian emir fell in love with a Scandinavian princess once and he took her to his palace to live. Although she loved him very much she missed her Nordic snows and landscapes and she was very sad. So he ordered that thousands of almond trees be planted throughout his domain. One January morning, when the princess looked out, she was amazed to see the palace grounds and countryside covered in almond flowers white as snow."

"Is that true, Mommy?" Jonathan asked, in a whisper because he didn't want Habib to think that he doubted the accuracy of his story.

"If Habib says so, it must be." Habib and I smiled into each other's eyes. I would miss his tall tales. I would miss him.

"Yes, we must all go home sooner or later," Habib said in a low, cheerless voice. He tilted his head and shrugged, as if to say the matter was out of his hands. His mouth quivered into an ambivalent smile. For a brief moment I too wished there had been enough love between us to keep us safely within his legends of jasmine and almond flowers.

"Yes, it is written," I said. It shocked me to think how casually we were planning to part. In spite of my carrying his child. I would miss him—our small room, our time together sheltered as long as we stayed within its four walls. But I didn't belong in that room. Or in Paris or Tunisia. I didn't belong anywhere.

Zine complimented me on my French. Habib agreed. "She has made incredible progress. But she will have to improve her Arabic."

"Way beyond my abilities," I demurred while Habib insisted on testing my vocabulary for Zine's sake. *Salam aleykum; labess; bismillah.* I knew many words and phrases but my pronunciation was obviously a source of amusement for the two men, their laughter resonating against the clatter of plates in the background. The people at the next table were smiling.

When it came time for Jonathan and me to leave, I signaled to the waiter. As he approached the table I detected a contemptuous line penciled around his mouth as he handed me the check. Perhaps he was annoyed because we'd stayed too long without ordering much. He then said something directly to me and I asked him to repeat it because I didn't think I could possibly have heard right.

"*T'as pas honte?*" he asked again. I didn't understand why he was addressing me in the familiar *tu*. I didn't know this person. Or why he was asking me if I was ashamed. Until he added, "*T'as pas honte, traîner les cafés avec des Arabes? Et avec ton gosse en plus?*"

Still, I couldn't be absolutely sure because of the scraping of chairs and the racket they made as they fell to the floor. Before I realized what was going on, Habib and Zine had the waiter by his shirt and were dragging him through the restaurant toward the front door. I yelled for them to stop, my cries lost in the commotion, everyone's focus on the two men who were now pounding the waiter's head against the glass panel in the door. Jonathan, perplexed and terrified, was screaming.

By the time I gathered my wits, grabbed Jonathan and ran outside, several men were trying to get Habib and Zine away from the waiter, a steady stream of blood from his nose spreading against his white shirt. Everyone was shouting frantically, especially Habib. "Go, Aimée. Now!"

A man came running out of the restaurant shrieking: "I called the police, no one leaves." He pushed his hand into Habib's face. "I called the police. Make sure the woman doesn't leave," his words barely discernible over the approaching sirens.

In the wagon taking us to the police station, huddled against me, Jonathan kept crying, "I want to go home now, Mommy."

"God, so do I, Jonathan. So do I."

The French police, either out of concern for Jonathan or, more likely, out of contempt for me, refused to release us unless we were in someone else's charge, either a lawyer or a husband.

Gilles came as soon as I called. He said nothing in the taxi, holding a sleeping Jonathan against him, the silence a hiatus into which we poured all our assumptions. Gilles presuming I'd lost whatever was left of my mind. And I, convinced I'd blown any chance of keeping Jonathan.

Gilles put Jonathan to bed, then went into the kitchen to mix drinks. He came into the living room where I was sitting in the dark and handed me a Scotch. He turned on a lamp, and said in that sensible, efficient voice of his, "I'm not going to ask you how you got yourself and Jonathan involved in a brawl. Your irresponsibility astounds me. I am going to tell you that it is not going to happen again. I have tickets for myself and Jonathan. We're leaving in three days."

Any resolve I might have had before this afternoon had frayed to a few fragile threads. "What happens to me?" I asked.

"I thought you had it figured out."

"No. Nothing figured out."

"Move in with Habib." It wasn't a question, but a foregone conclusion.

The two of us and a baby in his little room. I couldn't breathe. Fear obstructed my breathing. Not fear of Gilles, but fear of being left behind, fear of losing him and Jonathan. I squeezed my glass as hard as I could to stop my hands from shaking. "You know I can't do that." I was determined not to break down and cry. Only calm and clarity would get me through this. Gilles understood calm and clarity.

"Are you cold?" he asked, watching my hands. My pitiful state must have elicited some compassion. "Listen, you can stay in the apartment until the end of December. It's paid until then." He had thought of everything while I had exhausted all my options. He must have interpreted my silence as acquiescence. "So this is it. Jonathan and I are going home and you stay here."

There was enough doubt in his voice for me to muster the courage to suggest another possibility. "I'm not staying here."

"What are you planning to do then?"

"I want to go home."

He gave a long sigh. I wanted to believe it was a sigh of relief but I knew him well enough to detect the frustration behind the restraint. "Until Tunisia, I never suspected anything was wrong between us. Whatever you thought was wrong could have been worked out, Amy. But you couldn't even meet me halfway. There is one thing I've got to know. It's been eating at me and I've got to know."

"What is it?" Had he already guessed I was pregnant?

"I want to know if you lied to me in Sidi Bou Saïd when you told me it was over between you and Habib. Were you planning to see him all along?"

"No, I really didn't think I would see him again." Part of me had wanted to, I couldn't deny that. I had even planned to tell Habib I was pregnant. But when it came time to do it, I couldn't. Not only would it mean leaving Gilles but, since Gilles had threatened to fight me for Jonathan if I went to Tunisia, I would, in effect, be exchanging one child for another. It wasn't an option.

"But you did see him again. How long were you planning on holding on to this ... this goddamn fixation?"

I couldn't put it off any longer. "I know it sounds crazy, but I do love you and Jonathan. But something's happened. I've been wanting to tell you."

Gilles threw back his head and closed his eyes. He didn't say anything for the longest time as if he wanted to delay the inevitable. "What now?" he finally asked. The panic in his voice suggested the confirmation of a suspicion.

"I'm pregnant."

He didn't budge. "Since when?"

"Since Tunisia." I spared him the indignity of figuring out when we had last made love. "It's Habib's child."

He turned his face toward me, his eyes wide with incredulity. "Jesus fucking Christ." He seldom swore and when he did it was usually in French. "Weren't you using your fucking diaphragm?"

"Yes. It failed somehow."

"You stupid ... stupid woman. And I don't suppose this idiot ever thought of using condoms."

I said nothing.

"What does Habib think of this?" he asked.

"He doesn't know."

"You haven't told him?"

"No."

"You've been very busy with all your dirty little secrets. Well, at least he doesn't know. You weren't planning on telling him?"

"I decided not to." I suspected the next issue would not be as easy to concede.

"Good. You shouldn't have waited so long. It must be over three months," he said, fully confident what the next step should be. "Why did you wait so long?"

I assumed he was asking why I hadn't had an abortion yet.

"I can't believe you waited this long," he repeated. Then, as if struck by an inconceivable possibility, he turned to me, stupefied. "You weren't planning on having it, were you?"

I hesitated. "I haven't made up my mind." There was nothing left to risk.

"You can't be serious, Amy. Don't tell me you're thinking of keeping it. It's impossible."

I swallowed hard. "I'm not so sure."

"Why the hell not? Aisling got an abortion, why can't you?"

"It was right for her. The guy left her."

"So? Your two guys aren't going to be around either, are they?"

When I didn't say anything he asked, "Didn't you tell me Rose had an abortion once?"

"My mother and my aunts pushed her into it because he had four children and he was Native. I don't know the details. It was unheard-of for women in New Erie to have children out of wedlock."

"How do you plan to raise it on your own?"

"I don't want to raise it on my own." The words spilled out as easily as if I had rehearsed them. "I want you to be there."

He sneered. "No way. You're insane. This is every man's nightmare. You have no idea what it's been like for me these last few months."

I wanted to point out that the last few months hadn't been exactly a picnic for me either but he would only have reminded me that I had brought it on myself. When I said nothing, he said, "It would push me over the edge."

"No, it wouldn't. Of all the people I know, you're the one who could do it. You're always saying how your patients have to learn to mediate between the past and the present, how they have to learn to forgive and forget."

He glared, his face shattered in disbelief. "Don't throw my words back at me. This is different. I can't believe you're asking me to do this. I don't understand you." He shook his head. "In Sidi Bou Saïd, when I found Habib's belongings in our bedroom, I came across a folded sheet of paper tucked inside a book on the bedside table. Someone, I presume Habib, had written: 'Love cannot calculate. There is a core in everyone that no one can know through trying.' I thought it was pretty hokey at the time, but now I'm not so sure. I thought I knew you, Amy, but I guess I never have. I realized you were a little bored, having to stay home with Jonathan, but I assumed you'd work it out once he went to school."

"This has nothing to do with Jonathan. I did want to be with him the first few years. It's never been an issue." Which was true. I didn't want to leave him in someone else's care in spite of all the articles I kept reading about full-time mothers being little more than dimwit vassals who gave up all claims to selfhood. One of the articles hadn't even used the word "mother" or "father" once, referring to parents as "primary caregivers" instead.

"I want to keep this baby," I heard myself repeating to Gilles.

"Keep it if you want, but you have no right to ask me to help you bring it up." He stared into his empty glass.

"I know I don't, but I am asking just the same. You're the only one who can help me through this." I had no right to ask yet I knew I could. Wretched as I felt for having created such an impossible situation, I wanted to comfort Gilles. Put my arms around him and reassure him that everything would be all right somehow.

He began pacing, empty glass in hand, his face registering a gamut of emotions. "What makes you think I would ever agree to this? I can't think of one single reason why I would."

"I can think of several."

"Name one."

"Jonathan."

"People don't stay together because of a child."

"He wouldn't be the only reason. There's still us."

He caught his breath. After a few seconds he shook his head again, more in defeat than disagreement. "Us. Do you know how much I hate you right now? I worry about what will happen to you, but I really despise you for what you've done to us." He raised his arm and hurled his glass against the wall, sending the room into suspended animation. "Us …" His voice trailed in a murmur. "There is no us, Amy. It's over. We'll never have it again."

The sound of breaking glass had woken Jonathan. "Mommy," he called from his bedroom.

"We could have it again, but it would be different," I said as I left the room to see to Jonathan, trying to maintain some sense of calm and composure.

"I'll say," I heard Gilles mutter.

When I returned to the living room he was picking up pieces of glass from the carpet, concentrating on finding all the slivers. "We'll have to make sure Jonathan doesn't walk around barefoot, I don't know if I got them all." Then, still combing the carpet for glass, he said, "I'll help you for a while but only because I feel sorry for you. And only on the condition you don't see Habib again, you don't sleep with him, and you don't tell him about this kid. Until I figure how we're going to deal with this, I won't have him interfering. He can't be in our lives."

"What if the child wants to know who its father is later on?"

"That is not my problem. Right now you agree not to see him or tell him about this baby, or Jonathan and I are gone."

I saw no reason to hold on to the little dignity I had left. I was willing to agree to anything. "I guess I have no choice."

"You made your choice. Now live with it."

The next three days reeled into resolute frenzy: a reservation on the same flight as Gilles and Jonathan, packing, restoring the apartment to its original state. It was just as well. The ache I hauled didn't allow any free time to think. My heart had become much too large for the space around it.

A few hours before we were to leave, Madame Renée knocked at our door. I hadn't seen or heard from Habib since the incident at the restaurant, although she had made a point of telling me the day before that he'd been kept in jail only overnight. She had just seen M. Gérard go out with our son. Yes, I said, they were going to buy Jonathan his last chocolate croissant. She looked past me, into the apartment, to make sure Gilles hadn't miraculously materialized, then she retrieved a letter from the pocket of her concierge's smock. A letter from Habib. When I burst into tears she hesitated, extended her arm and squeezed my shoulder. "*Allons, allons, Mme Gérard, tout va s'arranger.*"

Yes, it would all work out, but how long would it take? "Would you tell Monsieur Habib I can't see him, but that I say goodbye."

"Certainly, madame."

My dearest Aimée,
Mme R. tells me you are leaving today. How terrible to have to end our adventure like this. I will always regret the month we will not have together, a month that should have been ours.
For two days I waited upstairs in the hope you would come to

say adieu. *But you decided not to. For two days I imagined you standing before the door, the gentle way you always knock, twice. I opened the door but you were not there. How will I stay in this room as empty and sad as my whole being? Tonight, I will lie on my bed and wait for you to knock again. And tomorrow morning. I will do it every day until it is no longer painful. Will there be such a day?*

You must go now, Aimée. Take the new road of your destiny with courage. We will go on, separately, because we know that our love is larger than the mere events that make up daily lives. I will watch you from afar. You are the love in me that never dies.

Your faithful Habib

Une aventure. In French, a love affair is called *une aventure.* This is what he undoubtedly meant. I might as well have been run over by a truck.

As we loaded our suitcases into the taxi, I sensed him watching from the small window on the fifth floor. But I didn't turn around in case it was only my imagination. We left for the airport. *Salaama,* goodbye.

Rémy

WE NAMED OUR SECOND SON JEREMY.

Not everything went well at first, especially before he was born. Days on end when I convinced myself I'd made the wrong decision, then thinking up ways of inducing a miscarriage. Until I heard Wassila's voice as she told us about her mother when she was expecting her. "Mother, there is no other world but here." I'd come this far, there was no turning back.

After Jeremy was born, Gilles's interest was perfunctory at best, his concern aimed mainly at my well-being, never the baby's. Aisling came from Vancouver as soon as the spring term ended. She took her role of godmother to both boys very seriously and became one of those childless aunts who assume the inalienable right to fuss, indulge every whim and buy all the useless presents. I was never so happy to see anyone.

For the first two months, Gilles couldn't bring himself to even hold the baby. I often saw him staring into the crib and once I asked, "Do you want to help me bathe him?"

"No, I have an appointment. I have to get going," he said and rushed off.

I picked up Jeremy then and held on to him as tightly and as long as I could, hoping to convey enough surrogate love for two absent fathers.

It didn't take long before Aisling started to complain about Gilles's indifference, first to me, then to Jeremy. When she didn't get any response from him, she laid down a challenge with her usual aplomb. "What the hell do you think you're doing?" she asked him. "You'd think a psychiatrist would know how to handle the situation better than this. I'm going to take Amy and this baby home with me if you don't smarten up. And Jonathan too since you don't seem to understand what it means to be a father."

Gilles must have known I would never agree to such an arrangement, but he must have also understood Aisling's reasons for overstating her case. "Amy and the boys are wanted here," was all he said.

That night he came into my bedroom and walked over to the crib. His stance had changed. He no longer stared at Jeremy from an uncompromising distance. After a few minutes he said, "I do care for him, Amy. I didn't expect to, but I do."

"You can't even hold him, it's cruel."

He sat on the bed. "The truth is, I don't know how to love him."

"He's a baby. There's no right or wrong way to love him, you just do." Giving birth to Jeremy hadn't been any different from giving birth to Jonathan. I'd gone through the usual highs and lows, the elation and the pain. As I'd said to Aisling, "After all the pain, you've got to love the little buggers just to make it all worthwhile."

"Aisling is right, I should be handling this better," Gilles continued. "I see the black hair and I can't help thinking of you and Habib. He must remind you of Habib all the time."

"Not really. I don't see Habib in him at all. I love him for himself, the way I love Jonathan for himself. Jonathan can't take your place any more than Jeremy can take Habib's place. It doesn't work that way."

"Habib still writes to you."

"Yes, he does." For the first month after returning to Canada, Habib had written almost every week, then once a month or less. I hadn't heard from him in at least six weeks when he'd sent a postcard saying he was now in Tunisia permanently. I wrote even less, partly in deference to Gilles, partly because I couldn't write the kind of letters he wrote to me. "My letters to him are quite …" I couldn't think how to describe them to Gilles. "Quite innocuous, you know."

"Do you tell him you love him?" he asked.

"No, I don't," I said, which was true.

"Does he?"

"Yes. All the time."

He thought about this for a while. "You're very spoiled," he finally said. "So many people loving you."

"So are you. You have as many people who love you as I have." I sat beside him and took his hand, the most physical contact we'd had in almost a year. He didn't pull away.

"When Aisling delivered her stupid ultimatum today," he grinned, "I realized how ridiculous I was being. How can such a little guy be so threatening?"

"Diplomacy has never been her strongest suit." We chuckled and I was so grateful to Aisling.

"Then it struck me," Gilles said. "If I can't handle this, if I can't do it right, everything in my life is going to be a sham. This helpless little guy is the measure of everything that's important to me and if I'm not up to the challenge, then nothing in my life will have any credibility. He scares the shit out of me."

"He scares the shit out of me too. I'm going to have to tell him the truth eventually. It would make it easier for him to know that, regardless of what happened between his mother and his biological father, someone else cared enough to be there for him."

"You really think I can do this?"

"I've never been more certain about anything." I needed to believe this as much as he did.

He confessed he hadn't given much thought to Jeremy's name but now he wasn't keen on it. He preferred Rémy, which his relatives also adopted. Mine stuck to Jeremy and another line was drawn between the two families. Jonathan compromised and settled on Jerry.

It took a few more months, but Gilles gradually became as devoted to Rémy as he was to Jonathan: baths, walks in the park, the mandatory photographs. Those he took of Rémy were almost indistinguishable from those he'd taken of Jonathan at the same age, candid shots before children become conscious of the camera. I also began taking more pictures than I ever had: Gilles with the two boys but, more often, Gilles with Rémy. Gilles probably suspected what I was trying to do: fixing an image of him and Rémy as father and son. Gilles also gave in to the less spontaneous time-exposed family shots. One that he framed for his desk had the two of us leaning against each other, watching Jonathan making faces at a puzzled Rémy.

Rose began to spend more time with us. Visits meant to last a week invariably grew to three, her reluctance to leave always apparent. Because of my father's failing health, one of my brothers had taken over the farm and moved in with his wife and children. Rose complained she was only getting in everyone's way. Gilles suspected she might be depressed. Whatever had been denied her all those years was now plainly visible in her face.

It was during one of these visits that I told her about Jeremy and Habib. I had, until then, avoided examining the entire affair too closely, and talking about it with Rose, going over the details, was peculiar. Somewhat like telling a story about a woman I didn't always recognize, a woman involved in a plot I didn't always understand. She was either too acquiescent or too conniving, too sentimental or too cynical. Certainly too earnest, with little sense of irony, like most people when they fall in love. There were the memory gaps I tried to fill in as best I could, but the details were not always accurate. I was tailoring my story to make it more accessible to Rose, but also to make it more accessible to myself.

As I spoke, she either clapped a hand over her mouth, trying to curb her astonishment, or kept repeating, "No! No!" as if to deny some fallacious rumor being spread about her niece. Until, satisfied I was indeed telling the truth, she cradled her head in her arms on the table and began laughing uncontrollably. "Lordy me! There is justice after all!" And she started laughing again until tears ran down her cheeks. "Will you be telling your mother?" she wanted to know. "And the others? Surely, it's too good to keep from the others."

"Maybe eventually, but not now. Let's keep it to ourselves for a while. If it's retaliation you're after, Rose, it's even better if we don't tell." We laughed until we ached.

"Gilles! What about Gilles?" she wanted to know.

"He wrestles with it, but he's coming around. It will take a while."

"Saints alive! Next you'll be telling me there really is a heaven." And she'd be off again, wiping the tears from her face. "And the young man in question? Tell me about him."

"A real looker, Rose. A nice man. But too romantic for his own good and mine."

"You're not going to tell him about his own baby?" She obviously didn't approve.

"No. I promised Gilles I wouldn't, not until Jeremy is older. I think it's better this way."

"But the poor young man, he'll be missing out on so much." She seemed genuinely grieved for Habib. She never once asked if he was Arab, or a Muslim. I don't think she even thought of it.

"Yes, he will be missing out on a lot. He'll probably chalk it all up to destiny if he ever finds out. He's pretty big on destiny. I guess I have to do the same."

"Does your friend Aisling know?"

"Yes, she's been in on it from the beginning."

"And what does she think about not telling the young man in Tunisia?"

"Oh, she approves." I told her about Aisling's experience with the man who left her when he found out she was pregnant, and her having to get an abortion on her own.

"She is still upset then, is she?"

"I'm not sure upset is the right word, Rose. Virulent would be more like it. I can't say I blame her, do you?"

Rose thought for a while then asked, "Do you remember the story of Scheherazade I read to you when you were little?"

"Of course I do. What about it?"

"Scheherazade's sentence, 'Nothing will shake my faith in the mission I am destined to fulfill'?"

"Kind of. Her mission was to tame the monster. But I don't know what this has to do with Aisling or me."

"Scheherazade never tried to convince the sultan that he was a monster or that his actions were loathsome, but that his view of women was too small. It is something for you and Aisling to consider."

"I'm afraid Aisling will need a lot of convincing before her views on men change. As for me, Jeremy is my main concern right now. Keeping Habib out of it for the time being is the only way I know to handle this." I couldn't let any doubt or regret creep in. Nor could I break my promise to Gilles. He deserved at least that much. "If Habib finds out, he might insist on seeing Jeremy, even take him to Tunisia. Worse, he might make some half-hearted attempt to know him, then lose interest. That would be devastating for him. I can't take any chances, Rose."

I didn't want to argue these points with anyone, not even Rose. Only Gilles and I had the right to decide what was best for Jeremy and for us. I needed to change the subject.

"What about you, Rose? You've always had other people's views imposed on you."

"Oh, I have only myself to blame for that," she said. She reminded me of Habib's faith in willing surrender.

"And my mother? Is she happy? Do you think she likes her life?"

She thought about this for a few seconds. "Why, I suppose she does," she said, having arrived at an unexpected conclusion. "Your mother always lived for her children and her husband. I guess she never needed a larger view than the one she's always had." She chuckled. "It kind of makes you envious, doesn't it?"

"Yes, it does, but it doesn't excuse all the biases. Even so, I had no right to judge her the way I did."

"Nonsense. Children have a right to judge parents, and readjust their judgment if necessary. Keeps parents on their toes." Her eyes crinkled as she grinned. She was about to reveal an important, undivulged fact. "Your mother is very proud of you, Amelia. She loves your spunk. I can't tell you how many times she read and reread the cards you sent from France and Tunisia, showing them to everyone, boasting how you and your son were alone down there, in that foreign place."

"Except I wasn't as alone as everyone thought." We laughed. "Rose, Gilles and I think you should come and live with us. It's high time you changed your view, and it's time I finished my thesis. Gilles is talking of buying a larger house, which I'm not sure I can manage, and I need someone to help me with the boys." I stood a better chance if I framed my request as a favor. Gilles tried to get more involved in the boys' daily care and upbringing but, ultimately, he left much of it to me. Not because he didn't love them, but because of the old dilemma so many men fall into: a family to support and a career to advance. In this respect, Gilles would never change and I wasn't sure I wanted him to. "So, how about it, Rose?"

"Of course I will. To tell you the truth, I was sort of hoping you would ask."

When Rose moved in, her entire possessions consisted of one suitcase of worn, hand-me-down clothes, a hope chest full of quilts, and the five old books she was still hanging on to.

I hadn't realized the extent to which she depended on relatives just to get by. In spite of her protests that, "My room and board is all I need," we planned to give her as much money as we could afford, and more once I finished my thesis and found work.

"How attached are you to those books and quilts, Rose?" I asked her as I helped her put her things away.

"Not very. Not any more. Why?"

"Because we are going to sell them and open you a bank account. We women need our own money. Anyway, it's time you read new books."

She didn't believe the books would have any value, let alone her quilts. When an ex-classmate of mine, a co-owner of the Art and Craft Gallery in Yorkville, agreed to take the quilts on consignment and sold two within one month, Rose was baffled. "Aren't city people a daft lot," I heard her say over the phone to my mother and her sisters, a boast disguised as criticism.

To her greater astonishment, the owner of the Antiquarian Book Shelf in the Annex found a buyer who offered her $12,000 for her illustrated Chaucer, of which, he said, there were only a few still in existence. She bought herself two complete outfits and a winter coat, the first new coat I ever saw her wear, and, with the balance, she opened her first bank account.

Our house on Palmerston Gardens was much too cramped for three adults and two boys. Within a few months of Rose moving in, we bought a grand old rooming house a few blocks away, on Palmerston Avenue, and converted it back to a single-family home. We let Rose have most of the third floor except for one room, which became my office. It was walking distance to the university. Several faculty members lived within a few blocks of us, and every once in a while I recognized some prominent artists. William Morris would have approved of the stained glass window of our front room.

The boys readily took to Rose. As Jeremy got older, we gradually introduced the idea that I was his birth mother but that

Gilles had adopted him. This made him very special, we assured him, hoping he would perceive his situation as unique but not so unusual as to sabotage his childhood or, for that matter, his entire life.

He did complain a few times, when he started school, that he wasn't like other children.

"What ever do you mean?" I overheard Rose ask.

He thought about it for a while, racking his little brain for differences that would stand out, but the only one he could come up with was his hair. It was black, unlike anyone else's in the family. I too worried sometimes about this cryptic correlation between his black hair and a father he didn't know, but neither Gilles or Rose thought it serious enough to worry about.

"What rubbish!" Rose chided as she tousled Jeremy's hair. "Children all over the world have black hair! The only thing that makes you different around here is all your moping and belly-aching. It isn't very winsome." Jeremy stared at her, trying to figure out what *winsome* meant.

Winsome and *loathsome* were two of Rose's favorite words. Jonathan often used them to tease her. "Winsome and loathsome Rose," he called her.

Six years after Paris, Chafia wrote to ask if I would come to Sidi Bou Saïd for a few weeks because Wassila was gravely ill. We wrote one another now and then, making promises to visit, but never did. Most of the factual news about Habib came through her. Although Habib still sent the occasional love letter or postcard, he seldom wrote about his life. It was Chafia who informed me of his marriage.

I didn't immediately understand why she wanted me to come and I declined her invitation. I had just miscarried, losing a daughter in my sixth month, and the experience had been extremely difficult for both Gilles and me. I was also busy with part-time work that threatened to develop into a career. I had completed my thesis: "An Ordinary Day in Women's Aesthetics," which examined the art of women such as Betty Goodwin, Mary Pratt, Kim Ondaatje and Lucy Lippard, artists who either explored the spaces they lived in or transcended lives of unmade beds, dirty dishes and diapers. My thesis supervisor, sensing that I was still at a loss as to the kind of work I wanted to do, had proposed that I translate a French article on the history of art in Quebec. Before I knew it, one project had led to another—translations of art books, essays, criticism. When Chafia phoned, her voice broken by sobs, I was working toward a deadline. Wassila was dying of cancer and Chafia's family and in-laws thought it inappropriate for her to tend to an employee. I would be her pretext when she needed to care for Wassila. I decided I should go.

"Are you going to see Habib?" Gilles asked.

"If he's around." I tried to sound casual but he obviously needed reassurance. "If I do see him, I promise you, it won't be to sleep with him."

"You won't say anything about Rémy? He's doing so well, we don't want to jeopardize him now."

"I wouldn't dream of saying anything. Don't worry." I kissed him on the nose to remind him of the place we'd hewn for ourselves in the last few years.

It was particularly hot in Sidi Bou Saïd that year, the late August landscape desiccated, not at all as I remembered. But then nothing was.

I hardly recognized Wassila, her slim body reduced to opaque skin stretched over bones. Her mother and two blind men came every day and stood by the bed, the heat absorbing their strength and their tears. Until Wassila's dark eyes obliterated any response and all trace of recognition disappeared, her landscapes and stories vanished in an emptiness as desolate as the desert.

I saw Habib for a few hours over lunch at a restaurant in

Tunis near his work. He seemed happy to see me but distracted. He was flying off to Mali on business later that evening and complained there wasn't enough time to be together. "You should have told me you were coming," he scolded. Then, out of the blue, "Come with me. It is only for three days. Chafia won't mind."

"Chafia needs me here, this is what matters now."

"Come with me," he pleaded.

"You're crazy. And shameless. We are both married now." A stupid argument since marriage had never been an issue before. "I must have been mad to fall for such a rascal," I said.

"What is this … *rascal?*" he asked.

"*Un très mauvais sujet,*" I said in my best upbraiding voice.

He laughed. His English had not improved, in fact it had deteriorated, his accent more pronounced. But he could still reduce the world to a circle where no one else existed. What would he have done if I had taken him up on his offer and gone with him? Would it have been only another episode, *une aventure*, like the one we had that summer? Or if I told him about Jeremy?

As I sat across from Habib, it occurred to me there might be another reason for not wanting him to know about Jeremy. An ill-defined motive that had nothing to do with my promise to Gilles and which I had avoided whenever it threatened to surface. It had to do with retribution. Not so much against Habib, but against his definition of love. It was too narrow to include the ordinary lives of mothers and children.

Except for the odd letter and card I received from Habib once or twice a year, he seldom entered my thoughts anymore, except in relation to Jeremy. Their eventual meeting dangled over Gilles and me like an oscillating pendulum, so we tried not to dwell on it. Oh, every once in a while a certain word or image from that summer appeared out of the blue to remind me how easily one's world can turn upside down. But then, like the fabled contents of a mirage, ethereal and distant, the world regained its equilibrium.

Our lives in Toronto were busier than ever. Gilles with teaching and a growing practice. He was also revising and editing lectures and papers delivered over the last few years, to be gathered in a book. Some dealt with the research he'd done in France, others with various Freudian models and their clinical ineffectiveness. In one, Gilles argued that Freud didn't like children very much because he didn't know them except as theoretical inventions. Because of Rémy and Jonathan, he had earned the right to make such statements.

My translation work also kept me busy. I enjoyed it. One language yielding to another, the transfer of sense between tongues, as when people of different cultures speak to one another. When certain passages resisted translation, I spent hours manipulating words and sentences, trying to extract meaning. As I had done with Wassila's story about her mother, when I encountered words whose definition I didn't know or understand. To this day, I'm not sure if the translation of Wassila's story was correct. But then, perhaps this is what communication is—improvising to make other people's words fit your own.

When I was asked to translate a series of books on artists who had lived most of their creative lives in France, I jumped at the chance. One of the artists was none other than Constantin Brancusi. The assignment required me to go to Paris to meet with the publishing house, Paroles.

It had been seven years since I had seen Habib, and it would be seven more years before Jeremy would decide whether to meet him or not. Gilles agreed it was time to see him again. I wrote to ask if he could come to Paris, for old times' sake, and informed him of the day and flight and where I'd be staying. When he didn't respond I assumed he wouldn't make it. But when I landed in Paris, he surprised me at the airport.

"You know I still think of you *that way*," he teased over dinner, with the same old seductive mischief.

I doubted very much that it was me he still thought of *that way*, but rather the memory of an insatiable longing. The moment always yearning to renew itself. In fact, when I laughed him off and said I was getting too old for that sort of thing, he didn't insist. I thought he looked relieved.

We talked late into the night. His mother was gravely ill. He himself had suffered a heart attack the year before.

"You never mention any of this in your letters or your cards," I reproached him.

"I don't want to worry you," he said, but I knew this wasn't the reason. His private or daily life wasn't part of our old romance.

"It's important I know what happens to you. What if you were to … disappear?"

"No, no. Chafia will let you know if I disappear. It is a small town." His offhandedness suggested he would be around forever.

"You're too young to be having heart attacks." He looked too heavy.

"I work hard," he acknowledged. He managed a consulting firm and negotiated building contracts throughout the Arab world. The traveling wasn't good for his health or his family life, he complained, but little could be done about it. "I wish my personal life was as successful as my business." He was in the process of getting a second divorce.

The next day we walked about Paris, revisiting the places that held our past. Robert Schumann Square. The Bois de Boulogne. Names inhabited by other versions of ourselves. The shops where he had worked and where he had offered me figs. One of the shops had changed owners, and the horse-meat store was now a Vietnamese restaurant.

Much of the Paris I remembered had given way to twentieth century expediency. A highway cut through the Bois.

Brancusi's house and studio had been moved once again and cowered in a corner of the progressive architecture of the Centre Pompidou, the new complex housing modern art.

"Are you happy, Aimée?" he asked as we stood before Brancusi's *Kiss*.

"I suppose so. Not very exciting, is it?" I seldom worried about happiness, as reliable an indication as any that I wasn't unhappy.

"This was us once," he said as he nodded toward *The Kiss*. "At least we have the memory."

"Yes. We have the memory. But I think I prefer the alternative," I said.

"What alternative?"

"To be happy enough with the present, so you don't need to be always returning to the past."

"You think this is possible? Memory is memory. You can't efface it."

He meant *erase*. "We never remember things as they were, not really. The more we try, the more space it takes. Too much space." A boundless elsewhere, a desert with shredded mountains, dead rivers and trapped seas.

"I lost part of myself when I let you go, Aimée. I should never have let you go."

His sincerity moved me. I locked my arm in his. "I couldn't have stayed, Habib. The loss would have been greater for both of us if I had stayed."

"I know. That's why I didn't ask. I wanted to, you know."

"I know."

"You still loved your husband. And there was Jonathan."

"It wasn't only because of Gilles and Jonathan. We were wonderful together, but we would never have survived the real world."

"Perhaps we should have tried."

"There was too much at stake. It's been over twelve years, Habib, we can't keep pining for something that might have been. We have to believe this was the best possible ending. A happy ending. We should be pleased about that." As we walked arm in arm toward *The Newborn*, I asked, "What about this piece? Do you like it better now?"

He barely glanced at the egg-shaped sculpture. "I still prefer this one," he said, pointing to *The Kiss*. "At least those two lovers will never have a change of heart," he said and kissed me briefly on the lips.

In the evening we walked to the apartment building where we once lived, his arm held tightly across the small of my back like a sash. Light shone through the dormer window of the small room on the top floor.

"Whoever is up there hasn't covered the shade," I said, referring to Habib's habit of placing scarves on lampshades to mute the lighting.

"Remember when the scarf caught fire?" he asked, and laughed.

"No. That must have been with someone else," I said.

"Ah!" he exclaimed, and grinned as he remembered an occasion that hadn't included me. I always suspected I wasn't the only woman with whom he'd had grand love affairs.

Light shone through the French windows of the living room of the Roussels' apartment and Habib suggested visiting them, but I refused. I had never met them and it was much too late to drop in on anyone unexpectedly. Nor did I want to do anything that could potentially embarrass Gilles. All this rummaging in the past was making me weary. I wanted to go back to my hotel and telephone Gilles and the boys. I missed them.

La Saison Tunisienne

AFTER JEREMY TURNED TEN, he began to ask more questions about why Gilles was his adoptive father. We explained, as best we could, that Gilles and I had lived apart for a while, before he was born, and my relationship with another man had led to his birth. I wasn't sure how well he understood the implication of what we were saying, but he would figure it out soon enough. There was no point in providing too many details yet. I wasn't even prepared for the next question.

"Can I see him?" he asked.

"I'm not sure where he lives any more," I said as vaguely as I could.

"We can look up his address," he suggested, his voice so hopeful.

"He lives in the desert. There's no address in the desert. But later, when you're big, if you still want to find him, we will. But not now. You're busy growing up now. Okay?"

"Okay…" he said with such acceptance I wondered if Habib's casual surrender to fate wasn't an inherited trait.

The subject of finding his father did resurface a few times but, surprisingly, he never pressed it, never seemed obsessed by it. Until Jonathan gave him a series of books on different Arab cultures for his sixteenth birthday. For his seventeenth birthday Jeremy asked Gilles for Arabic lessons and progressed at such a rate that we agreed to private lessons. If he still perceived himself as different, he treated it more as a challenge than as a limitation.

"Do you know how many English words come from Arabic?" He loved flaunting his new vocabulary: "*Admiral, algebra, chemistry, almanac.* Like the farmer's almanac at Grandma's house."

It was chance and Jeremy's determination that finally forced our decision to go to Tunisia. The spring he turned nineteen he found an art magazine in my study. Not an uncommon occurrence—I received art periodicals all the time—but this one announced an upcoming celebration of Tunisian culture throughout France. *La Saison Tunisienne*—an entire summer devoted to the art, crafts, literature, archaeology and history of the country.

Habib had sent it to me. Another seven years had gone by since we'd last seen each other, our letters getting scarcer, and he hoped we could meet in Paris and take in a few events of *La Saison Tunisienne.* No one he knew would get as much enjoyment out of it as I would, he wrote.

Before I had a chance to respond, Jeremy announced he was thinking of going to *La Saison Tunisienne* and then perhaps on to Tunisia to feel his way around before deciding whether to meet this other guy, as he usually referred to Habib.

I had, over the years, envisioned the circumstances of their meeting, the proper place and time, but I had never foreseen such an independent decision. "You're not going there without me." I was indignant.

"Why not?"

"Because your other father doesn't know he has a son, for starters. You can't just barge in and spring this on him. Anyway, we have to find him." I was still under the impression that Jeremy believed Habib was lost somewhere out there in the Sahara.

"I don't think this is going to be a real problem, do you?" he asked defiantly. It always astounded me to discover that my children knew more than I surmised.

I ignored the implication. "You've never traveled on your own. Do you think we'd just let you go off to Tunisia alone?"

Considering his age and maturity, I must have sounded ludicrous.

"I won't be going alone. Jonathan is coming with me."

It annoyed me to think of my two sons plotting such a crucial event without consulting me first. But if anyone could help Jeremy through this it would be his older brother. The two J's, as everyone called them, behaved so much alike, no one ever suspected they weren't full brothers. Or so I assumed. "I'm not giving you the money to go to Paris and Tunisia, Rémy. If you go, I go."

The time had finally come. After much discussion and too many arguments, it was decided the family would go to Paris for a week and look into *La Saison Tunisienne*. Rose would come too, since she'd never been to Paris. If Jeremy still chose to, the boys and I would go on to Tunisia. Gilles would visit with a few colleagues, maybe rent a car and take Rose on a few days' tour.

I wrote to Chafia and asked if she could make reservations for three in the one hotel I knew of in Sidi Bou Saïd, without specifying that one of the children was a young man I'd never told her about. I would explain later, in person. I sent my regrets to Habib, told him Gilles also wanted to go to Paris for *La Saison Tunisienne*, but it would be possible for me to meet him in Sidi Bou Saïd where I was planning to spend a few days.

Jonathan still had a vague recollection of Habib and the summer in Tunisia, especially the filming of the bar scene in *Star Wars*. He'd seen the movie half a dozen times, and had named one of his dogs Luke and his cat Yoda. Even now, when he was twenty-four, part of him still wanted to believe that the darkest forces of human nature could be defeated simply by inhabiting imaginary planets and wearing outlandish costumes.

"We should go to Matmata," he said. "I hear they're filming a prequel."

"We won't have time," I said. I couldn't imagine ever going near that place again.

On our first night in Paris, Gilles suggested L'Entrecôte for the steak dinner. We were disappointed to discover it had become part of a chain with flashing neon on the roof. The food was more or less the same, except there were no creamy heart-shaped desserts this time. Jonathan ordered an *île flottante*, billowy meringues floating on caramel custard. "It looks more like an archipelago than an island," he said, when the dessert was placed in front of him.

After dinner we picked up *Le Monde* and a *Pariscope*. *Le Monde* reported that thirty-eight Muslim militants had been arrested on charges of helping Algerian Islamic rebels stage a recent wave of bombings that had resulted in two hundred people being injured, and eight deaths. A young Maghrébin had drowned after being tossed into the Seine by two young Frenchmen. Half a page was devoted to a former minister who was once accused of deporting more than 1,500 Jews to Nazi death camps during the war, and who was now facing renewed allegations concerning another atrocity that had taken place in the sixties: the massacre of hundreds of Algerians, in the center of Paris, by police under his command. It was the incident Habib told me about the first time we met. He knew about it back then, yet the paper claimed the massacre had been successfully covered up through the co-operation of the French establishment. I put the newspaper away so Jeremy wouldn't see it.

No one could agree on what to see, so Gilles suggested that each person choose one event to which everyone would go.

Jeremy was given first pick. He chose a club featuring Tunisian singers, one of them a rap artist. Jonathan had heard of a controversial film by a Tunisian director accused of betraying his country by portraying young men who slept with tourists for money. Rose glanced at me and winked. She chose a concert by a musician who played an antiquated lute-type instrument and everyone moaned. Jonathan and Rémy teased her constantly about her taste in music. When she first bought Pachelbel's Canon and played it non-stop for days, they would say, loudly enough for her to hear over the music, "There goes the Taco Bell Canon."

Since receiving the magazine from Habib, I wanted to see the exhibition on Carthage at Le Petit-Palais. Rooms filled with artifacts from the ancient city, many from the Bardo, which we had seen: jewelry, sculptures, coins, a tombstone bearing the sign of the goddess Tanit to whom children were sacrificed. And on one of the floors, cordoned off to protect it from being trampled, a mosaic of Oceanus, each small and blue mosaic beaming as on a sunlit day.

Everyone, even Rose, balked at Gilles's selection: a day at the Institute of the Arab World, a new and modern cultural center and museum. "Why an entire day?" they lamented. They'd had their fill of cultural events and historical artifacts.

Gilles tried to convince them. "Because it's a pleasant walk from the hotel to the quai Saint-Bernard where the Institute is located. We'll be able to take in the oldest part of the city. The evening will be yours to spend as you please," he promised, but to no avail. The boys insisted on another free day. They'd heard of a "pomo" museum that they said was "neat," not because of the art inside but because of the square around it. It was always packed with students, artists, skateboarders, fire-eaters, tourists. "That's where I want to go," Rose said.

They were describing the Centre Pompidou. I hadn't thought about the Brancusi sculptures once, nor did I feel inclined to visit the studio again.

I was feeling very apprehensive about what lay ahead, so it was just as well that Gilles and I were left to ourselves. We enjoyed a quiet morning viewing a contemporary art exhibition at the Arab Institute, then lunched on the terrace with a view of Ile de la Cité and Ile Saint-Louis. By mid-afternoon we were both getting tired and decided to spend only an hour or so taking in some of the Institute's permanent collection. In one of the rooms, to my great surprise, I came across an instrument called an astrolabe. It was different from the one I'd read about as a girl in Rose's illustrated Chaucer. This one looked scientific and efficient. Invented over a thousand years ago by a Muslim named Nastulus, it consisted of six parts: limb, tympanum, sight rule, sight vane, spider, and a main component called *la mère*.

"Even ancient machines have a component meant to hold everything together," I complained to Gilles. "Why does it always have to be a mother?" I felt a thousand years old.

He put a protective arm around my shoulder. "If tomorrow is too much for you, I'll go instead," he offered. "You know I don't mind."

"No. I think Habib needs to hear it from me. I got us into this, I'll get us out."

"Remember, Rémy is still not sure he wants to go through with this. He's only going to test things out. He may change his mind."

I suspected this was only wishful thinking on Gilles's part. He wasn't ready for another man to replace him as Rémy's father.

"You'll always be his dad," I tried to reassure him.

"I know. Let's get out of here," he said.

Bunkers

NO SOONER HAD WE CHECKED into the hotel in Sidi Bou Saïd than Chafia called to invite us to her house. Jeremy was nervous and moody, especially after I introduced him. Chafia recovered quickly, but not before everyone detected the shock on her face.

Jonathan and Fatma vaguely remembered each other. Fatma had inherited her mother's grace. Jonathan was clearly smitten and a little disappointed to learn she was to be married in a few months. She'd refused two of her father's candidates for her husband and, with Chafia's blessing, was engaged to a man she'd chosen herself.

When I telephoned Habib's office, his secretary informed me he was away, but expecting my call. He was due back in Tunis the next day and had already made reservations for lunch. It gave the two children and me the afternoon to relax, do a little sightseeing, stroll along the shore. Recollections that had idled for so many years suddenly all came flooding back. Jonathan talked about the fishing boats, the periwinkles, his toes being painted, the details somewhat different from how I remembered them, distorted by the prism that makes up individual memory.

"So you remember him?" Jeremy asked Jonathan.

"Sort of. All kinds of things are coming back to me all of a sudden."

"What do you remember about him?"

"He told great stories. He dressed me up as Lawrence of Arabia once. He put jasmine behind my ear. There was a story about the jasmine, but I don't remember what it was."

I told them about the Tunisian custom.

"Sounds like a great summer, wish I'd been there." Jeremy's voice oozed with sarcasm.

"You probably were," Jonathan teased as he tried to push his brother into the water. "At least a glint in Mom's eye."

They jostled awhile, until Jeremy pressed for more details, his questions confirming he'd been more preoccupied with the events of that summer than he'd let on. Had we been so much in love then, me and this other guy? Why hadn't we stayed together? Exactly where was Gilles during this time? Difficult questions since I had never answered them satisfactorily even to myself.

We couldn't have stayed together, I explained, because I still loved Gilles.

"So you loved Dad more?" Jeremy insisted.

"Differently, maybe." How could I speak about such matters to my son? How did a mother explain desire to her child? "It wasn't a matter of loving one more than the other, Rémy. I think Habib thought that whatever love we did have should be lived on some other plane. At a distance, so it wouldn't be destroyed. You know, Rémy, having two fathers is not that unusual. When I first met Chafia, she told me about a friend of hers who had two fathers. Instead of blaming her mother, she saw it as a blessing."

"A lot of guys at school have more than one father. It's no big deal. Pépé Gérard says if it was good enough for Jesus, it's good enough for me."

I gasped, not so much at the Jesus reference but at the thought that Gilles's father knew. "Pépé Gérard knows?"

"Everyone knows, Mom," Jonathan said. They glanced at each other, cunning written all over their faces.

I never suspected everyone knew. Rémy going along with the charade because he sensed how important it was to me, tailoring his reactions to protect me. All his life he had adjusted to the unforeseen and now it was upon him.

"Except for my father, I guess," he said, referring to Habib as his father for the first time.

"It was the only solution. I'd made a mess of things. I was desperate, but one thing I was absolutely sure of: I wanted you and Jonathan with me." We stopped walking. I took his hands in mine. "Rémy, I chose you and Jonathan." I had chosen a source of love that would be unchanging, at least on my part. "And Gilles, the four of us together."

"How did you know Dad would come through?"

"I know him. Habib is a wonderful man but he lives on some other plane, where the grass is greener...."

"Even in the desert?"

"Especially in the desert."

"I'm not sure I'm ready to meet him. I don't know if I'll ever be ready. I like the way things are."

"Nothing has to change. Tomorrow is only a first step, you can take it from there. He's a loving man. You'll like him. Maybe you'll even grow to love him."

"I don't know.... Love is a day-to-day kind of thing, isn't it?" he said with the conviction of a nineteen-year-old who has just stumbled upon an indisputable truth.

"I doubt Habib ever measured anything on a daily scale. He's an idealist." I remembered him saying he wished he could have been a Sufi. "He believes in perfection, whatever that may be."

"Yeah, well, I may not be perfect enough for him."

"We're being too judgmental. Idealism is not entirely a bad thing."

"Dad says it is."

"Your father never said any such thing."

"He said that idealizing people prevents us from seeing who they are."

"Well, that does sound like your father. And Pépé Gérard. That's where he gets these ideas."

"He said he got it from you," Jonathan said, and they both began to laugh. The two conspirators.

"Anyway, Dad accepted me for who I am, his adopted son. Habib is more like an invented father, you know?"

"Habib is real, Rémy."

"Not to me. I don't want him taking over my life."

"He won't take over your life." Not any more than he already has, I wanted to add. "Maybe this is too much for you to take in all of a sudden, it's not normal."

"We're not a normal family, Mom." For a brief moment his smile took me back to Robert Schumann Square. "But I like this better." He bent over and kissed me on the cheek.

I imagined this meeting with Habib so often over the years. His delight at discovering he had a son, his dismay at not having been told sooner. The light and shadow in his eyes, the warmth and coldness they summoned from one second to the next.

As soon as I saw him sitting at the restaurant table, the conversations I had carried in my head all those years vanished.

"You've cut your hair!" he exclaimed as he kissed me on both cheeks.

"It's easier," I said.

"It is too bad," he said and for a second I wanted to belt him. It wasn't as if he hadn't aged too. His face lined in spite of the added weight.

"You're looking well," I replied as I sat down. "A few more lines perhaps. The prosperous businessman worked over by the winds of the Sahara."

"Or by twenty years of trying to forget. It is good to see you, Aimée."

He motioned to the waiter to open a bottle of champagne in a bucket beside the table.

"You drink alcohol now?" I asked.

"A little champagne on special occasions." He lifted his glass to mine.

I could hear myself frantically asking one question after another. He lived in Tunis but was building a dream house in

Sidi Bou Saïd with floors of Italian marble. Yes, he did buy a fishing boat, as he once said he would, in case his career failed, which, of course, it never did. In spite of a successful career, he said that he held me responsible for his private life. He was on the verge of a third divorce. He traveled extensively because of his work, especially throughout Africa, and spent a great deal of his time at subsidiaries in Paris and Milan. I was reminded of Chafia and her husband.

"What about you?" he asked. "You are teaching now?"

"Yes. Translation got lonely. I needed to get out of the house."

"What do you teach?"

"Art history and theory. At an art and design school." I was trying to buy more time. "Nothing too exciting." Except for a son who resembled him even more now that he was a young man. "What about you? What does your work consist of exactly?" I asked.

"Contracts. I negotiate contracts between companies and governments."

"It sounds important. What kind of contracts?"

"Building in developing countries. In Africa. The Middle East. A few months ago I negotiated a contract for a water plant in Mali."

"That explains all the postcards from different countries."

"Yes. I meet interesting people. Important people. A few years ago I negotiated the building of bunkers. It involved many millions of dollars."

"The building of what?"

"Bunkers." He pronounced it *bonkeur*, as in *bon coeur*, good heart in French. He could see I still didn't understand. "*Une casemate,*" he explained. "A fortified refuge."

"Oh, bunkers. Whatever for? Where?" The only bunkers that came to mind were shelters for soldiers. And the bunk beds the boys slept in when they were young.

"In Iraq," he said. He became very animated as he explained

the crucial role he'd played in negotiations with the Iraqi government. "I don't know where they are. I was only the negotiator. Except for the builders, the locations are kept secret. But I hear they are solid, the Americans could never penetrate them." He relayed this with as much pride as if he'd built the damn things himself.

"Bunkers used during the Gulf War?" I asked.

"Yes, yes. Protection from the American offensive. Their Desert Storm."

Little convulsive outbursts escaping from my chest and throat threatened to wipe out any composure I'd managed to feign until then. The situation was too absurd. A Canadian housewife and mother, sitting in a restaurant in North Africa, learns that the father of one of her sons negotiated contracts involving the Gulf War. It was yet another example of how far this man could take me from my ordinary life. "Bunkers." I thought of Rose, who envisaged life as a panorama and stressed the importance of acquiring as large a view of it as possible. "Not much of a view from one of those," I said and began laughing again.

"Why are you laughing so?" he asked.

"I'm not sure." I took a deep breath. "I think, generally, Canadians thought this was a pretty wacky war."

"Wacky?" he repeated.

"Crazy."

"Are you laughing at my English?" he asked, annoyed at my lack of self-control. How collected he always appeared, how unruffled, except for that one time in the restaurant in Paris. Even then his reaction, spontaneous as it was, had seemed oddly rehearsed, his responses always matters of personal dignity.

"No, your English is fine. I'm sorry. It's odd to be speaking to someone who has such a different slant on that war. What was Tunisia's position? Did they support it?"

"Absolutely. There were manifestations in Tunis, and not only by students, against Mitterrand and Bush. The French and the Americans had no business in Iraq or Kuwait. It concerned only the Arabs. What about Canada?"

"I'm not sure Canada thought it really concerned us. But our government supported the Americans."

"It should have concerned you. Canada is next door to the most powerful aggressor in the world. What about you, what did you think?"

"I'm against war. I would do everything and anything to prevent my children from going to war. Gilles and I thought it had more to do with oil than anything else," I added.

"Yes. Arab oil," Habib said.

Whose oil needed to be secured and for what motives were of little consequence to me but I did want to know the answer to one question: "What about you, Habib? Would you have let your son fight in this war?"

He shrugged. "You know I am against war, Aimée," he said, as if stating the obvious, when, in fact, I knew nothing of the kind. "But you have to defend yourself against aggressors." It was a poor justification for an answer he knew I didn't want to hear.

"You would have let a son of yours fight in that stupid war?" I asked in disbelief.

"What I would have done is irrelevant, Aimée. Tunisians did not fight in this war and I have no son."

"One of your daughters then. Would you have let one of your daughters fight?"

"Daughters do not go to war," he sniggered. "At least, not in our country. We do not place women in front of tanks. It is barbaric."

"No less so than men."

"Ah! You would send a mother to war! You have become a feminist," he exclaimed as if he'd finally corroborated his suspicion of a major character flaw.

"I wouldn't send anyone to war, least of all my children. If I had the choice between staying at home to protect my children or going to war to kill other people's, I'd stay home. But this is not the point. I want to know what *you* would have done. Would you have sent a son to fight a war as financially motivated as in Kuwait? It's important that I know."

"Sometimes we do not have the choice. It's a matter of principle."

Oh, spare me your fucking principles, I wanted to shout. I didn't want to hear about some abstract code of honor, I wanted to tell him about a child, his child. "We always have a choice, Habib." What else could I say to this man who was as attached to his idealism as he was to his fading image of himself as a lover. His face still handsome in spite of the weight and the lines. Yet there was no compulsion to reach over and touch it. The time had passed when he could silence everything around him: voices in a park or a busy restaurant; the lonely scraping of forks and knives on plates.

He pointed to a box I'd brought with me. "What's in there?" he asked.

"Nothing important."

"Not a present for me?" he teased.

"No. No present this time. Sorry."

I put a protective hand on the box. I had, in fact, along with a few photographs of Jeremy, brought his old letters. I planned to give them back to him as a symbol of the new relationship we were about to begin. But the timing was all off. He wouldn't know what to do with them, wouldn't know how to react. In telling him I didn't want to receive his letters anymore, didn't want to keep rereading the old ones, I would be robbing him of the one role he wanted to hold on to. Everything between us measured against the background of a love that was meant to last forever. Without it, what use would this aging lover be?

"It's nothing important," I repeated. "Do you have pictures of your daughters?"

He took out his wallet and showed me worn photographs

of three young girls, one of them barely a toddler. "I thought they were older," I said.

"They are. Seven, twelve and sixteen. These are old photographs."

"They are amazing, Habib. Do you tell them those wonderful stories you used to tell Jonathan?"

"Yes, when I see them, yes. They live with their mothers." Even his daughters he managed to love mainly at a distance. "Why didn't you have another child? Wouldn't you have liked a daughter?"

"I would have liked a daughter. I had a late term miscarriage about fifteen years ago." Talking, or even thinking, about it still upset me.

He looked perplexed. "You never told me about this."

"No. I must have forgotten." It wasn't part of our history, mine and Habib's, it was mine and Gilles's.

"And Jonathan, he is still in medical school?" he asked as he put the photographs away.

"Yes, third year."

"He will travel in his father's shoes?"

"Follow in his footsteps? Not entirely. He plans to specialize in pediatric oncology."

"What is it?"

"Children with cancer."

"This is very good. I regret not having a son."

"Would it have made a difference, do you think?"

The question surprised him. "Of course. It is best for daughters to remain with their mothers. I would have been closer to a son."

"I'm not sure that's necessarily the case. Anyway, it's never too late. Maybe it can still happen." My heart pounded so wildly, it was a wonder he couldn't see it from across the table.

"No. I would have to marry again. It is too exhausting, this marriage and divorce." He waved a hand in circular motions to indicate a chain reaction.

"Maybe you wouldn't have to marry again." The few bites I'd had for lunch threatened to come hurling up. "What if you already had a son?" The words were wrong, certainly not the ones I'd rehearsed. Or, more likely, there were no appropriate words with which to spring such news on an unsuspecting man.

An interminable silence followed. I sat motionless while my heart palpitated out of control. He stopped signing the credit card slip, looked up, questioning what he'd just heard. Until I finally said what I'd wanted to for nineteen years. "You have a son, Habib."

It still wasn't registering. "Pardon?"

"You have a son," I repeated.

"I have a son," he said, mechanically, without conviction. "What do you mean?" His eyes darted about, scrutinizing my face as he struggled to keep his own from contorting. "What do you mean?" he repeated calmly, his eyes two black stones hurled into mine.

"When I left Paris that November, I was three months pregnant. He's nineteen years old. He's here, his name—" Before I could finish, he'd jumped up, his hands in the air warning me to stop, his chair falling backwards. The same clatter, the same commotion as in the restaurant in Paris, everyone frozen in the middle of a sentence or a mouthful of food. But this time his reaction did not look rehearsed. He was in shock and terrified. Yes, it must have been dreadful to learn in such an impersonal place, in such an unexpected manner, that he was the father of a nineteen-year-old. Still, I wished this time his reaction could have been different.

I should have been better prepared for his inability to withstand the irreversible truth that is a child. Instead, I found myself numb with fury as I watched him storm out. So flustered that he forgot his credit card slip and his pen. A Mont Blanc. I picked up the pen, walked out of the restaurant and hailed a taxi back to the hotel.

Jeremy wasn't particularly surprised or disappointed when I told him Habib had not returned from his business trip and his secretary had sent his regrets. "Actually, I think it would be better if he learned about you in a letter. It would give him time to adjust to the idea." It never occurred to me all those years to relay such an important matter in writing, but I probably should have. It would have given Habib more time to accept the consequence of our illusions.

"Yes. That's what we should have done in the first place," Jeremy agreed. He probably suspected I wasn't telling the truth, but as he had done so many times before, he went along. We booked seats on the first plane to Paris for the next morning.

A Trace of Jasmine

NOW THIS LETTER. For a few seconds I consider tearing it up without reading it. Chafia telephoned to warn me that Habib had come to her house the morning the children and I left. He thought we were staying with her and he was very upset, insisting Chafia tell him everything she knew about a so-called son. Accusing her of conspiracy even though she kept telling him she'd known nothing about it until a few days ago. She finally told him he might still be able to catch us at the airport.

An overwhelming apprehension invades me as I open the envelope with his silver letter-opener. I almost wish I hadn't told him, except it is no longer my decision but Jeremy's.

The envelope contains a folded card, a reproduction of a watercolor of a town. A penned-in arrow points to a name, Mahdia, and beside this: "Where I was born." I always assumed he was from Tunis or Sousse.

The letter does begin with the same words as all the others:

My dearest Aimée,
I hesitate to tell you I love you for those words no longer make sense. You have never believed in my sentiments and you will think this another drama written by a rascal or a con artist as you have called me before. As you see, I have learned the idiom of your language well.

It is not the first time I sit to compose a letter to you, but it is the first time I write to beg and I am begging you now. I am entitled to the truth. I suspect you have already told me the truth about this

*young man you say is my son but I must know why you never told
me about him and why you have chosen to tell me now.*

*Before I met you at the restaurant in Tunis, I heard rumors.
Someone I know saw you in Sidi Bou Saïd with two young men. One
of them spoke Arabic, my friend said. I thought he might be a friend
of Jonathan's or, I will confess, I imagined he might be a young
lover of yours. I didn't want to be indiscreet when we met but I
thought you were trying to relive our past with another Tunisian
young man. So when you told me who he was, I could not understand why you would invent such a monstrous lie. It took me all
night to face the significance of what you told me. I rushed to
Chafia's the next morning, thinking you were staying there, but she
said you were either at your hotel or had already left for the airport.*

*When you saw me at the airport you were confused and
alarmed. You were with two young men. I recognized Jonathan, he is
the young boy still who resembles his father, except for your hair.
The other young man also was familiar, but he did not look like
your husband. He has my hair, my eyebrows, my nose. No one can
deny that nose! Then I heard him call you "Mother." He bought jasmine from a vendor and placed it behind his ear. "Look, Mother," he
cried out, "I am the jasmine man." I knew by your expression, the
way you pushed him and Jonathan past the gate towards the air-
plane, that you did not want him to see me. I suppose it is all I
deserve after behaving so badly.*

*Aimée, I am not the only one who has behaved badly. If this
is our son I cannot understand why you kept him from me all
these years. You sent photographs of Jonathan, but never of this
son. Why have you kept him a secret for so long? You know how
much I always wanted a son. I love my daughters but I wanted
to complete my life with a son. You knew this and I cannot
comprehend the cruelty of your deceit.*

*I do not know if you are back in Canada. I tried to telephone but
I get only an infuriating machine with Gilles's voice saying no one
can take calls and to leave a message. I cannot bring myself to leave
a message of such importance to a machine. I have considered*

*coming to Canada but I don't want to create problems for you or our
son. I must proceed correctly in this matter. So I beg you to telephone
me or write to me as soon as you get this letter. You have always
been so rebellious, Aimée. I love this about you, but now I must
insist on less rebellion on your part. I never wanted to hurt you and
I beg you not to hurt me with your silence.*

*If you do not answer this letter, if you ignore my questions, I will
come to Canada and stand at your door until you open. S'il te plaît,
Aimée. Telephone or write immediately.*

   Habib who loves you still
   and who always will

I must answer, he deserves at least that much. But assuming Rémy was my lover! Wait until I tell Aisling. I can just hear
her. "Men and their silly misconceptions. Everything always
comes down to the penis, doesn't it?" Apparently, she had
acquired a chew-up-men-and-spit-them-out reputation on
the west coast, a reputation she didn't mind encouraging, as
far as I could tell.

I pick up his Mont Blanc pen, which I will soon give to
Jeremy, along with the silver letter-opener.

Dear Habib,
*Indeed, an explanation is in order. But first, I want you to know
how much your letters have meant to me over the years—receiving
a few words now and then from someone who cared enough to send
them, giving me the opportunity to write to someone who cared
enough to read about my uneventful existence, my trivial joys and
complaints. No matter how many months went by, I knew I would
hear from you eventually, to remind me that beyond family and
home, the world is not a faceless place. For this I am grateful. And
for much more.*

*I have rehearsed writing this letter so many times, so many
replies to the questions you now ask. Even so, my first impulse
this morning was to deny everything and tell you I had lied, that*

I had let my imagination run wild. For a few seconds I even considered telling you that the young man you saw at the airport was indeed my lover. But there's no point in harboring this secret any longer. Yes, the young man you saw at the airport is your biological son. But you must understand, he is above all my son and Gilles's. His name is Jeremy.

You ask why I never told you. When Gilles learned I was pregnant with your child, he agreed to help me on the condition I not tell you until the child could decide for himself. I agreed because it was the best solution for everyone concerned. When I left Paris, you were in no position to take on the responsibility of a child and his mother, and I was not about to give him up or Jonathan. I wanted them both with me and the only way I could do this was to come back to Canada with Gilles. Jeremy has always considered Gilles to be his father, although he did learn eventually of another father he would meet someday if he wanted.

We went to Tunisia this last time to give him the opportunity to meet you if he wished. After our disastrous meeting I told him you were away on business. I don't think he believed me, but I didn't have the courage to tell him the truth. I did find your reaction disgraceful but, in view of the circumstances, it was to be expected. You may think my conduct has not been any better. To this, I can only say, I did what I had to do.

I understand how cruel all this must seem to you, how utterly bloodless. But please understand, my sons' welfare has always been my main concern. When I left Paris, I knew that every detail of Jeremy's upbringing would have to be charted with the utmost care. It wasn't without challenge. By the time he was old enough to realize the full implication of what it meant to have another father, I think he had already accepted his parents' eccentricities, especially mine.

Jeremy is a well-adjusted young man. He already speaks some Arabic and he has registered for an advanced course in the language at the university and another in Arab history.

Habib, you once wrote that marriage destroyed love. In a way you were right. It destroys the kind of love we once dreamed of in your little attic room. How I longed for that room after I left Paris. Until it dawned on me. Marriage is infinitely more than the love we imagined to be so perfect within your room's four walls. Marriage is what is left when obsession finally wakes up from the stupor of its longing.

I had planned on giving you back your letters once I told you about Jeremy—they were in the box you asked about in the restaurant but the timing and the circumstances weren't right. I then considered giving them to Jeremy, but certain areas of parents' lives should remain strictly theirs, don't you think? So on the morning I left Sidi Bou I walked to the isolated part of the beach where we bought fish so long ago. It was early and I sat under the warmth of the same rising sun that once singed my bones, a warmth that will remain with me always, a comfort when I'm old.

One by one, I tore up your letters and cards, scattering the pieces across the water. The fishermen coming in must have thought I'd gone mad as I stood knee-deep in water, fragments of paper swirling around, some gliding toward their luminous backdrop, others floating for such a long time I had to close my eyes to make them disappear. Raucous seagulls everywhere. One of them, tumbling on outstretched wings, swooped down to recover one of the pieces, perhaps to build a nest somewhere. The other fragments surrendering to the sea. My dear Habib, our story is no longer written.

There is another story waiting to be written, if you wish. One that is infinitely more enduring and important than ours. The story between you and your son.

The letter I received from you this morning is more indicative of your feelings than any you have ever written me. If you were to write to Jeremy with this same conviction, I know he would respond. You alone can convince him to meet with you.

My dear Habib, twenty years ago I sought through you an otherness shielded from everything I knew. Until this otherness curled up inside me and became my flesh and blood. I suppose this is where otherness resides, close to the heart.

It isn't without sadness that I say goodbye to the lovers we once were. If we meet again, I suppose it will be as the aging mother and father of an extraordinary young man! Imagine.
    With deep affection,
    Amelia

I reread the letter several times, made a few changes here and there, rewrote it, then sealed it in an envelope and mailed it before I could change my mind.

A few days ago, in one of Jeremy's books on Arab and Persian myths, I came across another illustration of an astrolabe. This one was different from Chaucer's or the scientific astrolabe at the Institute of the Arab World. Whoever gazed at the stars through this Persian astrolabe could never escape their fascination. So the king ordered it thrown into the sea, where it stayed for centuries until a fisherman retrieved it accidentally. It had been in the water for so long that it had become encrusted with coral, phosphorescent seaweed, shells, fossilized fish. The fisherman, not knowing what it was or what to do with it, instinctively placed it against one ear. To his astonishment the astrolabe began relaying the stories of all the people who had peered through it before it was thrown into the sea, each tale more mesmerizing than the last. The fisherman said it was like stepping on the other side of sleep where the unfolding of dreams takes place.

This is what my summer in Sidi Bou Saïd seems to me now, a dream. Because of Rémy, it is a dream from which I awaken again and again.